The Game

...........Short Stories About the Life

This is a work of fiction. The authors have invented the characters. Any resemblance to actual persons, living or dead, is purely coincidental.

Compilation and Introduction copyright © 2003 by
Triple Crown Publications
P.O. Box 7212
Columbus, Ohio 43205
www.TripleCrownPublications.com

Library of Congress Control Number: 2003104725
ISBN# 0-9702472-3-0
Cover Design/Graphics: Vickie Stringer & ApolloPixel.com
Editor: Joylynn M. Jossel
Consulting: Shannon Holmes and Vickie M. Stringer

Copyright © 2003 by Triple Crown Publications. All rights reserved. No part of this book may be reproduced in any form without permission from the publisher, except by reviewer who may quote brief passages to be printed in a newspaper or magazine.

First Trade Paperback Edition Printing April 2003

Printed in the United States of America

Triple Crown Publications Presents

THE GAME

Players in The Game

The Warning

In the street there is a school of thought that most hustlers scribe to, and that is: "Be True to The Game and The Game Will Be True to You." Ummm, sounds good don't it? I can't begin to count the number of times I've heard or said that (or various other slick sayings). I, for one, lived my adolescent life by these very words and wound up giving the system some of the best years of my life, my formative years.

No matter how successful I've gone on to become, I can never get back that time. In all actuality, "The Game", or "The Life" as they call it, is true to nuttin' or nobody. You're a fool if you believe otherwise. Too many times we're misled or led to believe these ghetto false hoods. Too many times our attention has become captured by the glitz and glamour (material things) this so-called *game* brings. We're never presented with the whole truth, the cold hard facts and the consequences. We're never given the flip side of *the game*.

The same person (probably ya friend, brother, cousin or so-called man) never told you that the odds are against you succeeding in this *game*. The deck is stacked and the cards are marked. Well, since he didn't pull ya coat, I will. This so-called *game* is like a bottom-less pit that can never be filled. Decade after decade, year after year, month after month and day after day, it devours countless lost souls. It feeds off of the young, old, foolish, stupid, and the ignorant. Its appetite is insatiable. Too much is never enough.

For those players who participate in *the game* willingly and unwillingly, directly and indirectly, behind the scenes and on the front line, ya life is on the line (whether you know it or not). The threat of death or imprisonment is merely a phone call away

i

for ya family, fa you it lies in wait (right 'round the corner). Think not? You know it! You seen it time and time again. In the hood this type of damage is well documented (such & such got bodied last night or such & such got knocked yesterday).

The game has made countless examples out of endless hustlers around the way. The signs (and the talk) are everywhere, yet we choose to ignore them. Even when we do get a wake up call (a brush with death or the law) we slow down only momentarily, just long enough to reflect how messed up it was for the situation to go down like that, then we're back at it again. Never once do we heed the warning and exit *the game*.

Far too many times we take unnecessary chances with our lives with our involvement in this so-called *game* without so much as a second thought. We dive head first, relentlessly pursuing illegal endeavors, with every ounce of energy we got, in hopes of climbing that slippery street latter of success and in hopes of finding that road to the riches.

Those that are fortunate enough to last that long (to have a long enough run in the streets) to ascend to the upper echelons of *the game*, to have their names ring bells in the streets or kicked in the yard in jail, then comes the drama. Either death comes knocking at your door or "The Man" comes to pay you a visit. Needless to say, THE GAME IS OVER!!!! Ya Heard? You Lose! This ain't Pac-Man. You don't get two more men or one more life.

My man once said, "If we get $10,000 dollars and nobody goes to jail, then we won. If we get $100,000 dollars and one of us goes to jail, we lose." He was right, but only partially. THERE ARE NO WINNERS IN THIS GAME. ONLY LOSERS!!!

Some of us (myself included) catch case after case, proudly taking our L's, taking our lumps in *the game*, then coming back for more (like this is our rite of passage into the big time). All the while we're thinking in the back of our minds, "It'll get greater later." We hold on for dear life to this mind set and it becomes our downfall (been there and done that). Chances are slim to none that we'll ever make it, but we are more than willing to die trying. We always seem to think that we can out-wit, out-smart and beat *the game* (always taking that one last shot). But *the game* ain't played in ya mind. It's played in the streets, alleys, projects and corners. And it plays for Keeps.

The damage we inflict on ourselves, as well as the communities in which we live, is enormous. This monster known as *the game* has shattered more lives and caused more senseless deaths than you or I could ever imagine. And everyday the count keeps climbing (I don't just say this, it's fact!). Do the math.

You wanna know what's really crazy? We don't *fear the game*, we wholeheartedly embrace it. We don't run from it like we should. We chase it. At early ages we enter this strange workforce, preparing for a career in the life of crime. A career criminal is what some of us become. Going in and out, back and forth through the justice system's revolving doors. Let me be the first to tell you, those bids get longer not shorter.

Even the threat of death or prison can't deter us or reduce our hunger for *the game*. Some of us never seem to get it. We don't believe shit stinks.

Today, more than ever, the rules of *the game* have changed. To be more specific, there are no rules. There is no honor amongst thieves. I've seen a lot of strange things in this *game*, like friend killing friend for "short" money. I've seen good dudes die over nuttin', as well as no-good, rat bastards prosper (or appear to anyway). So whose to say you're gonna make it? Whose to say you're gonna get in and out of *the game* unscathed? How long can you hold it down? Huh? *The game* is funny like that, same thing (person) that helps you can kill you. As much work as you put in to make it, someone's working double hard to take it (Fa Real)!

THIS GAME IS NOT A GAME AT ALL, especially when the stakes being waged are our lives, our families, our communities and our futures.

I pose the following questions to you: Is it a *game* when ya people have to beg, borrow and scrap up money for ya bail or lawyer? Is it a *game* when 5-0 runs up in ya mom's crib, throws her on the floor and puts a gun to the back of her head? Is it a *game* when ya man turns state evidence on you? Is it a *game* when you gotta kill somebody you grew up with? And for what, a block, a spot that you'll never really own anyway? Is it a *game* when you get life in prison? Huh? What part of *the game* is that? If that's a *game*, then I don't wanna play no more and neither should you.

Count me out! Give somebody else my spot, dog. Some things ain't worth dying for. Do you know how many prisoners and dead men wish they could have not been a part of *the game*?... Too Many!

In this *game*, death and imprisonment are clear and present dangers that can strike at any moment. They come from some of the strangest of places, for good reasons, but more often than not, for no good reason at all (brace yaself).

I leave you with the immortal words of rapper DMX, "IT'S NOT A F#@CKIN' GAME!!!"

BLACK BUTTERFLY
Tracy A. Brown

Kaia and Symphany cruised along the Staten Island Expressway headed for the mall. Although the end of summer was approaching, it was still very warm. The breeze from the open windows felt good.

"So what's up with you and Sean?" Kaia asked as the opportunity presented itself to find out what she needed to know.

Symphany kept her eyes on the road and smiled.

"He's aiight," Symphany said. "It ain't serious, though." As always, Symphany was careful with her words.

Kaia pressed further.

"Why do you think Aaron would be going to see him today?" Kaia questioned.

Symphany took her eyes off the road briefly to look at Kaia.

"Well they're friends, right?" Symphany asked.

"Yeah, but today it seemed like he was going for a reason, like it was business. Do you know anything?" Kaia said determined to get some answers.

"Nah, Kaia. I know what you know. Sean hustles. He's on some straight up money making shit. We could draw conclusions about what type of dealings are going on with him and Aaron, but why bother? Right now you're pregnant with your soul mate's child. You got out of your mean ass mother's house and you have enough to worry about now. If Aaron says to relax and let him handle things, then you should do just that. Let him handle his business. You work on taking care of your baby and finishing school," Symphany preached.

Kaia let Symphany's words sink in. Symphany had always been wise like an old owl. Kaia decided to take her advice and she let herself enjoy the day's shopping spree with her friend.

The next six months were filled with joy for Aaron and Kaia. The baby was due in four weeks and Aaron had seen to it that they

1

had everything the baby would need. He bought a crib, a changing table, a stroller, a swing and more clothes than their child would probably ever wear. He gave Kaia money for bottles, bibs, diapers, rattles, and any other necessity. They soon realized that there was no need for a baby shower. Since Kaia didn't really need anything else for the baby, her friends, Talia, Symphany, and Giselle, agreed to alternate baby-sitting for Kaia once the baby was born.

The girls came by the apartment to visit Kaia daily. They would sit around and talk about the latest gossip and discuss their love lives. Kaia often wondered how long it would be before Keith, Aaron's brother, became annoyed with all the females in what had been his bachelor pad. But Keith never complained. In fact, he spent a lot of time flirting with Symphany.

Aaron bought a used car from a dealership on Bay Street. Kaia loved sitting in the passenger seat of their Mercury Sable while Aaron drove. Aaron promised that once she gave birth he would teach her how to drive. She was so proud to be with him. And they were beginning to feel like a real family.

Aaron went with her to every single doctor's appointment. When they went for the sonogram during Kaia's fifth month of pregnancy, Aaron was overjoyed at the sight of his baby's hands, feet and head. The doctor couldn't tell the sex of the baby, but to Aaron it didn't make a difference. He was about to become a father and nothing in the world could take the smile off his face.

Kaia returned to Curtis High School in September and had continued to attend classes even as her stomach began to grow. She tolerated the stares from her classmates and teachers and heard the whispers as she walked through the halls. A few of her teachers complained that having her in their classrooms with a pregnant belly was a distraction for the other students. Teachers whispered about her in the hallways. They said she'd never amount to anything and that she'd never graduate. She was just another statistic...a baby having a baby. But Kaia was proud, so very proud to be carrying Aaron's baby. She was proud because he loved her. He loved their baby, and no one could make her see this as a hindrance. It just felt right. Kaia was on cloud nine.

2

Now that she had entered her eighth month of pregnancy, the guidance counselor suggested that Kaia take home instruction. A teacher came to her apartment each morning and taught her the lessons that she would have been learning in school. Kaia got home instruction five days a week from 9 a.m. to 1:00 p.m. This allowed her time to get the rest that she so desperately needed since pregnancy was beginning to take its toll on her. Kaia found that she was always tired. She couldn't wait to have the baby so that she could feel like her old self again. The extra pounds she had gained made her feel like a fat cow.

Aaron did what he could to soothe her diminished self-image. Every chance he got he told her that she was the most beautiful woman he knew. Kaia knew he was bullshitting, but it made her love him even more. It seemed that Aaron was giving her all the love that she had never received throughout her life. It made her want to cry, and sometimes she did.

Aaron, on the other hand, was not without his share of dilemmas. Wayne, whom Aaron had implicated in a robbery a couple of months before Kaia got pregnant, had recently been released from prison. Upon Wayne's release and subsequent return to the streets of Staten Island, he had learned of Aaron's newfound wealth and he wasn't pleased. Wayne had voiced his displeasure to a number of people and this information had been relayed to Aaron.

Aaron had successfully steered clear of Wayne up to this point. He continued to hustle but kept a much lower profile. He had too much at stake to risk a run-in with Wayne. Aaron also kept the news about his beef with Wayne from Kaia. He didn't want to worry her during her final month of pregnancy, but Aaron worried about it plenty.

Aaron had managed to secure a sizable nest egg courtesy of his steadily increasing crack sales. He had lessened his chances of getting caught by not hustling on the street corner like so many of his peers did. He operated by pager only. The crack fiends beeped him and he made his deliveries door to door. Aaron figured that by now Kaia was aware of how he was making so much money. She was no fool. But he loved her for not questioning him about it. She never criticized him for it. She never mentioned it.

He kept his product at an apartment he subleased in the neighboring New Brighton Projects. The $500 a month rent barely put a dent in his pockets. He had a nice amount of money saved, and once the baby was born, he intended to take Kaia and the baby and move away from Staten Island. Aaron was uncomfortable with the idea of hustling so close to where he called home.

The one thing that brought Aaron joy, aside from Kaia and his unborn child, was the fact that he had finally been able to bless his brother, Keith, financially. His brother had sacrificed so much of himself so that Aaron would have all he needed. It felt good to be able to finally repay him. Aaron had given Keith the money to put a down payment on a car and now Keith was the proud owner of a Nissan Maxima. It warmed Aaron's heart every time he saw his brother behind the wheel of that car. No one deserved it more.

In Aaron's opinion, Kaia deserved the world. It was the night before Valentine's Day and as he slid into bed beside her, he smiled. He was going to fill the house with roses, balloons, candy and jewelry for her. Nothing was too much for Kaia.

Aaron pulled the covers back and kissed Kaia's belly.

"Hi, little one," he said to the baby.

Kaia laughed and said, "Every time this baby hears your voice it starts going berserk."

Aaron placed his hand on her stomach and felt his child moving around.

"That's right. Kick for daddy, baby," he said proudly as he lay beside Kaia and kissed her. "I love you, Kaia. Don't ever forget that, you hear me?"

"Yes," Kaia replied. "I love you too. You know that."

"Nah, I don't know that. I need you to prove it."

Kaia giggled seductively as she stroked between his legs. Aaron smiled and made love to her as if it were the last time.

The wind outside whistled like a freight train as Aaron awoke the next morning. He pulled the comforter over Kaia and him as he woke her with a kiss. She turned towards him and put her arms around his neck.

"Good morning, baby," she said in a voice that was heavy with sleep.

"Good morning to you," he said. "Happy Valentine's Day."

"Oh, I completely forgot, Aaron. I have to go to the mall and get you something." Kaia started to get out of bed, but Aaron pulled her back.

"Not now you're not," he said with a smile. "Today we're going to stay in bed all morning and fuck."

"Aaron!" Kaia laughed. "You're so nasty!"

"Yup, and you love it!" He licked his lips and rubbed his hands together as if preparing for a feast.

"You're right. I do love it," Kaia said. "But it's Valentine's Day and I want to do something special for you."

"Then put your lips..."

"Aaron, stop being nasty! I'm serious."

Aaron laughed and said, "Alright, alright. Let's get dressed and go get some breakfast at Perkins."

Kaia smiled and said, "Last one dressed is a rotten egg!"

Perkins wasn't too packed when they arrived. They found an empty booth to sit at and enjoyed an intimate breakfast. They talked about the upcoming birth of their child and about the latest gossip. By the time they finished eating they were both full and lazy.

As they drove away from the restaurant, Kaia stared out of the passenger side window at the cloudy sky.

"Aaron," she said. "If I ask you something will you get mad at me?"

Aaron frowned at her and replied, "You know I can't get mad at you, girl."

Kaia paused for a moment. "Aaron, when are you going to stop hustling?"

Aaron looked straight ahead. He knew he'd have to face this question sooner or later. But the truth was, money was better now than ever before, and things were only getting better. But he understood that this was not the life Kaia wanted.

"Kaia, I promise that once the baby is born and you graduate from school, I'll stop. I just want you to finish school."

Kaia prayed that he was telling the truth. She had a bad feeling about the amount of money that he was making. For some reason, she was beginning to think that Aaron would eventually find himself in big trouble. They rode the rest of the way home in silence.

When they arrived home, Aaron helped Kaia out of her coat and joined her in the living room.

"Sweetheart, don't worry about anything, okay?" Aaron said sitting beside her on the couch. "I promise that I will get out of this when the time is right. You're having my baby and you're going to be my wife. I'm going to take care of you and the baby always. You understand?"

Kaia nodded "yes".

"Don't worry about anything. I will never be away from you, okay. Trust me," Aaron said.

"I do trust you, Aaron. I just worry about you that's all."

"You don't have to worry about me, okay? Just sit back and watch TV. I have to run out for a little while, and when I come back I want to celebrate Valentine's Day the way I told you earlier."

Kaia smiled naughtily. Aaron leaned down and kissed her, then again and then again.

"I love you," he said.

"I love you too," Kaia replied.

Aaron grabbed his coat and walked out the door.

Kaia had fallen asleep on the couch after Aaron left. She awoke with a sharp pain in her stomach. Figuring it was a cramp, she took a deep breath until the pain subsided. Keith had returned home from work and she could hear him moving around in the kitchen. She stood up and began to walk towards the kitchen for some juice. But as she stood up a gush of water escaped her vagina. She looked down and found that her pants were soaked as if she had wet herself and there was a pool of water at her feet.

"KEITH!" she screamed.

Keith came running into the living room wearing a pair of jeans, Timberlands and no shirt. He saw Kaia standing in a puddle.

"What happened?" Keith asked.

Kaia looked scared and replied, "Beep Aaron. My water broke."

"You're gonna have the baby now?" Keith said looking just as scared as Kaia. He ran to the kitchen, grabbed the phone and frantically dialed his brother's beeper number. After paging him, he returned to the living room and found Kaia crying.

"What's the matter?" Keith asked her. "Are you in pain?"

"Yes," Kaia muttered through clenched teeth. "I want Aaron."

"I know, Kaia, I beeped him. I'm gonna call Symphany so she can meet us at the hospital. Where's your bag?" Keith asked.

"I don't want to leave without Aaron," Kaia said as she laid back on the couch.

"Girl, I like you a lot, but I'm not delivering your baby in this living room. Now we're going to wait for Aaron to call back and we'll tell him to meet us at the hospital. Then we're getting in the car and I'm taking you to the hospital."

Kaia didn't argue. She closed her eyes and prayed silently, *"Hurry up, Aaron. I need you so bad right now."*

Aaron drove slowly along Targee Street looking for Wayne. He hoped to catch the son of a bitch off guard and shoot him at point blank range. It was time he became the hunter instead of the hunted. His pager vibrated on his hip. Stopping at the stoplight on Targee and Vanderbilt, he looked at his pager and saw his home phone number and the code '911' next to it. *"What's going on?"* he wondered.

Once the light turned green Aaron pulled into a gas station and walked over to the pay phone outside. He dialed his home number and Keith picked up on the first ring.

"What's going on?" Aaron asked.

"Man, you're about to be a father, that's what's going on," Keith answered. "Kaia's water broke and she's having contractions."

Aaron's mouth fell open. "WHAT? She's in labor?"

"Yes, Einstein. She's in labor and I'm taking her to the hospital. Meet us there."

Aaron's heart raced. He was about to be a father.

"How is she doing?" Aaron asked Keith.

"She's okay, but she's in some pain. Just meet us at Staten Island Hospital. We're leaving now."

"Alright. Yo, Keith..."

"Wassup, man?"

"Thanks a lot for this. I mean that."

Keith smiled and said, "Don't sweat it. Just bring your ass on to the hospital so you can see your baby be born."

"Tell Kaia I love her," Aaron said.

"I will. See you in a minute."

"Peace."

Aaron hung up the phone and turned to walk back to his car. When he turned around he was staring down the barrel of a Glock 9. Wayne stared icily at Aaron as he held the gun in his face.

"I never liked a snitch nigga," Wayne said menacingly.

Thoughts raced through Aaron's head at lightning speed. *Should I reach for my gun? Should I try to run?* Figuring it was too late to do either of these things, Aaron stood still and stared at Wayne.

"I didn't snitch on you, man," Aaron said calmly.

"You was supposed to be my man and shit," Wayne continued. "I trusted you and shit. Now you act like you the man around here, driving through like you running things. Fuck you!"

Wayne cocked the gun, and as he did Aaron reached in his waistband and pulled out his gun. Ducking behind the pay phone, Aaron opened fire at the same time Wayne did. They exchanged gunfire as people ran for cover. As Wayne tried to duck for cover, he was hit in the leg.

Seeing Wayne fall, Aaron took aim and shot him in the chest. As Wayne lay sprawled on the pavement bleeding, Aaron stood back and whispered, "Happy Valentine's Day, motherfucker!"

Aaron jumped back in his car and sped off down Vanderbilt Avenue and turned onto Osgood. As the sirens blared in the distance he felt no remorse. He felt nothing at all. It was kill or be killed and the best man won.

As he sped down the narrow block he noticed the sound of the sirens seemed to get closer and closer. Glancing in his rearview mirror he saw several blue and white police cars chasing him. Before he knew it, there were police everywhere. They had him cornered and there was nowhere to run.

"Push, Kaia," Symphany coached her friend. She wiped the sweat from Kaia's forehead and told her to breathe. The nurse held one of Kaia's hands while Symphany held the other, and together they encouraged Kaia to push as the doctor instructed.

"Where is Aaron?" Kaia asked breathlessly during a break in contractions.

The nurse looked helplessly at Symphany. Kaia had been in labor for four hours and there had been no sign of Aaron. Symphany had run out of explanations and was now just as concerned as Kaia.

"He'll be here, Kaia, but right now you have to push this beautiful baby of yours into the world. Now focus and try to remember to breathe like the nurse said," Symphany said.

Another contraction began as the doctor announced that the baby's head was beginning to crown. Looking at Symphany, he said, "Do you want to see?"

Symphany darted down to where the doctor stood and was frozen in astonishment. She could see the top of the baby's head poking out of Kaia's vagina. She was amazed.

"Kaia, I can see the baby," Symphany said as her eyes watered.

Kaia managed a smile and replied, "Can you tell it to hurry up?"

Symphany laughed and said, "Kaia, your baby has a lot of hair. So much curly hair."

As another contraction began, the doctor told Kaia to push long and hard. Kaia obeyed and after a few more strong pushes the baby was born.

"It's a girl, Kaia," the doctor announced. Symphany stood with her hand over her mouth as the baby wriggled and cried. Kaia smiled, exhausted.

"Kaia, she's beautiful," Symphany managed as tears fell from her eyes.

Kaia was teary-eyed, too. Her emotions were mixed. She was overjoyed at the birth of her daughter. But where was Aaron? What could have caused him to miss the birth of their child?

The doctor turned to Symphany and asked, "Would you like to cut the cord?"

"Yes!" Symphany said as she followed the doctor's instructions carefully and snipped the umbilical cord. The nurse took the baby to be weighed and cleaned up. Symphany remained at her friend's side.

"Kaia," she said. "Aaron will be here soon, I'm sure. You did a really great job, girl. She's beautiful," Symphany said.

Kaia smiled through tears as the nurse brought the baby to her wrapped in a pink blanket. Kaia's face beamed.

"Oh, she's so beautiful. She's so precious," Kaia said.

Symphany nodded in agreement and asked, "Did you decide on a name?"

Kaia stroked the baby's sleeping face.

"Yes. Aaron wanted to name her Phoenix. I wanted to name her Grace, after his mother, so we compromised. Her name is Phoenix Grace."

The nurse came to take the baby while the doctor prepared to perform an episiotomy on Kaia.

"Kaia, I'm going to go now and when you wake up in recovery, me and Aaron will be there, okay?"

Somehow Kaia felt that Symphany was mistaken. She couldn't imagine what would make Aaron miss this moment, but she had a feeling he would not be there when she awoke. She watched tearfully as Symphany walked out of the room.

In the waiting room, Keith was pacing back and forth. Talia and Giselle sat in the hard waiting room chairs and tried to concentrate on the small television instead of wondering where Aaron was. Symphany entered looking both angry and exuberant.

"She had a girl," Symphany announced.

Keith smiled. Talia and Giselle were overjoyed

"Is Kaia okay?" Keith asked.

Symphany nodded, "Yeah she's fine. Where the hell is Aaron?"

Keith shook his head and replied, "I don't know where he is. I beeped him so many times and he never called back. When I spoke to him, he said he was on his way. I don't know what could be keeping him. I'm going to go home and see if he left a message, a note or something."

When they all reached the lobby they noticed Sean walking towards them with a sullen expression on his face.

"Yo, Keith, I gotta talk to you, man," Sean said placing a hand on his shoulder.

"What happened?" Keith asked. "Where the hell is my brother?"

Sean's eyes were glued to the floor. He finally looked apologetically at Keith and replied, "Yo, Keith, I've been trying to get in touch with you for hours, man."

Keith was puzzled and asked, "Get in touch with me for what?" Just as the words left his lips, Keith's heart sank and he began to put two and two together. Aaron hadn't made it to Kaia's bedside. He hadn't returned Keith's calls. And now here was his friend telling him that he had been trying to find him for hours. Keith's heart thundered in his chest.

"Where's my brother, Sean?" he asked.

"He got locked up, man. He shot Wayne on Targee Street and 5-0 got him."

11

Symphany threw her hands in the air and flopped down in the nearest chair. Keith stared at Sean in disbelief.

"Explain this to me, Sean, from the beginning," Keith ordered.

Sean recounted the story to Keith as Symphany cried uncontrollably. How was she going to break this news to her friend? Giselle and Talia looked dismayed. They all knew this meant that they'd have to really help Kaia with the baby now because Aaron could be gone for a very long time.

When Sean finished telling Keith what had happened, Keith was like a zombie. He heard the voices of everyone around him but he wasn't listening. All he could think about was the fact that his little brother, who he had promised his mother and grandmother he would take care of, was in jail for murder. His niece would probably have to grow up without her father. Kaia had nobody. How had he let this happen?

Symphany stood and walked over to the window. She collected herself and tried to get her emotions in check. She would have to face Kaia sooner or later. It might as well be now. But what would she tell her? What would Kaia do now? What about Phoenix? How had everything gone so wrong?

Kaia couldn't imagine what could have possibly caused Aaron to not show up. The baby cried softly in her arms and Kaia looked closely at Phoenix for any resemblance to her beloved Aaron. She held the baby's hand in hers and smiled. This child was their completion...the period at the end of their sentence.

"Maybe he decided that he doesn't want to be a father after all," Kaia's thoughts raced as she thought of a possible excuse for Aaron's absence.

Just then, a nurse appeared in the doorway accompanied by Symphany. Kaia smiled at her friend who stood in the doorway with tears in her eyes. Symphany managed a weak smile in return as she approached her friend's bedside and stroked her newborn niece's curly hair.

"Ms. Wesley, I will take the baby for her feeding so that you can have some time with your friend," the nurse said. As she lifted the baby out of Kaia's arms, Kaia noticed the knowing look the nurse exchanged with Symphany. Kaia sensed that something was wrong. Symphany sat beside her on the bed as the nurse exited the room.

Kaia wasted no time asking questions.

"Where is Aaron?" Kaia asked.

Symphany choked back the tears that threatened to plunge from her eyes. She couldn't look at Kaia. She couldn't face her knowing that the news she had to tell her would destroy her.

Kaia noticed her friend's struggle and her heart began to beat audibly. Something was terribly wrong. "Symphany, where is Aaron?" she repeated.

Symphany shook her head. She couldn't do this. Just as she was about to break down and cry, Keith walked in followed by Talia and Giselle. Kaia noticed his eyes were puffy as if he'd been crying. She sat up in the bed.

"Keith," she said in a voice barely audible. "Where is Aaron?"

Keith looked at Symphany and realized that the burden of delivering the news to Kaia would fall on his shoulders. He walked over to Kaia and took her hand.

"Kaia, there's no easy way for me to tell you this," Keith began. His voice cracked and Kaia's hands began to tremble. Keith continued, "You have to remember that we need you to be strong for your baby."

Kaia was sick of the guessing game.

"KEITH!" she yelled. "Where is Aaron? Tell me now!"

Keith took a deep breath and spoke, "Aaron was in Park Hill when I told him to meet us at the hospital. Wayne's out of jail now and he saw Aaron using the phone. After he hung up with me the two of them had a shoot-out."

Kaia gasped and covered her face with her hands.

"Kaia, Wayne died at the scene. But Aaron is alright. He's in jail though, and he's being charged with murder."

13

The room fell silent. Everyone held their breath and waited for Kaia's reaction. She sat frozen with her hands covering her face for several seconds. Then she cried hysterically. It was a sound that made Symphany's blood curdle. Keith held Kaia in his arms and rocked her as she cried.

"Noooooo!!!! What am I supposed to do? What am I supposed to do?" Kaia cried.

Nurses entered the room and attempted to calm Kaia down. Symphany cried as the nurses physically restrained Kaia, who was flailing wildly. Symphany wished she had warned Kaia sooner about the seriousness of the beef brewing between Aaron and Wayne. Symphany had heard that the word on the street was that Aaron was in danger if Wayne ran into him. She had hoped it wouldn't come to this. But she was grateful, for Kaia and the baby's sake, that Aaron had been the one taken away from the scene in handcuffs rather than a body bag.

"Kaia," Keith said fighting to keep his emotions under control. He had to be strong for Kaia. Aaron would want that. "Kaia!"

Kaia finally stopped fighting the nurses. Her body went limp and she lay on the bed in a fetal position. She moaned softly and tears cascaded down her face.

"Aaron," she moaned. "Why did you leave me? Why did you leave me?"

Keith stroked her hair. "He didn't leave you, Kaia. He would be here if he could." He paused. "Kaia, me and you have to be strong for Phoenix. We owe it to Aaron to hold it together for the baby."

Kaia lay silent. Her body continued to be wracked with sobs and she shook uncontrollably. The nurse gave her two pills to make her sleep and Symphany and the girls stayed with her until she drifted off.

Kaia woke up an hour later with Symphany at her side. She hoped that when she awoke she would find that it had all been just a nightmare. But it wasn't. Symphany smiled reassuringly at her friend.

14

"Hey, honey, are you alright?" Symphany said.

Kaia sat up slowly and said, "Can you call the nurse? Ask her to bring Phoenix." Her voice was flat and emotionless. Symphany had never seen her friend look so helpless, so lifeless and so empty.

Symphany summoned the nurse and asked her to bring in the baby.

"Kaia," Symphany said softly. "We're going to get through this. We're going to work together and we're going to get through this."

Kaia sat in silence. She didn't respond. So many thoughts were racing through her head all at the same time. When would she be able to see Aaron? How soon would he get out of jail? She had to find someplace to stay. There was no way she could return to Keith's house without Aaron. She didn't feel right burdening Keith with her and her child. She had no money of her own. She had no plan. All she had was pain.

The nurse entered carrying the baby in a tight bundle of blankets. Symphany stood up.

"Kaia, do you want to be alone with her?" Symphany asked.

Kaia nodded in the affirmative and stared at the beautiful newborn in her arms. Symphany left quietly followed by the nurse.

Kaia gazed at her child sleeping innocently in her arms. What a beautiful child she and Aaron had made together. She caressed the baby's tiny hands as her eyes welled up with tears.

"Hi, Phoenix," she said with her voice quivering. "Looks like it's me and you against the world."

Kaia held the baby close to her and cried silently. She faced the fact that the weight of Phoenix's world was on her shoulders. She had a huge responsibility and a broken heart to match.

Kaia thought about Aaron's words, "*I will never be away from you,*" but he was. He was so far away from her and she had never felt so hopeless.

The raindrops tapped the windowpanes like the rhythm of drums. The stillness that echoed through the storm calmed Kaia. It was the day of Aaron's sentencing.

She wore her hair pulled back in a ponytail. Dressed in all black, she donned her shades and prepared to attend the hearing at which Aaron's fate would be decided. He had pled guilty to voluntary manslaughter and weapons possession. He had originally been charged with second degree murder but had copped a plea at the advice of his lawyer. The evidence against him was too powerful for him to try to beat it. He knew that even with the lesser charge of voluntary manslaughter he was still facing quite a few years behind bars. When Kaia had spoken to Aaron after she and the baby were released from the hospital, he had sounded defeated...crushed. He told her that he loved her and that he never expected things to go so wrong.

Kaia was angry with him and felt sorry for him at the same time. She was angry because his decisions had cost them both dearly. Now she was forced to take care of the baby by herself and find a way to survive. But she knew that he had good intentions. He thought he was doing the right thing and he had always stood by her when it seemed the world had turned its back on her. How could she hold that against him?

Symphany held baby Phoenix in her arms and spoke quietly to her friend.

"Kaia, the car is outside. Are you ready to go?" Symphany asked.

Kaia continued to stare out the window.

"Can I have a minute?" Kaia asked.

"I'll take the baby to the car. You take your time," Symphany said shutting the door quietly behind her.

Kaia glanced around the room. This had been her haven. This room had been the place she'd given herself to Aaron - the place where they'd conceived their daughter. This home had been one into which Aaron had welcomed her with open arms. Now he was gone and she could no longer remain there. She had decided to move out. It would be better that way. Keith had protested, but

Kaia knew it would be easier without her being there to complicate things. She would miss this house as much as she missed Aaron. But she had to leave. She had to learn to stand on her own two feet.

Keith had given Kaia the money that Aaron had saved. Kaia wanted to share it with him knowing that Keith was as important to Aaron as she was. Keith wouldn't hear of it. He refused to take a dime. So Kaia took the money and used some of it to rent an apartment for her and Phoenix. She chose to remain on Staten Island so that Keith could maintain a close relationship with his niece and so that she could finish school. In four months she would graduate from high school and Aaron wouldn't be there. Kaia felt so alone.

She opened the window and let the February air fill the room. The wind whispered in her ear and nudged her cheeks. The cold air filled her lungs and Kaia wept.

She wept because fairy tales do not exist. She wept for dreams unrealized. She wept because she'd yet to see a sky dipped in blue instead of gray. Her tears were salty with the bitterness of heartache. Her body convulsed uncontrollably. Her hands trembled. The earth ceased to spin...and she wept...all the while wrapping herself in an invisible cocoon determined to survive the storm.

****

Tracy A. Brown currently resides in Staten Island, New York where she is writing her debut novel, *Black Butterfly*, which continues to chronicle Kaia's life and the affect the streets have on her.

𝓣𝓗𝓔 𝓜𝓘𝓛𝓘𝓣𝓐𝓝𝓣
The Urban Griot

April 1972

"A new day is here, brothers and sisters! And it's about God damned time!"

"Yeah, it is! It's been time!"

"Now we've been knockin' on Mr. Charlie's door for more than a minute now and it seems that we finally . . . finally kicked this motherfucker in!"

"YEAH! That's what we did?"

"Right on, brother!"

CLAP! CLAP! CLAP! CLAP! CLAP!

Gary Clayton Wills Jr. heard his father's thundering voice over the loud speaker system out at the park in his hometown of Cleveland, Ohio. His mother looked at him and thought of cupping her hands over his ears to save his innocence. But it was too late for that. Lil' Gary had already heard plenty of his father's fiery speeches. And at three-years old, he knew the words that seemed to get the crowds excited. However, his baby sister, Jackie, didn't seem to like all of the commotion.

"Whaaaaaaaaa!" she howled, tugging hard on their mother's left pant leg. She wanted to be picked up to safety and away from the rowdy grownups who towered around her in their Afros, dashikis, and butterfly blue jeans.

"It's okay, honey," their mother told her as she picked her daughter up and rocked her in her arms.

Lil' Gary watched the comforting of his little sister and nodded his mini Afro. He felt proud to be a little boy who could handle the crowd noise and the weekly drama of the grownups. And even though he could barely see his father up front at the wooden podium, he adored the rowdiness and the loud speeches. He felt at home there. But his mother never cared for standing up

18

front. That was where the overzealous people stood. She was
growing tired of the repetitive speeches anyway.

"Now Mr. Charlie got some reckoning to do. And we're
gonna make sure . . . I said, we gon' make sure that new business
is taken care of."

"Right on!"

"That's what I'm talkin' about!"

"YEAH!"

Lil' Gary got so excited that he yelled out with the crowd
himself, "Yeah!" and pumped his little brown fist in the air.

His mother looked down at him with Jackie in her arms,
and she was not impressed with his bravado. She didn't have to
say a word to him. The steely look in her eyes alone told him to cut
the shit out. And he did, but not without mumbling under his breath
in defiance, "Right on."

His mother went ahead and ignored it instead of smacking
Lil' Gary upside his head like she felt the urge to do. She reasoned
that boys would be boys, and besides, if he had complained to his
father about it that night, like he was learning to do, she would have
another trite argument on her hands about manhood and what was
needed to train black boys to fight against "the system."

Dinnertime

As soon as the Wills family sat down to eat their dinner that
night in their crowded little two-bedroom apartment, the kitchen
telephone rang and broke Mom's peace before she even took a
seat at the table from fixing everyone's plates. She still managed to
answer the phone with civility.

"Hello," she said.

"Yeah, is Gary there?" the caller asked.

She paused and took a breath before she answered, "Yes,"
and handed her husband the phone.

"Who's that?" Gary asked her. His mouth was already
jammed with food.

19

"It's Pauly," she replied.

Gary winced and took the phone from her.

"Yeah," he responded to Pauly gruffly. Then he calmed down a minute. "Okay . . . yeah . . . unh hunh." He looked up at the clock that hung on the kitchen wall and said, "How 'bout around nine or ten?"

His old lady shot him a look from across the table but she remained silent. Gary ignored her stare. He had shit to do. As soon as he hung up the phone, she was all over him.

"Haven't you done enough for one day? What do they want from you now?"

Lil' Gary sat there at the table picking through his food. He too wanted to know. What more did his Daddy have to do in one day?

Big Gary took a breath before he answered, "Look, you know we don't get no damn breaks in the struggle. Does the white man give you a break on the job? Yeah, a lunch break that he charges you for," he stated rhetorically.

His old lady took another breath and held her tongue. She then helped their daughter to eat her food before she dug into her own, becoming the last to taste the meal that she had prepared that night . . . as usual.

Lil' Gary sat there in his booster chair at the table and smiled. He was tickled by the entire scene. He loved how his Daddy handled his Mom's tart.

"What's so funny, boy?" Big Gary snapped to his son. The struggle wasn't some damn comedy routine. It was about serious business, and Lil' Gary needed to understand that even at his young age. So Lil' Gary swallowed air at the table and erased his grin.

"Nothin'," he answered his father.

Big Gary nodded his head and responded, "That's what I thought. Cause I ain't raisin' no damn circus clowns in this house, boy. You hear me?"

"Yes," Lil' Gary squealed out.

"We got enough of that clown shit runnin' around out here

already, Amos & Andy niggas. And you damn sure ain't gon' be one of 'em. You hear me, boy?"

"Yes," Lil' Gary answered, still in retreat.

His mother spoke up for him and said, "He's only a child, Gary."

Big Gary glared at his old lady again and snapped, "You know what I told you about that, right?"

She turned her eyes back to her daughter and mumbled, "Yeah, whatever." Before her man could respond to her she added, "Somebody told me we'd move into a house soon, too."

Lil' Gary nearly choked on his food as he tried to chew it down. What would his Daddy say now? He could feel the tension rising up in the room again. His Mom and Dad were always going at it and Lil' Gary wondered how long it would take before they got to whipping on each other like he had witnessed from some of the other grownup couples in their chocolate-coated neighborhood of human stress.

But Big Gary kept his cool at the table. He only nodded to himself and grunted. It was his turn to hold his tongue. And they all ate that night in a tense silence.

Late Night Drama

Lil' Gary awoke late at night and rubbed his eyes in the dark of the small bedroom that he shared with his little sister. Mom and Dad were at it again in the master bedroom.

"Don't lie to me, got'dammit, or I will take the kids and leave right now!" his Mom screamed at his Dad in their room.

Lil' Gary's eyes grew wide. He didn't want to leave his Daddy. No way! His Dad was his hero.

His Dad said, "Look now, Monnie, cut this shit out. You always jumpin' to conclusions."

"Don't you give me that shit, Gary! I can smell the perfume all over you. And it damn sure ain't mine. So which one was it this time? Hunh? Which one?"

"I am so tired of this shit!" Mom told Dad as Lil' Gary

continued to listen. "And my name is Monica. 'Cause I'm tired of that 'Monnie' shit. I'm not one of your silly-ass girlfriends. I'm your wife, Gary. Doesn't that mean anything to you?" Then his Mom broke down in tears. Lil' Gary could tell by the sound of her voice. She then continued, "Because if that doesn't mean anything to you, Gary, then I'm just ready to leave. I'll move back in with my mother with the kids."

Lil' Gary sat up and was wide-awake after that. He didn't like his grandmother much. She had too many old-school rules: "Wash your hands before you eat, boy. You put that toilet seat back the way you found it. Help your sister first, boy. Don't you touch my damn garden, and sit down here, boy, and let me comb that nappy-ass head of yours."

Yeah, Lil' Gary was just short of hating her. She spoke to the boy as if he was a grown-ass man already. But he didn't know if it was legal to hate a relative, so he put up with her. But his grandmother didn't like his Daddy at all, and they always avoided each other. So Lil' Gary knew what that meant. If they moved in with "Granny", their Daddy wouldn't be able to see them much.

His Dad spoke up to his Mom in their room and said, "You know I'm not gon' let you do that, girl. You're not takin' my damn kids anywhere. Are you crazy?"

"No, are you fuckin' crazy, Gary? I am tired of this shit. All I do is sit around here with these kids all day while you run the streets, talkin' 'bout some damn revolution and movement, and then you come home late smellin' like some two-bit slut. And you gon' ask me if I'm crazy. Nigga, you must a lost your damn mind!"

Lil' Gary's heart nearly jumped out of his chest and landed on the outside of his pajamas. No she didn't call Dad that "N-word." But Daddy used it all the time; "That nigga did this . . . This nigga did that . . . Aw, that nigga's just like the rest of them niggas . . ." But it was different when Daddy said it. He was the King of the universe. He could say and do what he wanted. And so what if he had an extra woman or two. They all seemed to like him. But now Mommy went and called him a "nigga" for it.

"Girl, I will whip your motherfuckin' . . ."

"Well, do it then, you . . ."

"WHAAAAAAAAA! . . . WHAAAAAAAAA! . . ."

Lil' Gary was paying so much attention to his parent's heated argument in the other room that he didn't notice that his sister had awaken. Her violent cries shot out at the perfect time to cool things off before an AK-Bomb exploded up in there, an ass-kicking. Before his mother marched into the room to tend to Jackie, Lil' Gary pulled the covers back over himself and tried to pretend that he had not been up already.

"Okay, baby. Mommy's okay. Everything's all right. Hush, baby, hush," Lil' Gary heard his mother saying to his sister.

Mushy girl stuff, he thought to himself in his young mind. His mother realized as much. She stood there with her daughter in her arms and stared at her precocious son until he opened his eyes.

"Mmm, hmm," she grunted at him once she saw the whites of his eyeballs. "I know your lil' ass was already up, Gary. Gonna try and play possum. You just like your damn father. And can't even tie your own damn shoes yet."

"I can tie shoes," Lil' Gary lied to himself as his mother walked out of the room.

As soon as his mother walked out, his father walked in. Lil' Gary just stared at him. He didn't know what he was supposed to say, nor did Big Gary know what to say to his son. He was confused about his own actions. Who said grown-ups had all the answers?

Big Gary sat down on his son's mini bed gently as not to break it under his weight. He took a breath and said, "Gary . . . being a black man . . . is one of the hardest jobs you ever gonna have in your life, son. And I wish I could lie to you about it but . . . it's gon' catch up to you eventually anyway. So you might as well know the truth."

He looked into Lil' Gary's sympathetic eyes and said, "Your Daddy ain't perfect, boy." But then he added, "And neither is anybody else's Daddy. We all have our own demons to deal with. So don't you let nobody tell you nothing differently."

Lil' Gary nodded his head to his father in agreement with him.

"Yeah, everybody has to fight demons, he thought to himself. Because demons are bad."

Government Jobs

There was no extended drama story in the Wills household. Big Gary had made enough noise in the city of Cleveland for some of the powers that be to want to shut his ass up. Jail and death wouldn't solve their problems with the Negroes, or Afros, or . . . Black Power peoples all of the time. Sometimes it was smarter, and less messy, to buy them off. After all, a married man still had to feed his family no matter what color or creed he was.

So, Gary Wills Sr. got himself a new job downtown in the tall buildings where the white folks worked. He began to go off to work in the mornings with a briefcase, suits, and clumsy ties that he barely knew how to wear right. Lil' Gary had no idea what his Daddy did downtown in his new government job, but before he knew it, they had moved out of their rundown two bedroom apartment on the east side of Cleveland, and into their first three-bedroom home in a much nicer neighborhood. Then Mommy's stomach got big. She was pregnant again.

"Do you have any names for the new baby, Gary?" his mother asked him. Boy was she happy in their new home. She even found her own job, helping out at the day-care center not far from where they lived.

Lil' Gary asked her, "Is it gonna be a boy?" He was five-years old by then, and the gender roles would never let him go. A boy his age couldn't even look at a girl too long or the other guys would think he was going sissy. So they all treated their sisters like a new scab on the knee, you just had to deal with them until they fell off and went away.

His mother asked him, "What difference does it make? You'll have to love it either way."

Lil' Gary nodded his head and cheered up about it. He

said, "Okay. I'll name 'em . . . Georgie."

"Georgie?" his mother asked him with a wince. Then she smiled at it. "Georgie Wills, hunh?"

It sounded good to Gary. It started with the letter G, like his and their Dad's name, and if Georgie was as fun as Curious George in the kid's storybooks was, then they would surely get into great trouble together.

By the time everyone had taken a seat that night at the dinner table, Lil' Gary's Mom had grown to like the new name. It had a catchy ring to it, Georgie Wills.

"What do you think about that, Gary?" she asked Big Gary at the table.

Lil' Gary wanted his father to like the name as much as he did, so he looked up with eagerness from his dinner plate. His mother had learned to cook a lot better now, and he was already stuffing his mouth with rice and sweet corn before getting to the chicken that was smothered in yummy brown gravy. But his father frowned at the name immediately.

"Georgie? That don't sound like no first name," he said.

"Well, you always called me Monnie?"

"Yeah, but that was a nickname. And you stopped me from doing that anyway."

"Well, I like it."

His mother looked over at Lil' Gary and said, "And your son gave me the idea."

Big Gary looked at his son and grunted before he went back to eating his food and drinking his water.

"You don't like it, Daddy?" Lil' Gary asked his father.

Big Gary paused for a minute. He wanted to explain to his son correctly. He had learned to pause a lot lately to make sure that he was more thoughtful about his words and actions. But Lil' Gary didn't know if he liked that too much. He liked the old Dad who would say whatever the hell was on his mind at the snap of a tree branch.

"That's just not a first name, son. George would be a first name. But that name sounds too old for a Lil' boy."

"I like it," Jackie chimed in from her place at the table.

"You like everything," Lil' Gary snapped at her. She was getting in the way as usual. Daddy was talking.

"Oh, cut it out, Gary," Mom told Dad. "Every man grows into his name just like every woman."

"Well, how would you feel if your mother named you 'Monnie' instead of 'Monica'?" his father asked his mother.

Lil' Gary was paying strict attention to the logic of his parents on both sides.

"Well, I would have just had to live with it. It wouldn't be as if I would know there was another name."

"Until you met girls named 'Monica', and then you'd start to wonder why you had been given a nick-name instead of a normal name."

Lil' Gary started to laugh. His father was right. So he no longer liked the name Georgie. He just didn't have a name to replace it yet. But by the time the baby was due, which was indeed a second boy, his mom was stuck on the name. So she named him George Wills, with the full intention of calling him Georgie.

"Do you like that, Dad?" Lil' Gary asked his father after the fact.

Big Gary seemed less concerned about it and responded, "What's done is done, son." And that was all he had to say.

Lil' Gary found some disappointment in that. His father no longer seemed to put his foot down in the house like he used to do. In fact, he had rarely put his foot down at all in their new home. Mom seemed to run the show now. Dad's new government job had changed him. Instead of giving fiery speeches about the "God damned white man" out in the public parks of Cleveland, Big Gary now seemed more inclined to read a newspaper and watch sports on television. What the hell had happened to him? So one day Lil' Gary decided to walk up to his father while he was watching an NBA basketball game on TV, featuring agile brothers in tall Afros floating from rim to rim, sinking pretty finger rolls and jump shots and ask him.

"YEAH! Break 'em down, Doc! Break him down!" His dad

shouted at the television.

It startled Lil' Gary for a minute. He had never witnessed his father get that excited about a sports game before. He had gotten excited only for the movement. But was there still a movement going on?

"Daddy? . . . Daddy? . . .Daddy?"

"Yeah, Gary, what is it. You see I'm watching this game here, boy?"

His son noticed a touch of the fire that his father seemed to have lost, but it was now directed to the television and away from firing up the people to fight against oppression, whatever that meant.

"Daddy, do we still need to fight the white man?" Lil' Gary came right out and asked his father.

Big Gary stopped and looked embarrassed for a minute and replied, "What?"

His son repeated the question, "Do we still need to fight the white man?"

There was that pause again. This one was even longer. Big Gary said, "Son, there are some things in life that each man is gonna have to decide on his own. And there will always be a struggle for every man on this earth. You hear me?"

Lil' Gary heard his logic, but he was confused by it. He was not asking about "every man," he was asking about the black and white man's struggles against each other, the same struggle that he had heard his father talk about incessantly for the first three years of his young life.

"But what about the black man and the white man?" Lil' Gary asked more pointedly.

However, Big Gary's attention was only halfway on his son. The other half was on the basketball game.

"Shit!" his father hollered at the television again. His favorite team was beginning to lose. He said, "Look, Gary, we're gonna talk about this later on, just not right now. Okay? I'll explain all of it to you."

The son stood there and was shocked for a minute. The

Daddy that he used to know would never put a conversation about the black and white man on hold for anything. He had changed and Lil' Gary didn't like it. He didn't want some bump-on-a-log Dad who watched six straight hours of TV. He wanted a father who was about action . . . the Daddy that he used to know.

****

Stay tuned for the next installment of The Militant, a novella by The Urban Griot. For more on The Urban Griot, view his Website at (www.TheUrbanGriot.com).

EVERYTHING AIN'T FA EVERYBODY
Shannon Holmes

As the 10 car, graffiti covered, northbound # 4 train, commonly referred to as the iron horse, sped down the elevated train tracks toward 174th Street subway station, it bought with it an unmistakable sound. It was a deafening, ear splitting and thunderous noise that echoed off the various closed stores fronts, car lots, factories and buildings that lined Jerome Avenue. The train made its designated stop at the station, depositing its minority residents back to their desolate urban neighborhood.

This section of New York City was known as the South Bronx. It was hit hard by a rash of tenement building fires started by greedy, unscrupulous landlords seeking a big insurance settlement from properties they deemed worthless and rundown. They figured that torching their buildings was more profitable than fixing them up. They never took into account the cause and effect that this crime would have on the buildings residents or The Bronx period. Irreplaceable personal items went up in smoke with these buildings. Lives were ruined and families were forced to relocate from their places of birth to even worst conditions like the city shelters or the projects.

Like a bad case of the chicken pox, this insurance fraud scam spread across the South Bronx landscape, making it resemble a ghost town in some war torn foreign country. Where buildings once stood and life once flourished, there was now vacant lots with mounds of rubble and abandoned and charred skeleton remains of buildings as far as the eye could see. Later, crack cocaine came along and finished off the job that the fires had started. It killed off any remaining hopes and dreams that the neighborhood had of recovery. This section of NYC was amongst the poorest in the country. The Boogie Down Bronx, the home of hip-hop, became known as the Burnt Down Bronx.

On this chilly fall evening in the South Bronx, a trap was being set that would bring about some deadly consequences. Parked in a car underneath the train station was Kenny Greene, a.k.a. Ken-Ken. He was a tall, dark skinned, well-built ladies man, whose specialty was strong-arm robbery. He was also one half of a husband and wife con team.

Ken-Ken's wife, Maria, was a gorgeous Puerto-Rican woman with long red hair that flowed down to the small of her back. She had a light trace of hair just above her juicy lips and a beautiful black mole that sat atop. It was the kind that women always artificially added in an effort to enhance their facial features. Maria was also blessed with a body that could stop traffic. She had a pair of firm breast that stood at attention, a butt big and wide enough to sit a drink on, a flawless caramel complexion, plus long sexy legs.

Dressed in a red-hot mini skirt with a matching leather jacket and six-inch stiletto pumps, she looked every bit like the hooker she was desperately trying to portray. Unbeknownst to everybody accept family and friends, Maria was seven months pregnant with the couple's first child. But looking at her one wouldn't be able to tell. Her pregnancy agreed with her. And besides that, men, tricks and johns were too busy lusting off her bodacious body to closely examine her stomach.

This entire operation was Maria's idea. With the baby on the way she wanted to stack all the money she could while she still could. Pretty soon she'd be way too big to even think about doing things like this. She came from a family where breaking the law was a way of life. It was accepted and maybe even expected. Both of her brothers and her father were currently sitting in various prisons in upstate New York for their parts in various crimes. Maria was taught the art of pick pocketing, or jostling, as it is known in New York, by her brothers. She in turn taught her then boyfriend, Ken-Ken.

Growing up as kids and living in the same building, these two couldn't stand each other. They argued constantly. Several times they almost came to blows. Older people in the building predicted that one day they would be a couple since they always fought like one. Sure enough, as they headed into puberty their hormones took over. They suddenly stopped fighting each other and became attracted to each other. Some called it animal magnetism because they couldn't stay away from each other. So after years of fooling around, dating, break ups and make ups, it was decided by Maria's mother that they should get married. The couple agreed and they got hitched downtown in City Hall. It was a small simple ceremony with only a select few friends and family members in attendance.

Ken-Ken hated the idea of having his woman in on a caper, having her in harm's way. But he had no choice. Maria insisted that she be included. They were a family that did everything together, literally. And besides, she was critical to the success of the trap. She was the bait. Maria lured the tricks to a secluded side block under the pretense of prostituting. Then Ken-Ken would arrive just before she was to perform some lewd sexual act, preferably while they were discussing a price, and knockout the trick. If things went according to plan or if they were lucky, the two would then relieve him of all his valuables, cash and credit cards.

As the commuters began to trickle down the train station steps, going their separate ways, a young black couple got into a heated argument. This scene captured Ken-Ken's full attention.

"Motherfucker, you ain't hardly slick," the young woman said. "I seen ya black ass staring at dat bitch on da train."

The young man replied innocently, "Whut girl? You buggin'! I don't know whut da fuck you talking bout!"

"Nigga, don't play dumb! Ya ass ain't as stupid as you look! Since you got amnesia you can forget about hittin' this tonight!" the young woman stated strongly, while picking up the pace of her walk in an effort to distance herself from him.

Unable to control his anger any longer, the young man ran up to the young lady and kicked her straight in the behind.

"Motherfuck you hoe!" He shouted at the top of his lungs.

The young woman stumbled from the unexpected force of the blow. Quickly she regained her balance. Instinctively, she bent down in the gutter and picked up a half-empty glass soda bottle, launching it at his head. Luckily he ducked just in time. The bottle went whistling by before shattering harmlessly on the ground.

Thinking to himself how funny this situation was, the young man began to laugh uncontrollably as he ran off in the opposite direction. He didn't care about the girl anyway. She wasn't his girl. She was just somebody he was trying to lay up with for the night.

"You bitch ass nigga! I'ma get my brotha ta fuck ya azz up! Watch!" she cried out at the fleeing figure. "You gon' get yourz!"

"Whateva, you fuckin' slut!" he yelled back over his shoulder, not the least bit worried about her threat. He had too much back up around the way to let anything happen to him.

Ken-Ken was very much amused as he watched this dispute from his car. But this distraction caused him to take his eyes off of Maria. It diverted him from the task at hand. This momentary lapse of judgment would prove to be critical. He would live to regret this. This was one instant frozen in time, one of those life altering moments that in retrospect if he could have done it all over again, he would have been on point. He would have paid closer attention.

A few feet up the block, Maria had flagged down a potential Vic. He was a thin white man dressed in a blue pinstriped three-piece suit, driving a burgundy 300E Mercedes Benz with New Jersey license plates. This particular strip on Jerome Avenue was frequented by white men from across the river that who were looking for black and Hispanic crack whores.

"Hey, good looking! What ya got cookin'?" The trick calmly asked.

Maria replied, "Name ya pleasure; HBO, head, booty and other things. I'll take you around da world and back again."

To Maria, this trick looked and smelt like money. He was probably some big business man from corporate America. She just knew he'd be loaded with cash and credit cards; Visa's and Master Cards with an unlimited line of credit. After this heist they were gonna be straight for a while, she figured. Maria was going to do a lot of shopping for the baby at the expense of this trick.

But what Maria didn't know was that this man was a demented regular customer out for revenge. He caught gonorrhea from some Hispanic crack whore a few weeks ago. This set off a chain of devastating events in his life. He in turn took it home and gave it to his wife of twenty some odd years. She then promptly filed for divorce. Now she was trying to take all his assets in court; the house, the three European luxury sedans and his six-figure bank account and all because he had to satisfy his insatiable craving for Puerto Rican hookers.

This homicidal maniac swore he'd find and kill the whore who burnt him, who ruined his life. And it didn't matter to him that he might spill innocent blood in the process. It didn't matter that Maria wasn't the one who burnt him, she'd do. In his mind somebody was gonna pay. He was motivated by revenge. It led him to strike out at the first Puerto Rican hooker he saw that night. And as fate would have it, that person was Maria.

Nervously the trick glanced around for any signs of the cops. He didn't want anything to interfere with his murderous intentions.

"Get in the car, sweetie. I'm trying to go around the world. You think you can take me there?" He grinned.

"Well, you gotta pay to play! No romance without finance, as they say. No whatimean good lookin'?" Maria seductively said while licking her lips. "First things first, let's see dat cash, honey."

The trick quickly complied, removing a large wad of money from his jacket pocket. He hoped that this would do the trick, that the sight of the money would entice her enough to get into his car. He would then take her to some seedy motel to rape and sodomize her before killing her.

By now Maria was bent over slightly inside the passenger's window. From this vantagepoint, she could see clearly that he was holding nothing but 100's, 50's, and 20-dollar bills. She flashed a bright smile at the trick as she began scratching her head. This was a signal to Ken-Ken that everything was good to go, that they had a winner. Unfortunately for Maria, Ken-Ken never saw her signal. His attention was fixed firmly on the young couple carrying on in the middle of the street.

Suddenly a strange premonition came over Maria. She saw her life flash before her eyes. For a moment she locked eyes with her would-be-murder. Staring into his cold blue eyes she saw no signs of life, just pure evil. His eyes betrayed the sly smile that spread across his lips. In an instant Maria quickly examined the contents of the car. From the dim streetlight she saw the glimmer of chrome from a gun. Even that didn't frighten or deter her. Maria decided to try her hand anyway, believing that the trick didn't have the heart to shoot. Acting instinctively, she quickly reached into the car and snatched the money out of his hand. Turning her back, she ran as fast as her high heel shoes could carry her. She ran directly towards Ken-Ken, her protection.

At that very moment Ken-Ken happened to glance up and see his wife running full speed in his direction. His gut feeling told him something was very wrong. Though Maria may have thought she was running very fast, in all actuality she wasn't. She couldn't out run a bullet.

Calmly the trick raised his 357 Magnum and took aim, lining her up in the gun's sight. He squeezed the trigger. The cannon roared and the muzzle flashed simultaneously discharging two rounds. The gun was loaded with the dumdum bullets. This was ammunition legally made to do the most damage to it victim. The bullets found their intended target. Two shots slammed into Maria's back, sending her crashing to the concrete.

In horror Ken-Ken watched the deadly scene play itself out, knowing that he was powerless to stop it. The sound of tires screeching snapped him back into reality. He had a decision to make. He could either chase the gunman or try to save his wife. Ken-Ken opted for the latter. At top speed he ran to where Maria lay sprawled out, almost motionless on the ground. Once he reached her he could hear the weak moans she emitted from her gravely injured body. Though he saw no evidence of entry wounds on her body, he knew she had been shot. It wasn't until he rolled her over on her back, placing her head in his lap, did he see the gapping exit wounds that the bullets caused. He was shocked at how badly she was hurt.

"Maria! Maria!" he cried, while starring into her watery eyes. "Hold on baby, it's gonna be aiight."

"Kenny... Kenny," she whimpered in her thick Spanish accent, still clutching the blood soaked money. "It burns! Kenny, it burns!"

"Mami, hang in there ya gonna be aiight. I'ma get ya ta da hospital and they'll fix you right up as good as new," Ken-Ken said wishfully. But he knew it was a lie. As he desperately tried to comfort her, her heart was pumping out an incredible stream of blood at a fast rate. Her lifeline was flowing out of her body, running into the gutter.

"Help! Help! Help!" Ken-Ken screamed frantically trying to attract some attention on the deserted block.

Fortunately, God heard his cries for help. A transit cop who happened to be patrolling the subway station heard all the commotion and radioed in for the police and an ambulance.

"Ken-Ken, I'm gettin' sleepy," Maria wailed while fighting to keep her eyes open. "I can't keep 'em.... They keep clossin'"

"Don't go ta sleep, Maria!" Ken-Ken commanded as if she could control it. The two bullets had started an irreversible trip into the hereafter.

Gently he began smacking her across the face. It was to no avail. Maria kept drifting further and further from the land of the living. Ken-Ken wanted to breakdown and cry, but he had to be strong for the both of them. This was all of his fault, he told himself over and over again. If only he had been on his job. If?

Suddenly, off in the distance he began to hear the wail from the sirens of the ambulance and the police cars. Ken-Ken began to get optimistic. By the grace of God, maybe, just maybe they might be able to save Maria's life.
Ken-Ken clung to that flimsy hope, because hope was all he had.

The police and ambulance arrived almost at the same time. Immediately emergency medical technicians rushed into action.

35

They placed Maria's limp body on the stretcher and wheeled it towards the back of the ambulance. Even though she had a weak pulse they knew she wouldn't make it. Their main concern was to try and save the unborn child. The mother's life was virtually over.

"Who shot her?" the policemen inconsiderately asked Ken-Ken, while he followed the EMT workers to the back of the ambulance in a daze. "Did you get a look at the shooter? What in the world was she doing down here? Do you know what she got shot with? Does your wife have a history of prostitution?" the officers badgered.

Ken-Ken shook his head no over and over again. He was going into a state of shock. He didn't even have the presence of mind to respond verbally.

The ambulance took off like a rocket with Ken-Ken and Maria inside. Having radioed ahead, a trauma team was on standby waiting on them once they reached their destination. Feverishly, the remaining EMT worked on Maria, placing an oxygen mask over her nose and mouth and running an IV into her arm. But secretly he knew, even before he started this procedure, that she was a goner. He had seen so many trauma patients over the years that he could just about predict who was going to live and who was going to die. And Maria was in bad shape. She'd lost too much blood. He was just going through the motions, fighting a battle that only God could win.

"Maria, don't die on me!" Ken-Ken begged her while holding her limp hand. But Maria was already gone and nothing could bring her back. The grim reaper had silently separated her soul from her body. "I love you, Maria! You hear me? I love you."

As the ambulance raced through the streets of New York, summoning all the horsepower the engine could muster, they finally reached the hospital. Coming to a smooth stop, the doors flew open and about a half dozen doctors and nurses were standing waiting to assess the damage. They began speaking medical lingo that Ken-Ken couldn't quite understand. But he obediently followed as they rushed her down the long hospital corridors and into the operating room.

"Sir, you can't go in there. That's a restricted area," an obese white nurse said.

"But...But dat's my wife!" Ken-Ken announced, not fully comprehending what she said. His only thought was to be by his wife's side.

The nurse responded, "I understand that sir, but the operating room is off limits to everybody except medical personnel. Don't worry, she's in good hands."

Her vote of confidence did nothing for Ken-Ken's nerves. He had managed to stop himself from entering the operating room against his better judgment. He came to the conclusion there was nothing left for him to do but pray. This horrific experience suddenly renewed his belief in God. He walked slowly to the waiting area and kneeled down and prayed, desperately trying to recall all those special Christian prayers he learned as a child.

Meanwhile inside the operating room, the trauma team and doctor performing the emergency surgery on Maria, after trying to resuscitate her, quickly realized she was dead and there was no bringing her back. So the decision was made to save the life of the unborn fetus.

By cesarean section the doctor delivered a premature baby girl. Under these strenuous conditions the baby appeared to be healthy, but the long-term birth defects were yet to be determined. After the successful delivery, the doctor went to give the grieving husband a mixed blessing, the good and the bad news.

Still on his knees, Ken-Ken never heard the physician approach.

"Excuse me sir. Weren't you accompanying the Hispanic young lady that we bought in here about an hour ago?" the doctor gently asked.

"Yeah!" Ken-Ken said as he lifted his head up out of the chair. "How iz she, doc? Iz she gonna be aiight?"

This was the part of the job that the doctor absolutely detested. This was the part medical school could never prepare him for. How was he supposed to explain to grief-stricken family members that their loved one had perished? Emotions tend to run high under these adverse circumstances. They overcome all rational thinking. Families wanted answers now. How and why did their love one die? And sometimes no matter how much diplomacy he used, it just wasn't enough to satisfy their inquiry. They thought that everybody that came through those emergency doors was supposed to make it. But he knew better. Modern medicine couldn't save everyone. The doctor knew that when it was your time to go, nothing could help you. Only God knows why some shall live but others shall die.

The doctor decided to give Ken-Ken the good news first, in an attempt to soften the blow. He took pity on him.

"Well, sir...," his voice began to trail off. "You are now the father of a beautiful baby girl."

"But...but what about my wife?" Ken-Ken asked, yet he dreaded the answer.

"Unfortunately, we couldn't save her. She lost a lot of blood. The bullets severed some major arteries causing extensive internal bleeding," the doctor solemnly explained, giving Ken-Ken the best definition of the extent of her injuries in layman's terms.

Immediately, heartbreak and anguish registered on Ken-Ken's face. Tears filled his eyes. He broke down and cried.

"No! No! Maria's not dead!" Ken-Ken wept. He never realized he could lose so much and gain so much all in the blink of an eye. But the game was funny like that. One day it will be your best friend and the next day it will turn on you like a jilted lover, stabbing you in the back.

The doctor came over and tried to comfort him by rubbing his shoulder.

"It will be alright, sir. It will be alright," the doctor softly repeated.

"Where's my daughter?" Ken-Ken suddenly asked. "I want to see my daughter."

The doctor gave Ken-Ken a hand up off the floor, then he placed an arm around his shoulder, and together they walked towards the ICU ward. There, Ken-Ken would get his first glimpse of his past and his future. He'd lay his eyes on his daughter. She was fruit of his blessed but short union with his lovely wife, Maria. As Ken-Ken made his way through the hospital's maze, from that moment on he promised himself he'd dedicate the rest of his life to his daughter. Even if that meant losing his own. He promised to move heaven and earth before he'd let his seed get hurt.

****

Shannon Holmes is the author of the Essence Magazine Best Seller, *B-More Careful*. Shannon currently resides in New York where he is working on his next Best-Seller, *Bad Girlz*.

BLACK ICE
K'wan

Welcome pimps, whores, and all lovers of vice. I'd like to put y'all on to my main man, Ice. With a long stretched hog and minks of all flavors, Ice is what you would call a true to life player. He had a stable of fine hoes, so his pockets were never uptight. But my ace boon, Ice, fell victim to the life.................

The wheels of the forest green El Dorado bent the rain streaked corner of 33rd and Madison causing a few of the pedestrians to jump back onto the curb. The angry late night partygoers began to yell and curse, but all sound was cut off at the sight of the "Mother Ship". That was the nickname for Ice's 68 hog.

It was a custom made stretch Caddy that easily took up two parking spaces in any lot. The grill was trimmed in gold, and on a sunny day you would swear it was glowing. The interior was lined with the hide of an authentic Bengal Tiger, giving it the most exotic look. The wheels were as white as the day they first left the show room floor. And to top it off, the car sat on solid gold deep dishes that were about 22 inches each.

The hog pulled up to the curb where a group of girls were standing, and that's when the real show started. The driver stepped out and was truly a marvel. He slid from the driver's side with the grace of a jungle cat. When he stood to his full height, he was easily six feet six four inches. The long yellow over coat that covered his lanky frame was made of giraffe, as was his wide brim hat. The shoes that peeked out from under his coat were lizard and dyed the same print as the coat.

Slowly the driver bopped over to where the girls were standing. The regular folk just stared at the tall coal skinned man as if he was an alien. The night lifers who worked those corners knew better. This man was more than an alien and the girls on the corner co-signed it when they all started squealing, "The Ice Man is here!"

Now all eyes were on Ice, so he had to make an impression. Ice gave the corner his warmest smile, exposing two rows of gold teeth, all with blue diamond cuts. When he was sure he had everyone's attention he threw open his coat and declared his dominance in the game.

The suit that Ice had on could only be described as "whoa!" It was so black that you couldn't tell where the three-quarter jacket ended or the wide legged slacks began. The fabric of the suit was made of some kind of fur that no one could guess. Some say panther while others speculate a sort of mink. Only Ice knew the truth, and he would never tell. The shirt was as white as clouds in springtime and further brought out the giraffe print tie that hung loosely around his neck.

"Ladies," Ice crooned, "Daddy has come bearing fruit. Gather around as Black Ice runs it down."

Out of all the girls standing around, only three strutted over to the tall black man: Rachelle, Chance, and Jet. They were few in numbers, but the most choice by far. They were one unit who lived to serve their general. But all of the girls were quite different. Jet, was the shortest of the three. She was a thick lil' broad who was as black as her name. She was about five feet on a good day, with an ass you could balance a cup on. She was the lil Pit Bull that Ice kept around to watch over the newer girls. She was dead nice with a razor and the 380 that she kept tucked on her wasn't no punk either.

Rachelle was the white girl that Ice had copped from another pimp named Willie. Ice was at the player's convention in the Chi. Willie was getting cats at a crap game, and had the whole crowd uptight. That was until Ice stepped in the place.

Willie started hating on New Yorkers and coming at Ice all kinds of side ways. Ice, being the nigga that he was figured, that instead of getting all uncouth and scrapping with Willie, he would hit him where it hurt, in the pocket.

Ice joined the crap game all smiles and friendship, but there was larceny in his heart. Faster than the eyes could follow, Ice switched the game dice with a pair of 'tee.' Once the game was in Sway, Ice proceeded to trim every sucker in the joint, including, Willie.

Ice took ol' Willie for everything. He got him for his money, all his jewels and his truck. As a last desperate effort to regain some of his self worth, Willie bet Rachelle. As a result, Willie went home damn near naked and whoreless.

Rachelle was a tall Italian girl with smooth tan skin. She was Ice's freak dog and one of his biggest earners. She had long red hair and demon green eyes. She had breast that would have made any plastic surgeon envy her. The best thing was, they were hers. This white girl was almost six feet tall in flat shoes, so with the stiletto heels on that she always wore, she looked like an amazon. Her biggest asset was her ass. She had a booty that had made many a black whore jealous. Rachelle was a girl that would go where most wouldn't. What ever a trick wanted, they got it. Girl on girl, anal, bondage, golden showers, whatever. She was 'bout it. Guess poor Willie lucked out.

Chance was Ice's latest cop. She was a tender 18-year-old young thang who had come to New York on a bus from Mississippi. She was looking for fame, and she sure nuff found it. But instead of the big screen, she found the big player. She wasn't too short and she wasn't too tall. She was just the right height. This girl was what one might call perfect. She didn't have huge breast like Jet, or Rachelle, but she had just enough. Her ass was well shaped into the form of an apple. Chance had skin the color of corn meal. It was so soft that if you touched it and then touched a piece of cotton, you damn near couldn't tell the difference. Chance didn't look a day over 15. When she looked at the tricks with those soft brown eyes, their wallets would open as wide as the pearly gates. These ladies played for Ice's team, and to be a part of that line up was truly divine, in the life.

"What kinda fruit you got for us, Daddy Ice?" Chance asked, in her most child like voice.

"Fall back wit that shit, bitch!" Jet snapped. "You know Daddy ain't gonna talk business in front of these so called *pimps*. These niggaz would love to kick shit on his good name."

"Daddy, can us unworthy bitches climb in your hog so you can further enlighten our ignorant assesses?" Jet asked turning her attention to Ice.

"Bitch, quit clowning," Ice said playfully slapping Jet on the ass. "This ain't the sixties. But if you want me to stomp on yo ass like them niggaz used to do, then bend over."

"Yea, I'll bend over," Jet said pulling up her short skirt and exposing her huge thong creased ass. "But I want you to do more than stomp it."

"Get yo thirsty ass in the car," Rachelle said playfully pinching Jet on the ass. "That dick will be there when our shift is over. "What's up, Daddy, 'cause a bitch need to get back on the track?"

Ice gave Rachelle a smile and a nod. Even though Ice had bust her out a few times, he didn't really care for white folks, but he had to respect Rachelle. Her pussy was the bomb, and her mind was always on his money. You didn't really find whores like that in this new age of pimping.

"It's all good, ladies," Ice said squashing the argument before it started. "This ain't no top secrete, Skinny. I could give a shit if these square ass niggaz out here knew what was going down. I' am the Black Ice, and you are my ladies. We are unstoppable, unapproachable, and unmatchable. You can quote me on that one."

The few pimps or whores who were within earshot of Ice's little speech shoot him dirty looks. Ice was always flossing. Although they shot him shady looks, they couldn't deny the fact that Ice was the truth in the game.

Ice climbed into the hog followed by his three ladies of leisure. The green monster pulled away leaving a slew of angry bystanders and a few sour pimps. They could be sour, it was all good. They just had to respect the game.

"Okay, Daddy," Rachelle began, "now what's this all about?"

Ice took his time before answering, cause that's just the kind of nigga he was. He slowly lit a Newport, and commenced to coasting. They had actually gotten about four blocks before he even bothered to answer Rachelle's question.

"Well," Ice said blowing out a cloud of smoke, "it's like this. Remember how I was talking about washing up some of that dirty whore money? Well I've finally got a plan to do it."

"We going legit, Daddy?" Chance interjected.

"Nah, baby." Ice said with a wave of his hand. "We gonna have the best of both worlds. It's too much money in them streets to go cold turkey. We always gonna be in this here game from now until ya pussy is rotted out or falling apart. We gonna be hustlers."

"So, what's up then, Daddy?" Jet asked innocently.

"Well, baby girl," Ice began, "I got a partner over in New Jersey who's about to open a strip mall, and shit. Now for a small fee, my friend is going to be so kind as to let a nigga eat. To make a long story short, ya daddy bout to buy into some property. I already got a spot pegged for a hair and nail shop."

"Oh, Daddy," Chance squealed. "We gonna own something of our very own?"

"Hell, nah," Ice said with a bit of an attitude. "I'm gonna own something of my own. But you know how the Ice Man do. What's yours is mine, and what's mine is mine."

"That's right!" Jet co-signed. "Talk that shit. Let these lame whores know who's running the show."

It was times like these when Ice appreciated Jet's company. She wasn't the sharpest knife in the drawer, but she was good for his ego. Every one knows how average men love their egos to be stroked, but it was even worst with pimps. These so called money managers were the absolute worse as far as vanity went. To be a boss pimp you had to walk around like you were God's gift to women, and actually believe it.

"I'll tell you like this," Ice continued, "by tomorrow morning Black Ice will have one foot planted in the square world. With the

44

money I make off the streets, plus what I milk out the strip malls, I can tell them crackers to kiss my black ass. Now check it out, bitches. Being that I'm the good hearted nigga that I am, I'm giving you whores the rest of the night off. Now, you can go on about your business and do what ever it is you do when you ain't out selling ass, or you can come on out to the set and party with the Ice man. Now, can you dig it, bitches?"

The girls jumped and squealed for joy. Amongst the people of the night, selling ass was a full-time job. There was no vacations or sick days. It was just grind hard, 24/7. For a pimp to give one of his ladies a day off was damn near unheard of. But Ice was just a good nigga like that.

"So," Rachelle cut in, "where is the almighty Black Ice kicking it tonight?"

"Ain't nothing special," Ice assured her. "They having this lil thang uptown. I'm gonna roll up and through there, have a few drinks and pop some shit with these hard leg ass niggaz. You know I gots to have my team wit me so I can stunt on these breezy ass niggaz on the set. What's really good wit y'all, lil' mamma's?"

"Daddy," Chance started, "I can't speak for the rest of these bitches, but I'm wit you on that there. Lets do the damn thang and show these lames what's good."

"I know that's right," Jet co-signed. "I ain't shook my ass in a hot minute."

"I hear that hot shit," Rachelle added. "I'm going up in the joint, and try and catch me a trick. Y'all bitches get drunk and shake yo assess till they fall off, but a hoe like me is on a paper chase. We can't keep Daddy fresh if we don't do the do. Y'all need to get ya minds, and Daddy's money, right."

After hearing Rachelle's lil speech, an ear to ear grin spread across Ice's face.

"You see," he began, "that's why I can fuck wit you, ma. I mean youz a cracker wit a black bitches mentality. As long as you keep your mind on my scratch and up out of my mix, we ain't gonna never have no kind of misunderstanding. That's what's up," he said looking at Chance. "You need to get on Rachelle's page. She could teach you hoe's a thing or three."

Even though he was looking at Chance, Jet knew the comment was directed towards her. Unlike the rest of the stable, Jet had a special attachment to Ice. Back in high school, Ice and Jet were "fuck buddies". They were free to see who ever else they wanted, but when either felt like a good raunchy fuck, they would hook up. Jet wanted Ice to be her man, but he had other plans. Ice was determined to pimp, and having a girl friend would complicate his life too much.

From the first time Ice saw his late father check his nightly trap from one of his whores, Ice was hooked. His father used to always tell him, "Johnny, only a sucker goes out there and bust his ass to make another nigga rich. This game here is what's up. But if you wanna be a player, you got to pimp hard and pimp strong. Having a bitch always nagging you and stressing about who you wit and where you're at is for squares. I love yo mamma dearly for bringing you into the world, but I got to get my money right. Marriage just ain't in the cards for ya old man."

That speech would be forever etched into Ice's brain. Even when some young whore's brother parted Johnny Sr.'s skull like the Red Sea, Ice never forgot what his daddy used to tell him. His daddy was a good pimp, but old age dulled his senses. It would be a cold day in hell before some youngster would take Black Ice out the game.

$ $ $

Ice pulled his hog to the curb on west 41st Street, but there was no sign of the other girls.

"Where the fuck?" Ice said to no one in particular. "Now I could've sworn I dropped them heifers off on this block."

"You did, Daddy," Jet spoke up from the back seat. "There go Sheila over there," she said pointing to the all night diner across the street.

Ice turned around to see what Jet was talking about, and there she was, sure enough. Sheila had her wide ass parked on a stool, talking to a sharply dressed young cat. Sheila wasn't the prettiest girl on his team, but she could do amazing things with her mouth. Everything about Sheila was big, her ass and her chest. She even wore her hair in a big weaved out style. She was a big girl, but she wasn't fat. She was big boned and cute in the face, not pretty, just cute.

His first instinct told him to go in there and snatch her ass off that stool, but Ice was too cool for that. If he wanted, he could've acted all crazy and made a scene, and he would've been dead right, but that ain't how players do it. He was gonna test her out.

"Here," he said handing Jet a bag of weed and a cigar.

"Twist that for me, baby." Jet rolled the weed and the four sat in the hog and got bombed.

About a half-hour went by and Sheila was still flapping her gums with the young cat. Ice decided that enough was enough. He got up out of the car and made his way over to the diner. He was mad as hell, but he couldn't let his ladies know that. He had to play it cool. He strolled across the street like he didn't have a care in the world.

The inside of the diner was relatively full for it to be so late. There was a blend of night people and squares alike. The lesser-known pimps nodded to Ice, but didn't dare approach him. To these lil fish, Ice was the great white shark of the game and they didn't wanna come across lame.

Ice was right behind Sheila, but she still didn't see him. Had she noticed the look he was giving her, she would've probably broke and ran for the door. Now if Ice was a gorilla ass nigga, he would've slapped the taste out her mouth for spending all this time with the cat she was talking to, let alone for free. Time was money, and Sheila was fucking with his finances. But Ice wasn't no gorilla. He was a gentleman pimp, so he just tapped her on the shoulder.

Sheila spun around on the stool ready to get smart, but when she saw who it was tapping her, she almost dropped a load in her big ass panties.

"Daddy," she squealed, hopping off the stool. "I didn't expect to see you so soon. Is everything okay?"

Ice looked at her stone faced and said, "If you got my trap straight, then every thing is mellow, baby."

"You know I got your money on time, Daddy Ice." Sheila reached down into her 46DD bosom and produced a wad of crumpled bills. She handed the money over to Ice and proceeded to run her yap about something or the other. Ice didn't really know what she was saying. He was preoccupied counting his money.

When Ice was done counting he looked at the money like someone had taken a shit in his hand.

"Bitch," he said through clenched teeth. "You been down here since 7 o'clock, and all you got for me is a funky $200 dollars?"

"Daddy," she pleaded. "It's been slow down here and the tricks ain't really been rolling like that."

"Oh, really?" he said sarcastically. "How the fuck would you know? You been in here flapping yo mafuck'n gums for the last half hour with this square."

"Oh no, Daddy," she corrected him. "He ain't no square. This is Blood, and he's a pimp."

Ice had to keep from laughing in both their faces.

"A pimp, huh?" Ice said.

For the first time, Ice took a good look at the cat that called himself, Blood. He was a handsome cat. Ice had to give him that. He had smooth dark skin and not a trace of hair on his face. When he stood up to Ice's hand, his powder blue sweat suit hung loosely on his six-foot wiry frame. Ice just looked coldly as Blood's hand hung in mid air.

"They call me Blood," he said with a cockiness to his voice. "I just come up from Brooklyn 'cause I heard the whore money is sweet up here. I'm gonna be a king pimp, just like you."

"Like me?" Ice said with a chuckle. "You poor misguided, young fool. You can't be like me, lil nigga. I'm Black Ice."

There were quite a few snickers and giggles from the patrons in the diner. This only served to make Blood angry. Here he was trying to give a nigga his props, and Ice played him. But Blood wasn't going out like that.

"Nigga," Blood spat. "I ain't no punk. You better watch how the fuck you come at me. My gun go off, son."

The last statement wiped the smile off Ice's face, as well as everyone else's who had heard. Ice knew he had to put Blood in his place. Not really being one for violence, Ice decided to bark Blood down.

"Nigga," Ice started, "you must've fell and bumped yo head. Ain't you heard what the fuck I said? They call me Black Ice, wit a capital 'B'. I got five bad hoes, and they all chose me. My heart is coal black, just like my skin. And a feud wit me, is something you can't win. Now go on and step, while you still can. Cause its pure suicide, fucking wit the Ice Man."

Everyone in the place stood up and clapped after Ice laid his game down. He bowed graciously and blew kisses to the whores in the diner. While Ice was busy receiving his applause he didn't notice the steam raising from Bloods head.

Blood reached up under his shirt, but Ice had already peeped him. He smashed his elbow into Blood's nose and sent blood squirting all over the bar as well as on Ice's coat. Before Blood could recover, Ice swept his legs out from under him knocking him on his ass. Ice leaned down over Blood and placed his 22 snub to in the boy's eye.

"Nigga," Ice spat. "I should blind you. This coat cost me more than it took to raise yo lil ass and you done ruined it. I'd be dead right, if I splatter yo lil ass pea brain on these mafuck'n tiles. But you know what? I'm in a good mood so you can live, at least until you try this shit on a nigga who ain't as seasoned as me."

Ice took Bloods gun and raised up slowly. With his right hand, he kept the pistol on Blood. With his free hand, he pushed Sheila towards the door. As Ice moved to join Sheila, he added insult to injury.

"Say, lil' nigga, find you some business and stay the fuck up out mine. Y'all have a good night."

By the time Ice got outside, his girls were on their way over to the diner, with Jet in the lead.

"Daddy," Jet said waving her pistol. "We saw the commotion and we thought it was on. I was ready to lay my hammer game down, for real."

"And that's why you my number one," he said hugging her. "It wasn't nothing. I just had to straighten out some ol' square ass nigga that your so-called wife-in-law thought was a pimp. But it's all gravy. We still gonna party."

"Party," Sheila said joyfully. "Where we going?"

"Bitch," Ice snapped. "We is French in your case. Now, Chance, Rachelle, Jet, Precious, and me are going to the jump off at Perks. You gonna take yo big ass round that corner and finish humping my scratch up. If you can managed to get me some respectable whore money, I might let you come home in the morning. Speaking of Precious, where the hell is she?"

"Here I is, Daddy," she said coming around the corner. Precious was Ice's show stopper. She stood at around five feet nine inches and had skin the color of a new penny. Precious had a mean ass, and legs like two baseball bats. Her eyes were jade green and her jet-black hair hung down to her ass. Precious was knocking everything out the box. Ice fell for her after she won first place at an amateur modeling competition in St. Louis. She could've easily been a professional model, but she chose the fast life. She was a girl who dug sporting niggaz, and so it was only right that she chose Ice.

"What's up, baby?" Ice said kissing her on the cheek.

"Catching these tricks," she responded, handing him a healthy knot of money.

When Ice was done counting the money, he smiled from ear to ear.

"This what the fuck I'm talking bout," he said waving the money at Sheila. "This is respectable whore scratch. This bitch done been down here just as long as yo dumb ass and she already clocked $800 fo a nigga. Y'all could learn something from this lady here."

"Well, we can't all be size six bitches," Sheila said under her breath.

"Keep talking," Ice warned her. "You say one mo thang and you won't have to worry about coming home in the morning, cause you won't have one. If you don't like the way I run things, step yo ass off. Black Ice don't keep no hoe's against they will."

"I'm sorry, Daddy," Sheila said.

"Bitch, don't be sorry, be careful. Now the rest of you ladies, in the car. We gonna swing by the pad to change, then we party."

$ $ $

Perks was jumping, as usual. Even though it was a weekday, the Harlem lounge was packed. It was mostly frequented by people of the night, and it wasn't like they had jobs to go to in the morning.

To the passer by, Perks looked like any ol' other lounge, but the inside told a different story. Perks was like a fashion show. Pimps, whores and hustlers from all walks of life drank liquor, sniffed coke and partied the night away. It was truly a rest haven for street people.

The hustlers and players inside Perks were sporting the finest threads from yesterday and today. But when Ice and his ladies stepped in the joint, they shut 'em down.

Rachelle was rocking a one-piece leather cat suit that dipped way down in the front showing off her healthy bosom. Jet stepped out wearing a tight fitting mini skirt that showed off her ass. Chance chose to down play it and just wore blue denim jeans with a pair of brown cowboy boots and a matching cowboy hat. The belle of the ball was Precious. She sported a white mink and a studded white ball gown that hung down to her ankles. The ladies were fine indeed and caught the attention of every man in the joint, but Ice stole the show.

Ice stepped in the joint and everything went silent. He wore a powder blue mink jacket that was so smooth it looked like it had a perm. He was tastefully dressed in powder blue slacks with a black turtleneck. Around his neck he had a 40-inch platinum chain with a flooded cross that swung above his crotch. Like Chance, Ice wore a cowboy hat, but his was mink.

"Okay you suckers," Ice screamed. "You mafuckas quit gawking and belly up to the bar. You niggaz is drinking on the Ice man!"

Everybody in the joint cheered as they mobbed the bar. Ice man and his girls drank, cheered and popped shit deep into the night. Ice was having so much fun that he had forgotten about the incident with Blood, that is until his man, Party Time, came up in the joint.

"Well kiss my black ass," Party shouted. "If it ain't my man, Black Ice. What's up wit you nigga?"

"What up, Party?" Ice said feeling a bit tipsy.

"Shit, Ice. You know ol' Party gotta be where the action is."

"True, true."

"But let me run down to you what I heard from a lil bird. They say you put the hurt on ol' Blood from outta Bedsty?"

"Yea," Ice said sipping his drink. "I had to put that lil nigga in his place. He was talking all breezy and shit."

"Ice," Party started, "you my main man so I got to put you up on game. That kid, Blood...that's one mean mafucka, and he knows how to hold a grudge. If it was me, I'd have shot that mafucka."

"Well," Ice said glassy eyed, "you my main man, so let me put you up on something. You ain't me. I'm Black Ice! There ain't another nigga on the face of God's green Earth built like me. My paper too long and my game too tight. That mafucka, Blood, would sooner crawl back up his mamma's ass, than fuck wit me."

Party Time just shook his head.

"Ice, I love you baby, and you know I do. But that liquor got you talking out yo ass. Blood done shot quite a few people to be so young. I'm telling you Ice, watch yo back."

"Good looking, Party. But I got this here. Go on and have a drink on me."

Ice and his ladies drank and partied until the sun started to peek and they called last call. As Ice stood up from the bar, he realized how drunk he really was. Jet and Precious had to help him out to the car.

Once the air hit Ice, he sobered up enough to walk on his own.

"Unass me, bitches," he said playfully. "I'm Black, mafuck'n Ice."

"Hey, Ice," a voice called from behind. Without even thinking, Ice turned around. The last thing Ice saw was the bullet coming at him form the barrel of Blood's 45.

Before Ice even hit the ground, Blood took off. He jumped into his Lexus, where Sheila was waiting with the engine running. The two conspirators rode off into the sunset, and Ice lay in a pool of his own blood.

At the funeral, players from all over came to pay their respects to Johnny 'Black Ice' Walker. Ice was a true-blue player, and many a tears were shed when the Lord called him home. That's just the way it goes sometimes, when you're caught up in the game.

****

K'wan is the author of the street novel *Gangsta*. Without a doubt he is one of this generations most talented and gritty writers. Born the only child of a poet and a painter, creativity was imprinted in him from day one. K'wan resides in one of New York City's most gang infested housing projects where he continues to create beautiful and touching novels. Be on the look out soon for K'wan's next novel, *Road Dawgz.*.

CAN'T KNOCK THE HUSTLE
Kenya I. Moses

"God, who could this be on my phone so early?" I don't know why folks mess with me this early knowing that I'm going to be in straight bitch mode. Easing my body from underneath the covers and stretching my five foot three inch frame, I reach out to answer my phone.

"Who is it?" I ask before giving the caller a chance to say hello. Rubbin' my eyes I hear the operator say, "Collect call from Reese Bashar from a Texas Correctional Facility. Will you accept the charges?"

Exhaling loudly I okay the charges.

"Come on, ma, talk to me," my ex-husband and baby's father begs.

I guess I should explain our history...Reese and I met when I was in junior high school. He used to come and pick his lil' cousin up from the school and scope out the younger chics. He was a ballin' ass nigga getting major paper on the grind. I was a fly caramel complexion D-I-T (Diva In Training). Hell, I couldn't stand the sight of him. I thought he was arrogant and cocky. I can remember the day we met like it was yesterday. It was April 11, 1990 and I was dressed to the nine, ready to get home so that I could get changed into something more comfortable than what I was sportin'. I was walking towards my bus when a hand reaches out and grabs me.

"Yo, ma, let me give you a ride," Reese said.

Little did he know his first mistake was grabbing my arm. I snatched my hand back, rolling my eyes.

"Eww, boy, if you don't get your hands off of me," I gritted through my teeth.

Flashing that million-dollar smile, he just laughed. As he turned me lose and I began to walk off he replied, "You gon' be my wifey one day. Your fine ass just don't know it yet.

Laughing as I continued walking, I thought to myself, *"Dayum he is fine."*

The next day at school, right before fourth period, my name was called over the PA system. I was ordered to report to the office. As I entered the office I saw this big bouquet of white and pink roses with the cutest teddy bear buried in them. Reaching for the card a tiny sparkle caught my eye. I covered my mouth as I removed the teddy bear that was wearing a two-carat tennis bracelet around its neck. Smiling, I read the card: *"Told you I'd make you my wifey"* was neatly printed. I couldn't help giggling to myself.

"This nigga crazy," I said as I walked away bearing the gifts. Admiring the gifts, but not really caring about the sender, I dismissed the idea of liking him back. I had done my research on Reese and he was what they called a balla in the hood. He was 24 years old with no kids. He started hustling just so he could get his granny a house, but I guess the game got good to him so he stuck with it.

Reese was known to get with many girls but never to be in a relationship with one. He should have known better than to have tried to add me to his collection. I had seen the street life from afar and wanted no parts of it.

The last bell rang at 3:10 p.m. and as I was rushing to get to the bus. As I walked outside of the school I see Reese posed up on a freshly washed Lexus.

"Ma, you gon' let me give you a ride home or what?" Reese yelled.

I couldn't help but smile and blush. He was too cute in his Girbaud jeans, white T-shirt and fresh pair of Air Force Ones.

"Yeah, I guess today's your lucky day," I replied.

I walked over to his car. He held the passenger door open and I proceeded to settle in. Getting into the car I could feel the envious eyes of my classmates as they all began to whisper. I already knew this was going to be da talk of the school tomorrow.

"So, Ikeda," Reese said planning to go into conversation.

"You can call me Keda," I said cutting him off.

Reese and I chit chatted like old friends the entire ride home. Over time, Reese and I became inseparable. Two years would pass and we were still together, spending all of our free time together talking about any and everything. I nicknamed him Bear 'cause of his height and weight. Reese stood six feet five inches and was weighing in at 215 pounds solid. He became my best friend and my first love. I shared with him secrets that would ultimately cost me everything.

I knew Reese was a hustler from jump, but sooner than later he captured my heart. At night, when he would come home late and tired, he would tell me about his day's events. I knew more about Reese than his partner Shydeem did. Shydeem hated the fact that I had pretty much replaced him in Reese's life. I knew where the dope houses were, who had what and where it was located. The one thing Reese withheld from me was the code to the safe that was hidden in the wall of the condo we now shared.

Rolling over tapping Reese's shoulder I whispered, "Baby." Shaking him a lil' harder I say, " Baby, get up. I need to talk to you."

"Yeah, ma," Reese replied as he rolled over.

I sat up against the pillows and Reese laid his head in my lap. Running my fingers through his long curly hair I say, "I think I'm pregnant."

Lifting his head, and now fully awake he asks me, "What did you say?"

"I think I'm pregnant, Bear. My period didn't come. It hasn't come in two months. I didn't tell you 'cause I didn't wanna say anything until I was sure."

That was all Reese ever wanted was a son to carry on the Bashar name. But my telling Reese I was pregnant seemed to be like what was the beginning of the end. So much shit started happening. It was a whirlwind of events.

Reese was becoming a major figure in the game. We had moved from our two-bedroom condo into a four-bedroom house in the suburbs of Missouri City in Houston. I had graduated up from a Honda Accord to a Lexus truck. My baby was due in two and a half months and Reese was expecting the biggest shipment of heroin yet, 50 pounds to be delivered in five days.

His Cuban connect was to have someone drive the goods in a meat truck. The old head that Reese normally used to help him out wasn't around. For some reason or another he had just disappeared from the streets. This wasn't unusual 'cause often he would go on one of his high binges and be ghost for a while.

In the middle of one of my many naps my cell phone rang. I dug inside my Louis Vuitton bag and pulled it out. Glancing at the Caller ID I see that it's Reese.

"Yes, baby," I answered sleepily.

"Baby, I need you to get the picnic stuff and bring it to the spot," he said. Picnic was the code word for money.

"Baby, I'm tired," I moaned.

"Happy Birthday!" Reese said before hanging up.

I knew something was wrong, .I could just tell. First off all, he knew I didn't know the code to the safe, secondly, Reese never mixed his personal life with business. His motto with me was the less that I knew, the less the po-po could ask me about. Unknowing that *they* had just had an earful of our conversation, I hopped in my truck.

With a Louis Vuitton duffel bag stuffed with all the money I could gather from the secret hiding places around the house, I drove off to meet Reese. Hitting the speed dial button on my cell phone, I call him to tell him that I was right around the corner.

"Aiight, ma," Reese said. "I'll be outside by the time you pull around."

Something was strange about the block that day, too many cars and not enough people. I can't explain it, but you could tell something just wasn't cool.

Pulling up to the curb I beeped my horn and Reese came out to the truck. Walking around to the trunk, I reached in and gave him the bag containing the money. Not paying attention to my surroundings, I heard screeching tires from all different directions. Turning to see what was going on, I soon realized that we were surrounded by DEA, ATF and undercover agents.

A female agent ordered me to face the car and spread 'em. Automatically getting defensive, Reese lunged for the officer only to be thrown against an undercover car and held down.

Hearing Reese yell, "Yo, man, my wife is pregnant. Why y'all gotta handle her rough," caused tears to begin streaming down my face. I was cuffed and shoved inside the back of a car. I couldn't believe what was happening as I was driven off.

I was processed and placed in a dark room where I waited to be questioned. I asked to use the bathroom since I hadn't been in hours. Passing the other holding cells I recognize Sam, the old head Reese often got to do lil shit for him. Just then shit started adding up. Sam disappearing all of a sudden, the DEA knowing the deal was going down and later knowing what buttons controlled hidden compartments in Reese's vehicles all began to make sense.

Spewing, "Fuck you," as I passed Sam's punk ass, I couldn't believe he turned state on us. My attorney, Mr. Epstein, came in to see me and told me what the case was. Sam had been the state's confidential informant for the past two years. What it all boiled down to was that he had given Reese up for immunity. Mr. Epstein read off the charges against me and told me what kind of time I was facing. I had federal charges such as tax evasion, trafficking, money laundering and conspiracy, against me. In total I had about 12 federal charges against me and was looking at 25 to life.

"What are my chances of being found guilty?" I asked Mr. Epstein.

"Honestly, Ikeda, the odds are against you," he said. "You guys have been under surveillance for a while. Had you not known about the odds and ends of the operation, you would have had a better chance at beating most of the charges. There is a good chance you're going to do some mandatory time."

I couldn't help but to break down at the idea of giving birth to my baby behind bars and without Reese by my side.

For the week I was in jail I was denied any contact or visitation with the exception of Mr. Epstein.

Reese and I wrote to each other. I knew he was worried about me and stressing about the baby. I was due in court for a pre trial hearing. Reese was my co-defendant, but we weren't scheduled the same day. I wept quietly as I stood there alone in the courtroom while my charges, along with the mandatory sentencing, were read. Feeling as though my life was ending, I passed out as Judge Guzman read my sentencing date.

When I came to, a rapid pain was shooting through my thighs, stomach and vaginal area. Feeling like a fire was engulfing me, I was rushed to Ben Taubb Medical Center where my baby daughter was declared stillborn.

Maybe it was God's way of punishing me for my lifestyle. Maybe it was just meant to be and written in the books to happen. The attorney let me know that Reese had taken the ordeal hard, withdrawing himself and not talking to anyone or accepting any visitor. I knew the pain he was feeling. I knew he felt that he was responsible and was beating himself up. That's just how my boo was. I knew 'cause he was my other half, as I was his.

Months passed and I was found guilty of all counts against me. I was offered a three to five flat sentence in a minimum-security facility if I turned state against my man. I turned down the offer and told them to go to hell. In turn I received 171 years without the possibility if parole. Reese received life without the possibility of parole. I guess it's true, love overcomes all. Reese and I knew the price of playing the game of *hustler* when we began. Even with all ending like this, the two of us serving mad time, you still can't knock the hustle.

I was freed on a technicality 18 months ago. The Prosecutors couldn't prove I was directly involved and the arresting officer failed to read me my Miranda rights. So after serving only 22 months of a 171-year sentence, I was released.

Reese and I are still loving each other. I'ma hold strong as he does his bid. I'm the Bonnie to his Clyde. I opened shop and did what I had to do to survive. I'm attending the University of Houston where I'm working on getting my Masters in Legal Administration. I visit my baby's, Amiyah, grave as often as I can, which is normally once or twice a week. The rest of Reese's family makes sure I'm okay and that Reese has what he needs. Through the grapevine I heard that Sam mysteriously ended up with one to the dome. I guess that's what happens when you cheat in *the game*.

****

Kenya I. Moses is a 26-year-old mother of two. She is originally from Louisiana but presently resides in Paterson, New Jersey. She's been writing poetry for about 15 years and is a true lover of gangsta novels.

POPPED CHERRY
Joylynn M. Jossel

"Where the fuck are my boys?" Dollar thought to himself as he held Cartel and his two dudes at gunpoint. The four of them, each with their own degree of fear, stood timorous in the middle of Woody's Garage. Satan and his advocates were probably taking bets on whose heart was beating the fastest.

"These niggaz are loyal at entertaining us," Satan most likely snickered with pride.

Dollar nervously handled the black semi automatic as he aimed it directly at Cartel's head. Beads of sweat expelled from Cartel's forehead and could be heard hitting the cement ground of the garage like water droplets from a leaky faucet in the middle of the night.

A bullet had already escaped the barrel of Dollar's gun and whirled pass Tone's, one of Cartel's dudes, dome. Dollar had ordered them all to stand idle with their hands in the air. When Tone dropped one hand to scratch an itch on his nose, Dollar had to fire off a warning shot to let them know he meant business. The bullet found its way through a can of red paint that was sitting on a work shelf behind where the three men were standing. The can bleed red paint that oozed in sync with the trail of piss that was running down Tone's leg.

Dollar kept at a couple of arms length in distance from the men. He had seen enough action movies to know that the closer he was to the perspective victims without pulling the trigger, the more chance he had in housing the bullet in his own skull. The slightest flinch made by any of the three dead men standing ignited a reflex causing Dollar to simultaneously point the gun at each one of them. Back and forth from one to the next the gun steered.

The steamy stream of sweat occupying Dollar's hand made it a challenge to keep a firm grip on the gun. It soon became the weight of a canon. Dollar was squeezing his hand so tight around the gun that his nails punctured through the flesh of the pit of his palm. The stinging from the sweat hitting the open cuts made Dollar feel as though he was holding a fistful of bumblebees.

He couldn't help but wonder if Cartel and his dudes could smell the fear rising from up out of his pores. If not smell it, he wondered if they could see it rising like the vapor from a hot apple pie fresh out of the oven. Dollar had on his game mask over top of his pusillanimous face, but he still couldn't help but wonder if they could sense that he was just a pup at this robbin' niggaz shit. He stood before these unlawful tycoons like a sixteen-year-old pussy that had never been fucked.

"Where the fuck are my boys?" might as well have been tattooed on Dollar's forehead. He gazed over at the door a thousand times hoping to see them walk through it. Through Dollar's actions, Cartel and his two dudes expected the company of some uninvited guest real soon. Not soon enough for Dollar though. *"Maybe they can't find the garage?"* Dollar thought. *"Maybe they bullshiting around or arguing or something. I know they didn't bitch out. Naw, them niggaz just lost."*

Woody's Garage sat in a back alley off of Cleveland Avenue near a housing project known as Windsor Terrace in Columbus, Ohio. The black and orange *Sorry We're Closed* sign was a permanent fixture on the building's entrance door. The garage was regularly closed to unsolicited guest but always welcomed those with an appointment. Cartel, who ran a shiesty hustle out of the Garage, had penned in Dollar to meet with him that night. Dollar had driven in from Indiana in order for Cartel to make good on a transaction in the matter of a stolen vehicle.

Cartel was the mastermind behind a car theft ring. Not so much a mastermind as a man who managed to induce some young and dumb thugs into doing his dirty work. For less than a 20% cut of the street market value, these wanna be Dons would heist whichever vehicle was Cartel's flavor of the month. The other 80% must have gone towards what is known as administrative fees. Little niggaz didn't care though. A quick grand for their misdeed satisfied their adolescent appetites for life's material wants. If they weren't lazy and put in work every week, a quick grand averaged out to $52,000 a year. How the fuck they never managed to make a come up out of the hood was beyond insane. Dollar was determined to get up out of the ghetto and he planned on taking his brother and his mother with him.

While growing up in Gary, Indiana, Dollar watched his mother leave their one bedroom apartment for work at six o'clock in the morning and not to return until after ten o'clock at night. At one point or another she had managed to work for every fast food chain in America just to keep a leaky cracked roof over Dollar's and his younger brother's heads. On most occasions she would work at two and three joints at a time. Once, she got herself fired from Burger King because she kept referring to the kid's meal as a Happy Meal.

In spite of all the long work hours, Dollar's mother made sure that she did everything she could to see to it that he and his brother did well in school. It didn't matter how late she got in at night. Going over homework was a must. Seeing their mother work so hard was probably what had kept the two latchkeys kids out of trouble the duration of their youth. The last thing they wanted their mother to have to worry with was two bad ass boys. She already had to tolerate the white man's franchise all day long.

When Dollar was about ten years old, one night his mother didn't come home from work as expected. They couldn't afford a phone in their household so it's not like she could have called to give a reason behind her tardiness. Dollar was too afraid to go out and use the corner store pay phone to call the police. He feared the boys in blue might take him and his brother away and put his mother in jail for leaving them alone in the apartment. It was after midnight when his mother's sister, the boy's Aunt Charlene, came knocking on the apartment door. Dollar scooted the footstool over to the door to make sure that the voice declaring it was that of his Aunti Charlene's actually was.

Their aunt ordered the boys to gather some clothes and their toothbrushes because they would be staying with her for a couple of nights. Come to find out, their mother had an accident while running after the city bus and had been taken to the hospital by ambulance. Their Aunti comforted the boys by assuring them that it wasn't a serious injury and that their mother had probably only sprang her ankle.

Apparently, Dollar's mother had been a little late leaving her first job. As she headed down the street to catch the bus to her second gig, with only one more block to hike, she could hear the roar of the bus trailing up behind her. While running to the bus stop, the edge of her shoe skid a small pebble. She skipped a step, losing her balance, and came down with all of her weight on her right leg. She could hear a crack and felt a horrendous jolt of pain. She cried out in agony while lying on the sidewalk unable to move. After an ambulance was called and it transported her to the hospital, she learned that she had broken her ankle and busted up her kneecap.

His mother, nor did Dollar, ever dream in a million years that ultimately she would end up losing her entire right leg. Initially her toe had to be amputated and shortly thereafter so did her foot. Dollar was too young to grasp all of the details but he knew it had something to do with his mother neglecting a prior diagnosis of diabetes.

After the initial amputations, only a few months went by before Dollar's mother ended up losing her entire right leg. The government had the nerve to deny her social security two times before finally giving in to her claim. Aunt Charlene had convinced Dollar's mother to hire a lawyer, who in the end would receive a third of the retroactive benefits awarded. By then Dollar's mom could barely keep toilet paper on the roll. Seeing his mother in such a helpless condition murdered Dollar's spirit.

Dollar and his brother did everything they could in an attempt to become instant millionaires. They had yard sales that consisted of their broken toys and old clothing. They even set up a lemonade stand. There was nothing more rigorous for Dollar and his brother than setting up a lemonade stand in the projects and trying to sell lemonade to people just as broke as they were.

Everybody wanted a free cup, didn't have any money period or wanted to use food stamps.

As the two grew older, Dollar's brother decided that he would use his mind to gain riches. His mother had always hammered the importance of education in her boys, s o Dollar's younger brother set his mind to acing school and earning a free college education. That is exactly what he would end up doing. His dream was to become a doctor some day enabling him a plentiful income in order take care of his family.

To Dollar, college was four years he didn't have time to fool around with. College meant four more years of being broke. He decided that, like his younger brother, he too would use his mind. He would use his mind to think up a way to get fast loot.

Growing up in the projects and watching his mother shuffle from gig to gig, Dollar learned at an early age that everybody has to have some hustle in order to conquer life. Be it legit or otherwise, everybody has to have a hustle. It's the only way to survive.

Dollar came to the conclusion that he would let the love of money put its mojo on mankind. He would let the bankers bank, the pimps pimp and the teachers teach. He would let the plumbers plumb, the thieves steal, the hoes fuck and the ballers ball. Then he'd catch them slippin' and rob all of them blind. This resolution is how Dollar would find himself with a firearm aimed at three men.

Dollar portrayed himself to Cartel to be this eighteen-year-old kid from Indiana who jacked cars on a regular. Dollar had never stolen a bike let alone an automobile. He convinced Cartel that he could present him with a white Benz with gold trimming and honey leather seats. He ran down his bogus resume of a life of car jacking and won Cartel's greedy ass over.

Cartel couldn't wait to brand Dollar as one of his little accomplices of the good life. He never saw this set up coming. He only saw dollar signs.

The garage door suddenly flinging open would finally bring about some relief to Dollar. It was Tommy and Ralphie. Dollar's backup had finally arrived.

"Where the fuck y'all been?" Dollar gritted through his teeth. "Eleven o'clock p.m. muthafuckas...eleven o'clock p.m."

"Nigga we here now and that's all that matters," Tommy replied pulling out a 9MM with Ralphie close behind doing the same. Tommy and Ralphie each stood next to Dollar like statutes with their leather glove covered hands gripping the guns pointed at the designated targets.

"Strip," Ralphie yelled to Cartel and his dudes as he walked towards them. The three of them looked at each other with their hands still in the air.

"Did you hear my boy?" Tommy asked. "Strip. Take your clothes off. What y'all niggaz waiting on, for us to throw y'all some dollar bills or some shit? Take all your clothes off and put them in a pile in front of you. Start by removing those pieces from y'alls holsters one at a time. Don't try no funny shit either."

The three men slowly removed the guns they were carrying from the holsters they had either around their calf or their waist. Thank God Dollar hadn't slipped up and given them a chance to go for their shit. They laid them on the ground as Ralphie walked over and stood behind them with his gun to their backs. They peeled their clothes off slowly. After a few minutes they stood butt ass naked displaying only their jewelry.

"Trick or treat," Ralphie said as he stood before them with a brown paper bag he had removed from his jacket pocket and popped open. "Check all that shit in."

The men began to drop watches, necklaces and rings into the bag. They removed their diamond earrings and bracelets as well. That's what they get for trying to show off. Bling Blingin' and ching chingin' was one of the tactics Cartel used to lure his employees into his ring. He wanted to show them the things they could end up owning. The bling ching to the baby thugs was the dead raw fish being thrown to the killer whale to calm him into doing tricks. Dollar had studied Cartel and his crew's game like it was a textbook. He knew their steelo and was prepared to get paid off of their vanity.

Tommy went through every pocket of the pile of clothes on the floor. Some contained money clips filled with one hundred dollar bills. There were loose wads of money also. The clothes were thrown to Dollar after they had been successful raided by Tommy.

Dollar balled the clothes up under his armpit and headed towards the exit door. Tommy scooped up anything that slipped from Dollar's clutches.

"I want all of you to count 100 Mississippi's before you even consider moving. I mean your dicks better not even get hard and start to rise or you're dead," Dollar shouted. "Start counting now!"

The three men counted aloud as Dollar, Tommy and Ralphie looked around making sure they hadn't overlooked anything of value. Ralphie spotted what looked like a couple of cell phones laying on the worktable behind the men and fell behind Dollar and Tommy to go back and retrieve them.

Ralphie picked up the cell phones and as he skimmed over the worktable Cartel looked to make sure that Dollar and Tommy's backs were still towards them. They were pretty much walking out of the door at that point. After confirming such, Cartel ran towards Ralphie in attack mold. His two dudes were right behind him. They had only gotten to 20 Mississippi, but this was their chance to beat Ralphie down for his gun, pump lead into Dollar and Tommy and get their money, jewelry, clothing and ego's back.

Dollar had held the door for Tommy to come through and Tommy had done the same for Ralphie. When Tommy discovered that Ralphie wasn't there, Tommy looked just in time to see the three men dashing towards Ralphie. Why not one of the parade of bullets Tommy let off hit Ralphie was unexplainable, but Cartel and his dudes dropped dead like flies.

"Whoa Wee...Hell yeah!" Ralphie shouted as he looked at the three bodies piled upon top of one another. "Didn't my boy tell y'all fools not to move until you got to 100? It pays to stay in school. You learn how to count and that shit would have kept your asses alive."

"Let's get the fuck out of here," Dollar shouted as he snatched the cell phones from Ralphie and threw them on the ground. "Who the fuck was you going to call man? We got bodies on our shit now and for what, some fucking cell phones?"

"Fuck," Tommy yelled still in shock at the sight of the dead bodies, one still grasping for one more chance at life. Tommy began to wipe down the place with a shirt she had in her hands. She wanted to make sure she didn't leave a single smudge of evidence behind.

Tommy threw Dollar the car keys and all three of them ran out of the garage to the rental car that Dollar had some chic back home cop for them. They sped off leaving nothing but tire tracks and three dead men full of bullet holes.

"That could have been my ass laying back there fucking around with you too late ass niggaz," Dollar said as he consistently looked in his rear view mirror for any sign of the police or someone following them. "I ought to fuck y'all up."

"Did you see that man?" Ralphie asked still hype from the gunfire. "Tommy laid them son of a bitches out flat. Holy Shit. I could hear those caps popping they asses...Pop,pop,pop!"

"Tommy Gun to the rescue," Dollar said. "But I still ought to beat the both of y'alls asses for showing up late. Ralphie, you need to take your own advice about staying in school. You learn how to tell time."

"You need to quit talking to me like I'm some dude," Tommy, who was sitting in the passenger seat, said removing the baseball cap from her head allowing her jailhouse braids to fall down her back.

"Awe, you know you like one of the guys, Tommy, so quit trying to play all sensitive," Dollar said lightly punching her on her shoulder with his fist. "I consider you to be like one of the boys."

"Well, I got the goods to prove I'm all woman," Tommy said rolling her eyes.

"Don't talk like that. I'm not trying to visualize you with a pussy," Ralphie yelled from the back seat as him and Dollar began to laugh.

"Both of you can go to hell. This pussy done saved y'alls life a many of times."

"See there," Ralphie said getting an attitude. "That's why I hate when a muthafucka save your life a couple of times. They think you always owe them something. They be throwing it up in your face and shit."

"Quit acting like a bitch," Dollar said. "We got over $200,000 in cash and prizes and you back there crying."

"Man, I'm just saying," Ralphie added.

"Well, don't just say shit. Tommy done had your back since she was whooping niggaz on the playground for your ass. You do owe her."

Tommy looked back at Ralphie and stuck her tongue out at him.

"Well," Ralphie said lightweight under his breath. "Just let a muthafucka die next time."

The three jumped onto the interstate that would take them back home to Indiana. This was their first stick-up and it looked like it would pay off well. It was the end of a life of have nots and the beginning of a life of having it all.

All Dollar wanted to do with his share was take it home to his mother. He hadn't thought of the lie he would tell her as to where the money had come from. If she knew what her baby was doing, if the lack of will to live didn't kill her, the truth surely would. She had raised her boys to never put themselves in a position to encounter any sort of brush with the law. Until now, Dollar had done his mother proud.

Tommy and Ralphie had engaged in some criminal activity before their stint with Dollar, but nothing of this caliber. Tommy had a hustle flipping bank accounts. She would get people to give her their check books and ID. She would make spurious deposits into the accounts right before the weekend. She would then spend the entire weekend on a shopping spree writing one bad check after another. She would purchase jewelry, clothing, food and electronics. She would use Ralphie on the instances when the owner of the checks was a man.

If the owner of the checking account was light skinned Ralphie could get away with it by wearing a baseball cap. But being a white dude with red hair, it was hard for Ralphie to pass as a brotha. Nonetheless, he and Tommy would flip and split.

After all had been said and done Tommy would pay the collaborator up to fifteen hundred dollars, depending on how much dirt she got away with over the weekend. Sometimes the collaborator would have special merchandise requests and Tommy would just shop for them in lieu of giving them money. Come Monday morning the collaborator was to report their checkbook missing to their financial institution. By that time Tommy and Ralphie had damaged the account severely.

When Dollar came up with the idea for the three of them to start robbing people, Tommy and Ralphie were game. They were ready for a real hustle. Dollar, on the other hand, had just gotten his criminal cherry popped with the Cartel job. He had successfully robbed three occupational criminals. It wasn't in the plan to see them dead, but circumstance always determines the outcome.

No longer a pup, on that night, July 4, 1995, Dollar became a dawg. Him, Ralphie and Tommy had set the stage to become career hustlers. They had no intentions of stealing petty stuff or holding up liquor stores. Their hustle would be taking advantage of and profiting from other people's hustle. They would make a life for themselves by straight out robbin' muthafuckas.

***

Over a two week period, Dollar, Tommy and Ralphie each either took the valuables they got off of Cartel and his dudes to the pawn shop or sold them on the street. Once all the material items had been transformed into cash, the three split the proceeds of the robbery. The three walked away with $63,000 each.

For his mother's sake, Dollar pretended to be going to work everyday. He would actually be hanging out over Tommy's house all day or with some chic on the block that had noticed his new sophisticated demeanor. Dollar had to let his mother think he was out making legitimate money so that she would take the $500 a week he gave her. He went behind her back and paid off every debt she had so that the bill collectors would let her live in peace. He paid her utility bills down including the excessive figures in her PIPP accounts. She never seemed to pay close enough attention to the billing statements to even notice their depletion.

Dollar deposited a lump sum into his little brother's bank account. Until then it had only had a balance of $203.52, of which he had earned from his paper route. The stipulation was that the money wasn't to be touched until his little brother graduated high school and went off to college.

Dollar wasn't worried about filling his own pockets with his profit from the Cartel robbery. He was planning out heists in neighboring cities and states that would give birth to his come up. He would get his, no doubt, but first thing was first. He had to look out for his family.

Dollar had become the man of the house at the ripe age of four years old, therefore he felt it was his duty to take care of his family. At the age of four is when his daddy abandoned them never to be heard from again. Word on the street was that he got into the pimping game and mastered it. Dollar's father treated pimping like it was a franchise. He supposedly let one of his partners man his hoes while he went to Detroit, Michigan to set up shop and eventually to Ohio. Over a period of time every hoe in the Midwest would want his name tattooed on their pussy.

The authority of having the power over another human beings body went to his head. He became one of the most crucial cats in the game. Bitches, and his so-called assistants, feared fucking up his money. Stories about Dollar's father and the pimp game were eventually over shadowed by success stories of the new entrepreneurial opportunity, slinging crack.

Dollar figured that the hustle in him was the only thing he had inherited from that sorry excuse for a man known as his father. Dollar was determined to do for his family what his father didn't. He would hustle, but only death or jail would keep him from taking care of his family.

Tommy, on the other hand, bought her a little house right outside the hood in order to get the hell away from her family. Her humble abode wasn't in the suburbs or anything but it wasn't suspicious either and that's all that mattered. Tommy didn't want anybody sniffing around trying to put the pieces together of her slight come up. She had to get a little job bar tending on weekends to prove she had an income in order to keep Uncle Sam out of her business. The house wasn't much, but it was better than the two-bedroom house she had been living in with her Mother, her mother's boyfriend and her Sister and her two kids.

Ralphie was tricking his new money with every hoe that got a whiff of it. Rumor was that Ralphie was snorting up the other portion of his cut.

Just as easy as the money came, it was going. The three couldn't resist spoiling themselves with some named brand fancies such as shoes, clothing and jewels.

Before Dollar could start working on setting up their next job, the police were beginning to link the trio to the killings in Columbus. Eyewitnesses had reported seeing the rental car leaving the scene of the crime. The plates were traced back to budget car rental where the vehicle had been borrowed.

A couple of detectives made their way to Indiana to question Bubbles, the girl who rented the car from Budget for Dollar. They shook her up so bad, threatening to charge her as an accessory and put her daughter in a foster home, that she gave them everything on Dollar except for his blood type.

When the detectives arrived at Dollar's mother's apartment she told them that her boy was at work. She told them that they would be wasting their time with any questions they might have had for him because her boy was a good boy and didn't even as much as hang out with a bad crowd.

The detectives waited outside the apartment until they spotted Dollar walking up the porch. They immediately approached him and asked him to come with them for some questioning. Dollar obliged and spent a total of 19 hours and 13 minutes being interrogated.

In the meantime, Dollar's fingerprints were being matched to those found on the cell phones in Woody's Garage. Once informed of this breakthrough it was time for Dollar to start talking.

The detective suspected that Dollar hadn't pulled off the robbery solo. No way did some young punk with no street respect take Cartel and two of his dudes down alone. The detective wanted the names of Dollar's accomplices. If Dollar didn't tell he would go down for a triple homicide. He would very well spend the rest of his life in jail. If Dollar did give up the name of the trigger man, he would go down as an accessory and walk away with a smack on the wrist as a first time offender. That was the deal.

Although Tommy was the one who actually pulled the trigger, Dollar knew that Ralphie would go down hard. Unlike Dollar, Ralphie wasn't in a position to be making any type of deal for himself. He had several strikes on his record that would guarantee him time in the slammer.

To Dollar, it didn't make sense for all three of them to go down. Besides, he couldn't see himself snitchin' on his partners and he especially couldn't picture Tommy spending the rest of her life in prison. He knew, without a muster seed of doubt, that if the shoe were on the other foot, both Tommy and Ralphie would do the same for him.

Dollar had learned quiet a few things about hustling. No matter the nature of the hustle, every hustle has the same rules. One can only get down with people whom they have 100% trust in. The clique has to be willing to die for the hustle and do time for the hustle. Dollar was willing to do just that...and so he did.

****

Joylynn M. Jossel is the author of *Please Tell Me If The Grass Is Greener*, *World On My Shoulders*, *Twilight Moods* (Daydreaming at Night) and *The Root of All Evil*. Joy is currently completing her Triple Crown Publication, *Dollar Bill*. "Popped Cherry" is the first chapter of the forthcoming novel *Dollar Bill* and is merely an appetizer of the literary feast it will bring to its readers. Expect the unexpected on every page.

BORN
Shere Washington

I guess some will say I was doomed from the start. Well, my start was swimming through my father who was filled with Wild Irish Rose and Heroin. He had just finished his gig at some local jazz joint were amateurs got together to act like they were the temptations, or even better, the O'Jays.

His girlfriend for the night, a.k.a. my mother, was at the bar drinking Rum and Coke thinking she was the bomb because her man was the finest one in the place. All of 15-years-old, with no street training, she stole her mama's stockings and pearls and headed for the big time, or so she thought.

Well, her story is pretty much the same as any other black girl raised by a southern family who moved to New York at a young age. As John Potter, my father who was better known as Suede, moved through the crowd of smoke towards my mother, there were gawking women and men. My mother could feel her heart swell up, and being as vain as she was at that age, she wanted the world to see just how bad she was.

Let's dance she said pulling him by the hand to the dance floor. Just then a woman came out of no where and screamed at my mother, ordering her to get away from her man. Before my mother could respond, the woman slashed her in the face with a straight blade razor. With all the blood and commotion, she passed out and later woke up in a dark room. She heard voices and saw shadows but could not make out the faces. Finally she noticed Suede and called out to him.

Suede raced to my mother's side and said, "Don't worry, Red (her given name is Ann, but she liked to be called by her nickname). I took care of everything. I spoke to your mama and she's very worried, but I told her I would take care of you. And that girl who did this to your face, baby...well, let's just say that you won't be seeing her again. The doctor says you will be just fine."

Suede continued as my mother simply laid there nodding.

"You only needed 26 stitches. With a little face make up you will hardly notice," he said rubbing her hand.

Suede took Red to his house. All Red could do was cry. The pain was unbearable. What the doctor gave her to ease the pain was useless. Because of her age, he didn't want to give here anything stronger, so Suede, being the dope fiend that he was, turned her on to heroin. After the first shot that he gave her, Red laid in the bed feeling no pain. Suede decided to take her body. Red tried to say "no" and push him away. She was a good girl at heart and believed in marriage before sex, but the dope had her so fucked up that she couldn't fight Suede off.

She screamed the words "no", but Suede was not trying to hear that. He tore into little Red like a lion. She screamed from pain and passion as she laid there becoming addicted and becoming a woman.

A product of rape, I was conceived, and that's only the beginning. I was born at the local hospital weighing only three pounds and five ounces. My dear mother hid her pregnancy and fed me dope. My grandpa saw to it that Suede married my mother by way of a shotgun, but by then she was already seven months pregnant and malnutrition. But by marrying my mother off, my grandpa didn't see it as his problem anymore.

My father was somewhat of a hustler via music and dope, and my mother, well let's just say that she wasn't the doting type. I stayed hungry all of the time. I remember as early as age five, me and Red going to the supermarket and her putting meat in my pants. All I could remember thinking was, "boy I am gonna eat good tonight," only to watch her sell it on the street.

"Don't look at me like that," Red would say. "You still have those cans of sardines in your pocket."

The only thing I could say good about my childhood is that I did dress nice thanks to my mother's boosting skills. Red would always take me with her on her stealing sprees and I too became a pro at it. I always kept up with the latest fashions. By the age of ten I was reading Vogue Magazine. As a matter of fact, that's all I was reading. My mother didn't encourage school so I only did what

I needed to do in order to get by. All Red was worried about was copping her next hit.

Things started getting real bad when Suede was diagnosed with full blown AIDS. He became too sick to go out and cop, so he wasn't making any money. Red started selling her body to get a hit, but hardly anybody would pay a decent dollar to a cut up face whore with tracks all over her body. Red had even worn out her vagina vein, so eventually she would resort to sucking dick for a three dollar fix. I had even witnessed her take it from behind to get a good fix. Red didn't hide anything from me. If I just happen to be in her presence when shit went down, then it was done right in front of me. I guess that's what Red called *keeping it real.*

Someone getting shot, stabbed, fucked, or sticking a needle in their vein was as normal to me as little girls playing with dolls. Some people ask how all of this is possible in this day and age of welfare and Child Protective Services. I'm here to tell you that there are major cracks in the system, and it just so happens that I fell through all of them. I guess those two little boys found in the basement malnutritioned, and one dead, is proof that the system is anything but flawless.

I suppose all was good because no matter what dope den we happened to be living in, I would take it upon myself to attend school regularly, until about the eight grade anyway. That's when Suede died. His body was so decomposed that the cause of death couldn't be pinpointed.

Sued had been staying with his brother last I had heard. Then one day, out of the blue, Red and me went to see how he was doing. That's when that mean old brother of his told us he had kicked him out a month prior to our visit. This was the same uncle who finally took my virginity at the age of eight. Before turning eight he would tell me that anything younger than eight wasn't ripe, so he would make me suck his dick until snot came out. But just as soon as I became *of age,* according to his standards, he would prep me for sex by opening my legs and licking my private in order to get it all wet with his spit. Then he would put it in. I will never forget that day and all of the pain I endured.

I told my mother about what my uncle did to me and she got so mad that I thought she was gonna kill him. Instead, she demanded money from him to keep him out of jail.

Once my mother knew that I wasn't a virgin anymore she came up with this plan to pimp me out. It started out small.

"Just show it to him," she would order me to do.

All of the men had these nasty little worm looking penises. It was disgusting. Finally it became "Just close your eyes and suck," Red would say. Then it became "Just open your legs damn'it. Can't you see I'm sick? Do you want me to die like your father?"

I would close my eyes and follow Red's orders. She would turn away, not watching her daughter perform sexual acts. When I was finished the men would pay her and we would pay a visit to the dope man.

That pretty much sums up the beginning years of my life. Red did eventually managed to get social services to get her an apartment right in the middle of the ghetto. Our home sweet home was yet another dope den.

I had my own room, which I bought a lock for because I was still boosting clothes and I didn't want dope fiends in my shit. And besides, my room was my only escape. It was where I would draw clothes and put different colors together. Shit, I loved that stuff. When I showed Red some of the outfits I had drawn she sarcastically said, "Oh please, Miss Hollywood."

Ms. Dismore, a teacher at my high school, loved the way I dressed and said that I should study fashion and design. That was my hope, but there was no time 'cause we had to get money for the next fix and that is what life was all about. I was the daughter of a dope fiend. I was all Red had. Life was hell, but I loved my mother no matter what she did. She was all I had and still, after all of this, I would not trade her for anything in the world.

One day, while in my room cutting out fashion ideas and thinking of the stores that were in the new mall that had just been built out east, Red knock on the door.

"I need you to do me a favor," she said signaling me to follow her into the living room.

I went into the living room and it was empty except for this woman who looked and smelled like a man.

"What do you want?" I asked Red.

"Well, baby, my friend here wants to spend some time with you alone. And look, she gave us $350.00. She wants me to leave you two alone. It's okay though, 'cause I know her good. I will be back. I'm just gon' go get something to eat and buy you something nice at that new mall.

"Ma, don't spend all your money on junk," I said. "Buy us some food. Don't forget Kool-Aid."

"Okay, baby," Red said hurrying out of the door. "You two have a nice time. Goodbye,"... and she was gone.

I looked over at this butch and said to myself, "What harm could this be?"

Then I said to the butch, sounding like a pro as I pulled down my pants, "Okay, come suck me off. That's what you want, right, baby...this pussy. Well come and get it, daddy."

The butch got up, walked over to me and slapped the taste right out of my mouth. I was shocked and mad as hell. I tried to attack her but I was no match. She picked me up and slammed me down onto the floor. I was dazed and out of it for a few minutes. The next thing I knew I was butt naked and this butch had tied me up. She removed her coat and underneath it she wore nothing but leather. From her inner coat pocket she pulled out a whip.

"Oh my God," I cried. "What are you gonna do with me? My mama is going to kill you when she finds out what you are doing."

The butch laughed, insisting that Red already knew about what would be going down. The butch strapped on the biggest dildoe I had ever seen before. It had to be 12 inches long. I begged her not to use it on me.

"I'm only 15," I pleaded.

"That makes it all the better," she said whipping me with the whip until I began to bleed. Once she saw the blood she stuck it inside of me, but not in my vagina. The pain was unbearable. I passed out. When I woke up Red was sitting there with buckets of Chinese food. She was as high as a kite. She had cleaned me up and put me to bed. On my nightstand was a tall glass of red Kool-Aid.

Red apologized endlessly.

"She said she just wanted to be with you. Baby, I had no idea she was going to do this to you," Red said as she witnessed my laying there in pain.

I didn't say a word to her. This was the first time my mother would ever offer me drugs, in fact, she insisted on it. I refused. I was never gonna fuck with drugs, not after what I saw they could do to a person. I would rather just deal with the pain.

I laid in that bed hemmed up for a few days. I thought about my life and my mother's life. I was gonna get us out of this shitty ass lifestyle one way or another.

I laid up in bed for days. I didn't leave my room and never returned to school. It wasn't too long before my mother was trying to get me out of the bed to get back to work 'cause she was getting too weak to even suck dick any more. She needed at least a bundle to keep her from being sick and another bundle to get her high…and it was all about the high. So once again I got up and hit the streets for money.

That's what I am, a child of the streets. I hooked in places you wouldn't think of like the mall, movie theater parking lots, the hardware stores and other place where I felt I could lure money. I couldn't work the local tracks because they were ran by pimps and there was too much competition from the regular hookers. Besides, police were everywhere and I couldn't risk going to jail. Who would take care of Red? So after a day's work I would cop two bundles and head on home.

While Red took care of herself, I withdrew to my room and designed clothes, matched colors and imagined going to fashion school just like Ms. Dismore said I should. But before I knew it I was interrupted by the shouting of Red and one of her dope friends.

"Run some cold water," one shouted.

"Fill it up with cold water," the other one cried. "Mike done gone and overdosed."

This was very common in my up bringing and I knew just what to do. When I heard their calls I didn't panic. I raced into the bathroom and filled the tub with cold water. I helped them place Mike's lifeless body into the tub in an upright position. I started slappin' him as hard as I could. If need be, I was prepared to give him mouth to mouth. I had learned that technique in my eighth grade gym class. I had paid close attention because I thought it might be useful just in case I ever had to save Red. It had come in handy a time or two.

In this case though, the cold water worked. Mike came to and started puking everywhere. I was used to this scene, especially since Red always throws up before and after she shoots up, so I started cleaning up the vomit.

The next day while I was out working the streets I passed a sign that read, "Enroll Now in the Fashion Institute-Loans Available if Qualified". I wrote everything down and stuck it in my pocket.

The night was slow and it started getting late. I knew Red would be up soon waiting for her medicine so I decided to call it a night. On my way home I passed a store that had a "Help Wanted" sign up. It was this fancy clothing store that I had always admired. I took a deep breath and got the nerve to go inside and inquire about the job. The position was for a mannequin and window dresser. There would be some sales along with some customer service tasks involved. The only problem was that I had no high school diploma. I knew math and how to read, but the position required at least a high school diploma. There was no way I could go back to high school. Maybe I could go to night school or something to get a G.E.D.

I had already wasted enough time fooling around with that job and its requirements. I had to get home and check on Red. She gets crazy if I get home too late.

As I walk around the corner I notice police cars and a ambulance outside of our apartment. I ran towards the action thinking, "Oh God, not my mother."

When I saw Red's face as she walked down the apartment steps I was so relieved.   What I hadn't noticed was her cuffed hands behind her back.

Behind Red was a police officer and behind him two emergency medical technicians were carrying a body out on a stretcher. I made my way through the crowd and ran towards my mother who was almost out of control. The officer continued ushering my mother down the steps and into a police car as I inquired the entire time as to what was going on.

I informed the officer that I was Red's daughter and he told me to stand aside, that someone would tell me what was going on shortly.

By this time my head was spinning out of control. I tried to enter my apartment but crime scene tape prevented me from doing so. The body, the blood, the detectives and camera clicking was all overwhelming, and Red, my poor mother was going to be sick. She would die down at that precinct if she didn't get a fix.

Eventually I found out that Mike, the guy who overdosed a while back, was at our apartment getting high with Red. Mike accused Red of stealing drugs from him and they started arguing. According to Red, he attacked her and she ran to the kitchen and got a knife to defend herself. She stabbed him 14 times, killing him.

While in jail Red started to go through severe withdraw. She was transported from the jailhouse to the hospital. After a few days in the hospital she was to appear in court where she would then remain at the county. At least she had somewhere to go. I had nothing, no home, no friends, no family and no Red. What was I going to do?

I walked around for what seemed like hours. The police finally allowed me in the apartment to get some things. I grabbed some clothes, some of my drawings and a picture of Red and me before she had lost all of her teeth.

I ended up staying at one of the dope dens that Red and I had camped out at when I was growing up. Nobody bothered me there and the place reminded me of Red.

The next morning, when I was out doing my thing, I came across a newspaper that had an article titled "The Job Core". After reading the article I asked myself, "why not?" The thing was, I needed to provide The Job Core with some information that only Red could give me.

Once I made my way to visit Red I couldn't believe my eyes. She looked better than she had looked in a long time. She told me that she felt good but had been diagnosed with both HIV and Hepatitis C. She was taking all sorts of medication including methadone. I told her about the Job Core and the information that I needed and, of course, she was unable to help me out. She didn't have my birth certificate or social security card.

On my way out I asked one of the female officers how I should go about getting the documents that I needed to provide to Job Core. She broke it down telling me that I needed to get this from here and that from there. After doing just that I obtained the items I needed to submit my application. But I soon realized that I had one more problem. I didn't have an address. I got the ideal to get a P.O. Box and use that as my mailing address. I did just that and submitted the application.

One day I went to get my mail and there it was, my acceptance letter into the Job Core. I was able to get my GED, but one day what I really wanted to do was go to school and study fashion and design, but I had to take it one step at a time.

I had to get a physical and go through some minor training. After passing everything I was notified that I would be heading to Albany, New York.

How can I leave Red now that she was clean, sober and getting ready to face eight to twenty-five years for manslaughter? I couldn't abandon Red. I couldn't get on that bus to Albany, New York. There has to be another way I can make something out of my life.

On my visit with Red I told her that I wasn't going to Job Core. She was speechless. Once I told her why I wasn't going she began to cry. That was the first time I ever saw Red cry.

"After all I have put you through from the time you were conceived," Red cried, "you are still loyal to me. I am done, baby girl. You still have your life. You have to get on that bus and go. If you don't, you will end up right here with me and I don't want that. I'm sober now and I'm seeing things a lot clearer. I have been high everyday for the last 18 years and for the first time in my life I want to live and I want you to live too. You have to go."

"But, Mama. I can't Leave you," I said. "You are all I have."

"No, baby, you have Jesus. Remember when you were a little girl and we would pass the church and you would always ask me who was in the church? I'd say, Jesus is in there. Well, I grew up in the church. I never missed a Sunday until I met your father. I turned my back on the church, but Jesus didn't turn his back on me," Red said. "Take this Bible and read it every night. You go on and do what you have to do. I will be here when you get back."

"No, I can't leave you, Mama."

"Yes you can damn'it! I have done nothing for you and if I have to, I will refuse your visits. Now get up and get the hell out of here.

On the ride to Albany I opened up the tiny Bible Red had given me. I read and read and I read 'till my eyes filled with tears. Before I knew it, I found myself talking to Jesus.

"Thank you, Jesus. I didn't know you were there by my side all of this time," I said.

After completing Job Core I was off to fashion school, but prior to that achievement I lost Red to her diseases. But I am happy for her. I now know that she is in a better place. And although she thought she never did anything for me she had. She gave me the most important thing that a mother can give her child, the love of Jesus.

****

Shere Washington is a 32 year old mother of two boys ages nine and thirteen. She is an avid reader and has quite a few good stories to tell. She is currently in the process of working on a novel that is sure to blow her reader's minds. Shere resides in Uniondale, New York.

THE LETTER
Vickie Stringer

Shaniquita,

    I hope this scribe finds you in the best of health and spirits. I am writing you to find out what in the hell is going on.

    I called the house and I hear your voice pick up and you don't accept my phone calls. It has been over three months since our last visit. At mail call I don't get any mail, nothing. A nigga threw bricks at the penitentiary to take care of you and this is how you gon' do me? Are you just gon' turn your back on me and walk away like I wasn't nothin' to you? I moved you out of the projects. I took care of you and your three kids.

    Dre' said he saw you riding around flossing in my ride wit' another nigga. When I see you I am going to kick your ass. You a foul ass triflin' ass bitch. These walls can't hold me forever and when I hit them bricks, my 12 is going straight up your monkey ass. You stank ass beatch!

Dink

Shaniquita, or "*Shay*" as she was often called, dropped the letter on the table next to a stack of one hundred dollar bills and passed the blunt to her girlfriend.

"Fuck dat mark ass nigga!" she said as she continued to polish her toes while sitting on the butter soft, cream-colored leather sectional sofa. Their laughter floated through the house and echoed off the 20-foot ceiling.

"Baby, I am about to bounce," her new man said as he walked over to the side of the sofa and kissed her on the forehead. Shaniquita looked at her friend and gave her a wink of the eye.

When the two ladies were certain that they heard one of the four car garage doors close as he exited the driveway, Shaniquita picked the letter back up.

"Can you believe this motherfucker talkin' shit?" Shaniquita screamed. Her girlfriend nodded in agreement.

"How much time he got?" Girlfriend asked.

"Motherfucker got twenty years talkin' about kicking my ass," Shaniquita said sipping on her glass of Mimosa.

"Shay, how he gon' do that with twenty years," her friend asked inhaling on the blunt and resting back onto the sofa relaxing.

Shaniquita picked up her notepad and a pen and placed a devilish grin on her face.

"I am going to write that motherfucker back and when I get finish with him, he gon' be on suicide watch," Shay cracked.

"Don't do that. Girl, just ignore him."

"No, fuck dat. Remember all the times he played me and I sucked that shit up cause he was PAID. Well it is my turn to floss on his ass."

Her girlfriend shook her head, not really giving a fuck. They had been spending his stash and she was getting free Coach bags on the regular. What did she care?

Dear Dink,

Or in your case should I call you *John*? This the letter you been beggin' for. Well, let's see. It would be virtually impossible for you to kick my ass, seeing as how you will be an old and gray bastard when you come home. Your dick is so little that I doubt you could ever wear a size 12. And since I like it up the ass, the thought of a size 12 in my ass excites the hell out of me. So, please don't tease me.

Don't you know by now that I never loved you? As quiet as it was kept, I didn't even like you. And your sex was horrible. Yeah, your boys see me flossing in your shit. I am flossing they shit too. Your dude

Chris eats pussy better than you ever could, and your partner Stan's cum taste like ice cream in my mouth. You hear my voice when you call <u>your</u> phone? And after today you will hear "I got a block" on all my phones. Don't try that three-way shit either 'cause I got caller intercept. Fucker just turn homo and die.

I got your loot, you took the case, now press that bunk and do that motherfuckin' time.

You the man, remember? You that nigga, right? This pussy is yours, wrong?

You a has-been and I ain't got time for no shoulda, woulda, coulda stories. You should have stayed free. Dumb ass, nobody told you to ignore the po-po on your tail. Nobody told you to trust a crackhead mule and get set up. Certainly, nobody told you to fall in love with me.

You snooze, you lose. You did all the work, now my new man and me reap all the benefits. The best thing you could have ever done for me was get locked up. The pimp game got flipped on your ass.

Now do the best thing for yourself, get you a boyfriend, let him suck your dick and leave me the fuck along.

Oh and before I go, the baby, he ain't yours.
Wake up! You played yourself. Charge it to da game!

That Sheisty Bitch!
Shay

Dear John letters are a part of the reality of the incarcerated inmate on a daily basis. If you don't think they come, then think again. If you think your girl won't do it, think again or better yet. Ask your cellie.

Approximately six months after Dink received the letter from Shaniquita, he got a letter from his attorney notifying him that he had won his appeal. That letter also stated that he would be released in thirty days with the processing of his paper work. His first plan was to visit Shaniquita.

****

Vickie Stringer is the ESSENCE Magazine Best-Selling Author of *Let That Be The Reason*. Vickie resides in Columbus, Ohio with her son, where she is putting the finishing touches on her sophomore novel, *Imagine This*, which is the follow up to *Let That Be The Reason*. Also, look forward to her Fall 2003 Triple Crown Publication, *Death Before Dishonor*.

SWEETEST REVENGE
Thomas Long

"Local drug kingpin, Charles "Slim" Jackson, was shot five times in an attempted murder plot outside a local nightclub!"

That's what the newspaper headline read on the front page. The story goes on to talk about how the police think that the shooting was related to a long standing turf war between drug factions in East and West Baltimore. According to the article, there had been a series of recent shootings involving members of Jackson's alleged East Baltimore drug cartel, "The Get Money Clique" and members of the "Mo' Murder Posse" from West Baltimore, allegedly run by Lamont "Ice" Braxton. Although the shooting took place in front of a crowd of onlookers, the writer states that no arrests had been made in connection with this incident.

As I'm sitting in my hospital bed reading the article, my mind is steady clicking on how to get revenge on Ice for bringing me a move like this. It's been about six weeks since the shooting and I'm about to be released from the hospital. Of the five shots that hit me, only two of them did any major damage, while the rest just passed right through my flesh. One of the two more serious shots hit me in the jaw and left a permanent scar on the right side of my face. The other one hit me in the groin and the doctor had to remove one of my balls. Now they say I'm not able to have any kids. *You know this nigga gotsta to pay for that shit!*

The time in the hospital had actually worked to my advantage. In the last few months, with all the heat that this so-called beef we had with Ice and his crew had been bringing to the streets, my down time in the hospital gave us a chance to get 5-0 off of our backs for a minute. I had instructed my soldiers to lay low and not to retaliate in any way. Getting at Ice was gonna be something personal for me and I knew just how to handle this situation to put his ass on ice for real. As soon as I get home, I'm gonna set the plan in motion.

It was summertime, on a Monday morning, when I got released from the hospital. My man, Stan, came to the hospital to pick me up in a limo. That was straight ghetto fabulous without a doubt, but that's how we do. He figured that since I was the boss of the family and had survived a plot on my life, that I should send a strong message that I wasn't going nowhere anytime soon. What better way to do that than to exit the hospital in style like only a true Don is supposed to do?

As we rode and talked, I filled Stan in on the details of my plans to hit Ice. Since I would be out of commission for a while, he was the one who was going to handle putting the plan into motion. Stan was only too eager because he never liked Ice any way. With him out the way, we could move in on the west side and take over the entire city.

Just thinking about why I got shot pissed me off even more. It wasn't over no turf war like the media tried to say it was, but this whole thing went down primarily over a bitch.

See, Ice caught feelings when he found out that I was fucking his favorite stripper, Mia, who worked down at the Cathouse Club. Mia had told me how bad that Ice was trying to get at her by offering to buy her all kinds of shit just to hit that ass. I mean this dude is supposed to be a baller and he wanna knock another playa off his grind over a chic that fucks for money. The sad part about it all is that she *never* gave the nigga any pussy no matter how hard he tried or how much money he was trying to spend. ***This clown motherfucker was gonna feel me for real after this shit!***

Growing up in the streets, I knew that if I was gonna put a hit on Ice, I would have to do it in a way that it couldn't come back on me. I had to make it look like another random act of violence on the streets of Baltimore. That meant that I had to bring in outside muscle to handle the job. I had the perfect crew in mind to carry out my plan.

My New York supplier, Hector, had put me down with a hit squad that he used whenever he needed someone erased from the face of the Earth. Hector was a grimy Colombian dude who ain't take no shit, but for some reason, he took a liking to me. It might've been because I made him a lot of money and never came up short on a payment. It really didn't matter because if Hector had the right team to get the job done, then I was down to pay, no matter what the price.

This crew that Hector used to do his dirty work was well known throughout Latin America for their craftiness and discretion when carrying out a hit. They were successful in knocking off several infamous drug lords in countries like Panama, Columbia, and Mexico. What made them so unique is the fact that they were *women*. Not just average broads, but Hector said that they were five of the finest motherfucking pieces of pussy that he had ever seen.

They called themselves the Murder Mamis (Double M for short) *in* tribute to their Hispanic heritage. The fact that they were fine as hell is probably why they were so successful. No one would ever think that women this fine could be so deadly. But in the streets, things are never really what they seemed.

I had Stan go to New York to meet with Hector to make the connection with the Murder Mamis and to hit Hector off with some dough for looking out for a brother. After Stan returned to Bmore, he told me that Hector sent his regards and gave me the 411 on when to expect to meet with the MM crew in person. After all the arrangements were made, I finally got a chance to see for myself what Hector was talking about. Man, these chics were banging!

Each of the girls were around five feet seven inches with long, pretty ass hair that hung down to the middle of their backs. Their bodies were off the chains and they were finer than anything I had ever seen walking down the streets of Baltimore. On the surface, they all looked like harmless schoolgirls that didn't have a devious bone in their bodies. However, inside their disarming exterior, there lied the minds of a pack of cold-blooded killers. After talking with them and telling them about my plan, I knew that I had the right crew to handle this business for me.

The leader of the crew was named Rosita. She was the oldest looking one in the crew, seemingly in her late twenties. You could tell that she was in charge by the way all the other girls responded to her and because she was the only one asking me any questions. She told me that the price for the job would be 100 grand, with half of it due up front and the other half due once the job was complete. I agreed and told them when and where to meet Stan to pick up the deposit.

To hit Ice wasn't a hard thing to do. First of all, he wasn't the smartest cat in the world because he always had a need to be seen. If there was a big party going down in town, expect to see him there making the most noise and spending mad money. That made it so much easier to track his movements and to get the drop on him. Secondly, he had a weakness for pussy that made him an even easier target. A cat that can't control his pussy habit is as bad as a dope fiend because he'll do just about anything to get his fix. With these two things to my advantage and a pack of fine ass gangsta broads to do the job, I knew that my plan would be on time like clockwork.

The plan was for the girls to start working at the Cathouse as strippers because that's where Ice and his top soldiers always hung out on Friday and Saturday nights. Ice and his boys were famous for the after parties that they would throw with the girls from the club. They would spend mad money every weekend buying the girls out of the club to fuck. Once they got a look at these fine ass Latino sisters, ain't no way in the world that they wasn't gonna try to include them in on the fun.

After the girls had been at the club for a couple of weeks, things went down exactly the way that I had planned. At first, the girls played hard to get with Ice and his crew just to make them want them more. After they teased them with the pussy for a while, they finally agreed to do a private party with Ice and his boys at the Marriott Hotel downtown. With the stage now set, I was ready to proceed with the next part of my plan.

Ice had taken a particular liking to Rosita. She said the nigga wanted her so bad that he was willing to pay her a grand just to eat her pussy. When she told me that, I almost laughed my ass to death thinking about how much of a sucker he was. But I knew that if she got him that open, then he wouldn't be on point and expecting the drama that I was about to bring.

The party was set for that Saturday night after the girls got off from working at the club, which was two o'clock in the morning. Ice and his boys were supposed to rent out the entire penthouse floor of the hotel so that every one of his boys had his own room with one of the girls. The rooms were adjoining so it would be like one big party until any of the guys might have wanted to have some privacy. Each of the girls was supposed to get paid two grand for the night. For that price, the guys could touch, feel, suck, and fuck anything and anyway that they wanted.

When the girls arrived, Ice and his crew were already partying by the looks of the bottles of Cristal, Belvedere, and Hypnotiq laying around. You could see clouds of smoke when you entered the room from all the chronic that they had blazed up. No doubt about it, them cats were stupid high and totally out of pocket.

When the girls came in the room they were all dressed alike in black, tight body suits looking like a Spanish version of En Vogue in their heyday. They all could have passed as models on a runway. Under different circumstances, I definitely would've been trying to make one of them my wifey for sure, but tonight, they were all about business, nothing personal.

The music was blasting and the ladies got down to doing their thing. They all slowly started to undress at the same time and began to dance seductively in tune with the music. They stripped down to their g-strings and now their breasts were in plain view. Wasn't no need for any push-up bras in this room because these young, supple-breasted sistas were flawless from head to toe. At this point, Ice and his group of clowns were wide open and down for whatever.

The girls continued to do their striptease show to get them all hot and horny. That was when each of them grabbed one of Ice's boys, who were all his top lieutenants, and proceeded to give them a lap a dance of the freakiest order. After they bumped and grinded on them for about thirty minutes, each of them led one of the guys into one of the rooms. I told Rosita to make sure that she picked Ice because I wanted her to do something special with him. Ice and his boys thought that they were gonna get fucked royally. If I had my way, they would, but not in the way that they thought.

After everybody was situated in their individual rooms, the ladies got down to handling their business. They fucked Ice and his boys all night long in every which way possible until they fell asleep. If these girls fucked any way like they looked, then I know for sure that them cats got their money's worth. I know personally how freaky them Spanish broads can be, but that's another story.

The plan was for the girls to kill them all in their sleep so that they never see it coming. Each of the girls was supposed to wait until they knew for sure that the guys were knocked out completely. That wasn't hard to do considering all the drinking and smoking that they had been doing. Damn shame them fools let themselves fall right into my trap.

Once they were sleep, each of the girls was to slit their guys' throat with a razor bade. Their deaths were to be quick and painless. I gotta admit that just the thought of Ice choking on his own blood did give me a sick sense of pleasure. I chose for them to use razor blades because even though it would have left a bloody murder scene, it was easy for them to dispose of the murder weapons. Plus, if they caught them in their sleep, there would be no struggle and no noise for anybody else in the hotel to hear. My plan worked to perfection as the girls executed it with precision, no flaws.

As for Ice, after Rosita slit his throat, I had her to do something extra special for his bitch ass. I told her to cut his dick off and stick it in his mouth. That was my way of sending a message to the rest of his crew to let them know that when you think with your dick, you make a dick of yourself. Even more so, I wanted them to know that shit was gonna really be on if they tried to retaliate against my team for knocking their boss off.

I know that when the police find Ice's ass with his dick cut off, they are gonna get the laugh of a lifetime off of that shit. For some reason, homicide cops seem to develop a sick sense of humor from being on so many murder scenes. I know because one of my homies that I grew up with is a homicide detective and he done told me some crazy, but funny, stories about some of his investigations.

Once the job was complete, the girls gathered up all of their shit and got the fuck up outta there through the emergency exit. Nobody knew who they were or where they came from. These chics were for real and sure nuff lethal when they had to put their murder game down. I definitely would be using their services in the future.

"It was bloody murder at a prestigious downtown hotel; notorious drug lord, "Ice" Braxton, and four of his top lieutenants were killed. There were no witnesses or suspects reported to this brutal massacre."

That's what the newspaper read the next day on the front page. The report mentions that some unnamed source at the hotel stated that he saw five beautiful, unidentified women go up to the penthouse floor the night before the incident, but never saw them leave. I just laughed because finding them chics would be like finding a needle in a haystack, almost impossible. After Stan met them in Delaware early the next morning to pay them the second 50 grand installment, they were long gone out of the country.

I expected for the police to come and question me for this shit. That's why I made sure that I had an airtight alibi and nobody associated with me was involved with the crime. While the girls were doing their thing with Ice and his gang of pricks, I was at home watching the Roy Jones fight with a house full of family and friends. They couldn't argue with a room full of witnesses who could verify my whereabouts the night Ice was killed.

Even though the streets knew what went down, the police ain't have any evidence to charge me with anything in this case. No murder weapon, no suspects, no witnesses, and no nothing. If they tried to bring me a move, all I would do is sick my attorney, Marcus Wilson, on their ass with a quickness. Marcus was Baltimore's version of Johnnie Cochran and he loved to shine the spotlight on the police for harassing a black man. I paid him a lot of money throughout the years to keep my black ass free and it was well worth every penny.

After a few months went by and the drama from Ice's death had passed, I was now fully recuperated from my injuries. It was now time for me to proceed with the second phase of my plan to expand my empire into West Baltimore. With Ice out of the way and his death just another unsolved murder in Baltimore City, taking over his territory was piece of cake. Without Ice around, the rest of his crew were a bunch of pussies that were no match for my GMC crew. The streets were now all mine and I had the keys to city. Now that's some gangsta shit for ya ass for real!

****

Thomas Long was born and raised in the streets of Baltimore City. This up and coming author/poet has had his eyes and ears open to the harsh realities of inner city life for quite some time. His first self-published book, *Reflections of My Soul*, is an insightful collection of poetry. In his second book, *For My Sisters: 7 Relationship Tips*, the author shows his sensitive side. Thomas Long is currently working on his first full-length novel titled *The Game Done Changed*.

BROTHAS ON LOCK-DOWN
Nikki Turner

I reflect over all of the times that I've heard my brothers, cousins, or guy friends talk bad about a sistah rolling out on him while he was doing a bid. I'm a female who has a chain of older male relatives. I was raised by an "old school" mother who was nurturing to everybody. We were always going to the jailhouse to visit my brothers, uncles or cousins when I was growing up. So I had no type of understanding of how a woman who claims to love a man reaps all of the benefits while he is on the streets hustling, but turns her back on him as soon as he goes to jail. That wasn't even an option for me.

My man, Poppy, we were together in an intense relationship for two years. He was "that nigga" for me. The way he walked, the way he talked, thought, dressed, the way he interacted with others, the way he handled his business, and just everything about him made me want him so badly.

I was attracted to him mentally, psychically and emotionally. When I would meet up with him just to get some quick cash or whatever token of his appreciation for me he might have, my pussy would get wet. He completely fulfilled me, so I submitted to him. He was my man, my all, my everything.

We spent a lot of time together and communicated pretty well. I made sure that he was happy at home. I made it known to him that I was in our relationship for the long haul. Being a man of the streets, he reciprocated the love as well as he knew how to. Although we were not legally married, we lived as happily as a married couple in love.

When I met Poppy he was a mediocre hustler, but he made sure all things were possible for us. He paid the bills. We went on weekend getaways. He took care of my schooling, car and pocket money. He took care of me fully. We ate good and lived well. I was definitely "wifey" material. I cooked, cleaned and loved him strong.

In return he cheated on me a countless number of times. Every time he cheated, he never took a step up from my caliber; instead he only stepped down to the filth, the grime and the guttersnipes. Poppy constantly went to strip parties, but stripers don't count, right?

You might think that I may have nagged him and drove him into the arms of the other women, but that wasn't the case. Until the hard evidence was in my face, I only used the information that I suspected to my advantage. When I would finally stumbled upon a situation catching him red handed, I wanted to end the relationship right then and there. Of course he begged, pleaded and bribed me to stay. Poppy would even promise me that he would never cheat on me again.

Following my heart, I went against my better judgment and I continued the relationship with Poppy, after all, I loved this man like I had loved no other. Then there came the day when he reached kingpin status. Mo' money brings mo' hoes. Pussy was everywhere, more plentiful than it had ever been. Faithful old "wifey" was not even a concern anymore.

My girlfriends would say, "As long as you getting' yours it shouldn't matter what he's doing in the streets." Well, sometimes the money and trips don't balance out.

Poppy's fucking around on me started toying with my self-esteem then it got to the point where he started talking to me any kind of way. Yeah, he still came home every night. He would be so burnt out from fucking them other chics though, that he wouldn't have the strength to make love to me. Some nights he'd even sleep on the sofa. Dressed in the sexiest piece of lingerie I owned, I'd be waiting for him to walk through the door and he wouldn't even touch me. This treatment made me start to second-guess myself and question what I had done wrong.

Eventually the way Poppy treated me caused me to get bitter, to strongly dislike him, to actually hate the fucking sight of him. My patience grew short with him and I eventually ended the relationship. I realized he was bringing the worst out in me. I was miserable. I had to move on with my life.

Immediately after the break-up Poppy was sited around town with all the chics that claimed they could fill my shoes. Them hoes had no idea how big the shoes were that they thought they could fill. All kinds of females went chasing after Poppy. There were those who appeared to be in a better situation financially or economically than I might have been. These were mostly the old hoes trying to get their groove back. Most of them had already acquired all of the things I was trying to get. Sure they may have their own $300,000 home, business and one or two, perhaps even three degrees, but there was something they lacked... loyalty, devotion, dedication and a genuine love for Poppy. These women didn't posses any of those qualities and Poppy would soon learn so.

Four months after the break-up the Feds came for Poppy. He caught a five-year bid and after he was slapped with the sentence, all his females fled, became missing in action, no where to be found, done, disappeared, departed, vanished, and never to be heard from again. They were already on the paper chase for new blood.

One or two may have hung around long enough to see what money or material possessions they could get. But one by one they fell off too.

I secretly kept up with his well being and location. I could have jumped in at anytime and completely held him down like no other bitch could. I was built for that type of shit. I was taught principles, stand by your man, criss-cross, holy cross, but never double cross.

The average chic knows none of the sort. But I waited before coming to Poppy's aid. He needed to know what it felt like to be abandon, forgotten, lonely, isolated and to have someone you care about turn their back on you.

See, I thought that this lesson would teach him to be more considerate, more appreciative, selfless and more understanding. After he had been in the joint for a while, I finally dropped him a card. We started to correspond through mail only on a friendly basis. Months later I eventually gave him my phone number, and a couple of months after that I filled out the visiting form.

Against the blessings of all my friends and family, I became faithful to him as I had been in the years before. The visits started flowing like clockwork, regardless of the weather or storm I was facing in my very own everyday life. See, it didn't make a difference to me that he was in prison, for my heart was with him where ever.

I was fully aware that he was the "forbidden apple", but at the same time I knew about all the shit that loving him came with. I knew all about his baby momma, his mother, kids, family, his ways, when he's lying, when he's telling the truth and what he is capable of. This was an advantage versus meeting somebody new, going out with them, finding out their bullshit, their lies and deception after dating them for three or four months. So I was what the doctor ordered for my poppy.

I sent so much mail that I blew him up on "mail call" everyday. I got to visiting hour on time and always had plenty of change or singles for the snack machine. I was always home when he called. I never brushed him off, even when he phoned at 6 a.m.

I was in the process of starting my own business and wanted him so badly to be a part of it. I sent him copies of every piece of paperwork involved so that we could make all of our decisions together. I endured the struggle and passed every test that was sent my way. And on top of that, I kept it tight for him...burning out numerous vibrators and sex toys.

All of that and it still wasn't good enough. Poppy questioned, bashed, and accused me of everything under the sun. For a while I welcomed the challenge. I thought every test I aced would bring him closer to me. In the end I thought Poppy would value my love and would have no choice but to offer me his unconditional love. But this only caused him to question my actions. He didn't understand just how I could still love him after he had done me so rotten when he was on the streets. He started taunting my motives. He even suggested that I was trying to make him get deep into me so that I could turn around and hurt him. I was certain that all of his wild accusations were his guilt talking only to realize that he was a selfish, thoughtless, unappreciative motherfucker. Unfortunately, I would learn the hard way.

One day Poppy called me and asked if I was coming to visit him the following day. I assured him that I was coming. He asked me would I bring his homeboy's mother up there. I told him that was no problem. Particularly, I liked to ride by myself because I didn't need anybody else's drama. I only did it on the strength of being submissive to my Poppy.

I had a hard time falling asleep the night before. The last time I had looked at the clock, 4:07 a.m. is what it read. At 7:20 a.m. the homeboy's mother was ringing my phone. I suppose that was my un-requested wake-up call.

I hopped out of bed, took a shower and got dressed. I stopped to pick the woman up, which was on my way to the jail. When I got to her house she asked if her daughter could ride along too. Her daughter lived about ten minutes away. I agreed to scoop her up. On my way to her daughter's house the woman realized that she had forgotten to bring her ID, which meant that I had to turn around to go back to her house so that she could get it.

After she got her ID we were off to pick her daughter up. We ended up waiting ten minutes for her to finish getting dressed. Once she finally came out of the house, she had two children and two different outfits on hangers just in case the prison didn't let her in with the tight fitting outfit she already had on. Once on the highway, the mother asked if we could stop to get some breakfast while the daughter was whining that she has to go to the bathroom. I obliged by stopping at a McDonalds.

The remainder of the two-hour ride, the daughter was going on and on to the mother about who got shot, who did it, who was having a baby and by whom.

Once we arrived at the prison, I was relieved to be able to get away from those people. I sat waiting patiently, longing to see my man who I had just seen only two days before. When he came out he embraced me. We talked a bit and then shortly after he went into the accusations drill. Some no-where ass nigga who just got to the compound saw a picture of me that Poppy had and claimed he knew me and that I was *an around the way girl*. Come to find out, the dude went to school with me. He was wack in school and lived his entire life as a bammer and a flunky junkie. The only reason he was even sitting in a Federal prison was because he got hit with some bitch ass gun charge.

I was born and raised in my hometown and have met and known a lot of people in my day, especially dudes. Not saying I have slept with all the dudes that I know, some I know through my male family members, some my girlfriends may have messed with or others may be just mere acquaintances.

What my Poppy never took into consideration was that I was there at that Federal prison to see his ass. I got searched down for him. I went through the bullshit of playing taxi for him. I consent to drug tests for him. I put all those countless miles on my car for him. I sacrifice so that I can have the necessary monetary funds I need to go visit him. I make visits a mandatory for him. I go by the post office every day to send off mail for him. I stepped up to the plate like no other woman had done for him. Still, I am still taken for granted.

My Poppy failed to realize that a pipe can take but only so much steam before it burst. A lot of brothas don't understand that it's hard for a woman to be out in this world trying to find herself. Women want to feel appreciated because little do these cats on lock-down know, a visit starts long before we get inside those prison walls. We really don't owe them niggas anything. So what if they left a few dollars behind for a chic to get by on for a minute.

All the while Poppy was bitchin', he never stopped to looked at all the other cats in the joint who didn't get visits, who didn't have somebody coming through with moral support, mail, phone calls or a picture. I hope no other brotha on lock-down makes the same mistake as my Poppy did.

Poppy's insecurity and selfishness caused him the royal life we could have had together. So now when I hear a brotha complain about how a woman left him when his back was up against the wall I have to ask, "What part did you play? Did you run her away?"

I can understand partially why some chics don't support a brotha when he catches a case, why some chics won't and why some just can't. I know it takes a strong woman to go through this type of tribulation with a man, but at the same time, be very mindful that a woman needs the brotha to be strong and a little compassionate, even behind bars. It takes two strong people in a game of tug-of-war. But my Poppy, well, he let go of the rope...he let go of me. So for my brothas on lock-down, keep ya head up. And if you got a woman like me on the outside holdin' it down, hold on to the rope. Don't let go. No storm lasts forever.

****

Nikki Turner, who has been crowned "The Princess of Hip-Hop Fiction", is the author of *A Hustler's Wife*. She currently resides in Richmond, Virginia where she is creating her next Triple Crown Publication masterpiece, *Project Chick*.

BETRAYAL
Chris Forster

"Aye, yo, son! Poppy got knocked and I need to put my hands on four cakes. I'm on my way up top and I'll hit you on your hip as soon as I touch down so we can holla, alright," said Mark "Lil Man" Washington using his best New York accent.

"Alright, peace," said Dakim.

Lil Man was calling Dakim from his cell phone while driving along I-78 East from Harrisburg, Pennsylvania. He was cruising in a forest green 1999 Lincoln Navigator with chrome trimmings that was sitting on 22" shiny chrome rims. He was in route to meet up with Dakim in the cocaine capital of the Northeast, New York, New York.

His hope was to purchase four kilos of hard raw powder. In his black bag sitting on the passenger seat was $80,000 in cash. Arriving in Brooklyn and paging Dakim to get directions to Linden Plaza was all that Lil Man could think about.

People called him Lil Man because he was five feet six inches tall and weighed only 145 pounds. Although he was only 18 years old, he had already received stripes from the streets. He earned his stripes by way of an attempted murder charge that he was acquitted of due to lack of evidence and witness intimidation. Lil Man was on the fast track to one of two places. Either a life sentence without parole, which means six feet under, or millionaire status.

While attending a party in Philadelphia, Lil Man met a charismatic gentleman named Dakim. During this meeting he determined that Dakim had the qualities he was looking for in a new drug supplier. Earlier that evening Lil Man's previous supplier admitted to him that the Federal Authorities had been following him and would probably pick him up soon, thus, Lil Man began his hunt for an alternate supplier.

Dakim was five feet eight inches tall and weighed 160 pounds and had black wavy hair. His demeanor was suave and confident. When he walked into the club, he commanded attention as he strolled to the booth that Lil Man and Tiana were occupying.

Present with him Dakim was the most stylish, beautiful woman in the club. She stood five feet five inches tall with long flowing, gold highlights in her brown hair. She possessed a body that most men would kill over. Her perfect sized 32C breast, twenty-four inch waist and hips and ass that came out of nowhere kept the men looking. To say that she was bootylicious would have been an understatement. She was known by many as "Goldie" for her smooth golden complexion and the expensive diamond and gold jewelry that always adorned her body. However, to her family, she was Tracey Richardson.

Tracey and Tiana were friends who met while attending Temple University in Philadelphia. Now they each hung out with Dakim and Lil Man who were their boyfriends from back home. Dakim was from New York and Lil Man was from Harrisburg.

Once seated in the booth, Tiana introduced the two men to each other and they spent the remainder of the night partying and discovering that they had a lot in common. Their conversations ranged from favorite rap artist to entrepreneurial dreams. They all agreed that in order to accumulate large sums of money, a person would have to be an entertainer, ball player, entrepreneur, and/or very educated. Education being the key was a constant theme.

Tiana was a 19 year old good-looking Business Major. She was in her second year. Tracey was a junior pursuing a degree in Accounting. Dakim had taken a few Business and Technology courses at a New York community college. However, most of his time was spent on the streets of Brooklyn. On the other hand, there was Lil Man who was awaiting the results of the GED test he had taken earlier that week.

After leaving the club the two couples went to the local IHOP to eat. The good conversation continued and the ladies were pleased that their men had hit it off so well. Before splitting up for the night the two men exchanged pager and cell phone numbers.

They agreed to meet the following day in order to go shopping at the huge King of Prussia Mall.

Meeting at a pizza parlor near Temple University, the friendly foursome decided to make the 40-minute trip to the mall in Lil Man's Navigator. Dakim's 1997 red SC 400 Coach edition Lexus Coupe was too small, especially with all the shopping bags they intended to accumulate. Dakim was very pleased when Lil Man started the truck's engine and "A Hard Knock Life" by Jay-Z came blaring through the speakers. He started to sing along, "Instead of treated we get tricked. Instead of kisses we get kicked. It's a hard knocked life."

After the days shopping, on the way back to Tracey's apartment, which was near the college campus, Lil Man continued rambling on about how the two men could make a few moves together. Dakim just smiled and shook his head in agreement while listening to Lil Man expose his entire drug operation. This wasn't a very clever thing being that they had just met and the ladies were listening. Dakim attributed this to Lil Man being young and a little naïve. No doubt he would have to school the young man.

The couples spent the remainder of that Saturday evening together attending a bowling alley and then a restaurant. The following morning they met back up for brunch before catching a movie. Since both of the ladies had schoolwork to complete, both men decided after the movie to head back to their respective hometowns.

While at Goldie's apartment gathering his belongings, Dakim pulled Lil Man into the kitchen for a chat.

"Yo, money, I like your style and I think we could become partners," Dakim said.

Without another word he reached beneath the kitchen table with two empty hands and produced a wad of cash with one hand and a small 380-caliber handgun with the other. Placing both objects on the beige circular table and looking into Lil Man's eyes he said, "Here is a $5,000 dollar down payment on *our* next score. Now, of course, you could take this money and never call me again."

Leaning forward and placing his right hand on the gun Dakim continued, "But that would be a mistake. You see, with my connections and your hustling ability we could make that down payment a hundred times over in just three months. In any partnership trust is imperative." Touching the money with his left hand, Dakim pushed the money closer to Lil Man.

"I'm willing to trust you, which, believe me is not common. I have to go to the bathroom. If the money is not on the table when I return then I will know that I have a partner. If it is on the table, then I know we don't have a deal."

Getting up and placing the gun in his pocket, Dakim disappeared into the hallway, grinning and thinking to himself, "*I have been watching too many Mafia movies.*"

Things were just as he imagined they would be when he returned. The money was no longer on the table and Lil Man was smiling. While shaking hands and looking in the direction of the women in the other room, Dakim said, "Let's keep this strictly between us. Everything ain't for everybody. Alright?"

"Yeah, true. When are we going to talk again?" Lil Man asked.

"I'll holla at you Thursday or Friday before I fly to Virginia. If not then, most definitely when I get back on Monday. We can meet here if my girl don't mind. I don't like talking business on the phone. So, when I ask how you're doing and you respond alright, I'll take it to mean everything is fine. Other than that no business conversation should be held on the phone."

Lil Man and Tiana left the apartment in good spirits. From all outside appearances they looked content, but on the inside, Tiana was having reservations about spending the rest of her life with a drug dealer, and not to mention the toll of a long distance relationship.

It was no secret that Mark was also screwing a young girl from the Hill-Top section of Harrisburg. Tiana was only putting up with the infidelity because of her feelings for him and the amount of money that he was spending on her. Besides, she was occasionally spending time with Ken Harris, the star basketball player from Newark, New Jersey.

When the weekend came around again, Lil Man made a surprise trip to Philly to see Tiana. Little did he know, the surprise would be on him. Tiana was on a date with Ken. Lil Man called the dorm several times but got no answer. He even tried paging her but he couldn't find a pay phone that accepted calls. Wanting to waste some time, he decided to go over to Tracey's apartment. This wasn't a far-fetched plan because he thought the two girls might be together.

Tracey was home studying when the doorbell rang. Wearing only her panties and a tight short T-shirt she wondered who could be at her door. Looking through the peephole she recognized Lil Man. She wondered why he was at her house because Tiana wasn't there. Opening the door she said, "What's up? How you doing?"

Lil Man, wide eyed, looked Tracey up and down and replied, "What's up, Goldie? Have you seen Tiana?"

"No, but I think she and a few friends from her class were supposed to go out to eat."

Tracey was aware of Tiana's date and wanted to be sure to look out for her girl as females usually do.

"Did you try paging her?" Tracey asked.

"I couldn't find a working pay phone. Could you page her for me?"

"I'll page her and let her know that you're here. First let me go get dressed, okay?"

"Thanks, but you don't have to put on any clothes. You look fine just like you are," Lil Man stated while reaching out to touch Tracey's long brown hair.

"Boy, you better keep those hands to yourself. I'll be back in a minute," Tracey exclaimed while heading to her room to put on a pair of jeans. The jeans of choice didn't conceal much because they were tight and her behind was phat.

A few minutes went by after Tracey paged Tiana before the phone rang. Tracey answered the phone and Lil Man listened to the short exchange. From what he gathered, Tiana was excited and would be at the apartment shortly.

Awaiting Tiana's arrival, Lil Man continued to flirt with Tracey. Enjoying the break from studying, she wasn't showing much resistance. Male attention raised her self-esteem so she seldom shunned the advances, but there was a limit to how far she would go. When Tiana showed up the flirting came to an abrupt halt. The trio sat around chatting for a couple of hours before Tiana pronounced her desire to leave so she could be alone with her man.

Once the couple departed, Tracey paged Dakim to cover herself just in case he set-up the whole demonstration displayed by Lil Man. "The Big Cat", as some people knew him as, was very clever and had a way of convincing people to do his dirty work. When Dakim called Tracey back, she immediately asked, "What's up with your little friend, Mark? He stopped by my place looking for Tiana. Can you believe while he was here he was flirting real hard with me? I don't think you should trust him one hundred percent."

"Oh, word! Shorty was trying to get at you, huh? Don't worry about that. I'll take care of it. How is everything else going?" Dakim inquired in a nonchalant tone.

Tracey expected the response because he hardly showed emotion. In fact, his emotionless demeanor was part of his character and what intrigued many people the most.

Everyday for the next week the two men spoke briefly on the phone talking about cars, women, and financial goals. Then on one Sunday morning Dakim received the call notifying him that Lil Man was on his way to New York in order to score four-kilogram's of cocaine. When the brief conversation was over, Dakim estimated that he had about two hours to put a plan together.

Calling a wild young hustler named Pop from Linden Plaza, a housing projects in East New York, Brooklyn, he formulated a plan. The unruly youngster was the key to his plan "A". An alternate plan was devised just in case plan "A" didn't work. Dakim was always prepared.

Pop and Dakim met in Don Land (street name for Linden Plaza) to discuss the intricate details of plan "A". Since many of its young male inhabitants wanted to impersonate the late great Teflon Don, John Gotti, Don Land seemed an appropriate nickname. Certain that plan "A" and "B" were understood by all parties involved, Dakim gave Lil Man directions to a neutral destination.

Knowing that he had to do some good acting, Dakim purchased a cold Heineken to drink on his way to meet Lil Man because once he picked him up, the curtains would have to go up for show time.

"Hey, what's going on, Lil Man. How was your trip?" Dakim asked.

"It was cool. I've driven it a few times," Lil Man replied.

"Yo, I talked to my connect and we won't be able to score until tomorrow. Do you want to stay at my crib or get a hotel room?"

"I'll get a room."

"Are you sure?" Dakim asked.

"Yeah. I like walking around in my boxers and don't want to cramp anybody's style."

"Do you want one of them fancy rooms in Manhattan or do you want to stay in Brooklyn?"

"Brooklyn is fine with me. Just make sure I'm near some fast food joints. You know a nigga gets hungry," Lil Man laughed.

"Alright. I know the perfect spot but it's in the hood."

"I don't give a fuck. I was raised in the hood!"

Just like Dakim figured, little cocky chump was falling right into his trap.

After checking into the Galaxy Hotel on Pennsylvania Avenue in East New York, Dakim and Lil Man sat in the room shooting the breeze. Before heading back out, Dakim gave Lil Man another $5,000 dollars and told him to put it with the rest of the money and to tuck his platinum chain inside his shirt so as not to entice the local stick-up kids. Lil Man lifted his shirt to expose a pretty nickel-plated Smith and Wesson 9mm and confessed, "I'm not worried about stick-up kids."

On the way out of the room they passed some shady looking characters wearing black hooded sweatshirts. Reaching for his gun, Lil Man was ready for action but nothing happened. A few hours later they pulled up to the world famous Tunnel, a nightclub located in lower Manhattan.

Scan'tily clad females were everywhere. Lil Man was enjoying the semi-celebrity status he was receiving. Every five or six steps closer to the club's entrance more men and women were calling out to Dakim to greet him and his companion. He hugged and gave dap to numerous men while introducing Lil Man as his new associate. There was no way possible Lil Man could remember all the people he met with names like Understanding, Everlasting, and Supreme.

Once inside the club, the scenery was unlike anything Lil Man had ever encountered. Funk Master Flex was dropping bombs while playing the hottest songs. It wasn't uncommon for little fights to jump off or people to get their jewelry snatched. All night long intoxicated females were practically stripping on the dance floor because of the mixture of intense heat and alcohol. Clouds of marijuana smoke hung in the air like a London fog. Huge $1,500 dollar magnums of champagne were being purchased and consumed. Rows and rows of smaller bottles were lined up on the bar near the section where most of the Brooklyn hustlers were hanging out. Women were coming through the section in droves. Some were there to get their champagne glasses filled while others were setting up dates for after the club.

When Dakim and Lil Man decided to leave the Tunnel, the time was 4:00 A.M. The two men jumped into the Navigator and headed to the hotel in Brooklyn where Dakim's Lexus was parked. Arriving at the hotel the two men proceeded to the room.

Approaching the room a knot began to form in Lil Man's stomach. He could see the door to his room was left ajar. Reaching the room his worst fears came true. All the drawers were open and the mattress was standing upright...a robbery. Lil Man headed to the spot where he had placed the black bag, but it was gone, nowhere in sight.

Dakim managed to lower and shake his head in disgust then said, "Yo! I told you the room was in the hood and to tuck that damn chain in. Plus the two cats who were lingering in the hallway when we left are some vicious stick-up kids named Toni and 'L'. They live in the projects across the street."

"Well, let's go over there and smoke them niggas because I'm out of a lot of money," yelled Lil Man.

"Hold on Shorty. It's not that simple. Remember the big, fat, dark-skinned cat that I introduced you to earlier named Understanding? Well, he is 'L's' brother and they know me, my family and where I live. I can't just go over there and kill them without starting all kinds of negative repercussions. This has to be done with some finesse," Dakim said.

"Well, those cats don't know me. I'll do it myself. Just show me where they live," Lil Man said.

Dakim was silent for a few minutes, thinking about his next plan of action. Suddenly he stated, "I got it! Toni was just released from prison a few weeks ago and did a little over two years on a gun charge. My little homeboy, Jay, from my projects and Toni have the same Parole Officer. They usually have to meet with the PO on Mondays. If I'm not mistaken, Jay will be going to see his PO tomorrow afternoon, which means Toni may have to go too. You can ride with Pop and Jay to see if he is there and if he is, follow him, put in your work and head back home. In the meantime, I will be going to meet up with my connect to put my hands on a couple of bricks. When I get them, I'll make sure you get your share in the 'Burg. What you think about that?"

"Yo! That sounds like a power move to me. I thought that I was going home without any product," Lil Man said.

"Naw, son, let me worry about the product. You just make sure that you handle your business. Let's get your things, get the hell up out of this room and catch some Z's at my crib in Plaza. When we wake up we can put this plan into action."

"Cool!" exclaimed Little Man.

At approximately noon on Monday, the sleeping duo began to wake. The sun was shinning bright through the white vertical blinds. Dakim was the first person in the bathroom to brush his teeth, shower and get dressed. Heading into the living room Lil Man was sitting up right on the gray pull-out sofa bed with his right foot near his mouth, biting on his big toe nail. Laughing hysterically Dakim asked, "Man what the hell are you doing?"

Looking embarrassed Lil Man said, "Old habit I have, biting my toenails. When I was young..."

Dakim cutting him off stated, "Man, I'm not trying to sit here kicking it, get up and get your ass in the shower. I don't want to smell your nasty morning breath. The bathroom is the first door on your left. Under the sink you will find clean towels and wash cloths. Holla at me when you're finished."

About thirty minutes later Pop and Jay were ringing the doorbell. The four men sat in the living room watching BET as they went over the plan. One problem kept resurfacing; Toni wouldn't be careless enough to carry a loaded firearm into the PO's office. However, Shorty was certainly going to be riding the 1999 Yamaha R1 motorcycle increasing the chance of escape from the planned ambush.

Discussing the different scenarios and possible outcomes took another 15 minutes. After concluding the strategy session, Lil Man's body conveyed its need for food by growling loudly. In order to suppress this condition Jay and Lil Man headed out for Chinese food.

Alone in the apartment Dakim asked Pop if everything was set up as planned. Nodding his head and grinning, Pop said, "Let's go up to my crib and see."

Leaving the apartment and heading upstairs three flights, they reached Pop's apartment. Once inside they headed to the rear room. Opening the closet door, Pop produced Lil Man's black bag containing the $85,000 in cash.

"I would say that everything is pretty much taken care of. Now hit me off with the $10,000 you promised," Pop said reaching out both of his hands.

"Here's your money but just make sure part two of the plan works out. I'm on my way to see Tito for two of them thangs. Page me as soon as y'all are finished. Alright... Peace," Dakim said.

Sitting in front of the Paroles Officer's building, on the sidewalk was Toni's blue R1. Pop and Jay exited the green Navigator so that Jay could attend his weekly visit. Lil Man remained in the truck focusing intently on the motorcycle. His instructions were to move when it moved, follow the bike until he was in a position to shoot, shoot and then immediately head to Harrisburg.

Ten minutes later a person carrying a colorful motorcycle helmet walked through the large double doors. Watching closely Lil Man observed the person putting on some black leather riding gloves as they walked towards the brightly colored motorcycle. Turning on the truck's engine and placing a bullet in the chamber of the nickel-plated 9mm, his adrenaline was pumping extremely fast. *It's on*! He thought to himself.

Meanwhile Toni was putting on the helmet getting ready to assume the riding position. Inserting the small key into the ignition and turning it, the engine began to purr. With the right hand, shorty turned the throttle slowly. The engine responded with a short VROOM. Turning the throttle again in a quicker and harder fashion, the engine responded with a louder and longer VROOM. Grabbing the clutch with the left hand, shorty pressed down on the shifter using the left foot. Descending off the curb in a slow manor, Lil Man was soon following behind.

Suddenly Toni began to speed up. It wasn't long before the R1 was doing 50 M.P.H. heading towards Atlantic Avenue. As Toni picked up speed so did Lil Man. Once on Atlantic Avenue Toni did a wheely extending a block. Upon returning the front tire on the road, the bike jolted forward at a quickened pace with the Navigator about four car lengths behind. By this time both vehicles were moving way faster than the 55 M.P.H. speed limit.

Traveling about 20 blocks the vehicle had to slow down. Up ahead the traffic light turned yellow then red. Unavailable was the chance to shoot because too many witnesses were in other cars nearby. The light turned green and the traffic moved ahead rapidly. Another ten blocks passed before Toni began to slow down. Making a right turn on a semi-desolate block, Lil Man had an opportunity to fire at his target.

Steering the large SUV with his right hand, Lil Man stuck his left hand out of the driver's side window. Squeezing the trigger, he discharged four bullets. Not wanting to be apprehended in a foreign locale he didn't wait to see his victim fall, but proceeded to leave New York City. Three hours later, arriving in Harrisburg, Lil Man was happy to be safe, free and able to prove himself to Dakim.

Meanwhile on the Land, Toni's Yamaha was speeding up the ramp. Shorty was looking for Dakim and Pop. Approaching a large group of people hanging out and playing Cee-Lo, Toni, taking off the helmet said, "Yo, Dakim and Pop, let me holla at y'all for a minute."

Proceeding away from the group Toni continued, "Yo, that little nigga in the truck bust some shots at me."

Laughing, Dakim and Pop said in unison, "Oh Word!"

"Lil Man is a wild nigga. Did he get arrested or something?" asked Pop.

"I don't know, but being shot at wasn't part of the plan," Toni said.

"I'm saying. I told Lil Man not to shoot if you stayed on Atlantic Avenue because the police would be all over," Dakim said.

"But I didn't stay on Atlantic. I turned on Saratoga Avenue and that fool started shooting at me. That shit shook me a little."

"See, I told you about thinking you're as hard as the men. Girl, these streets are dangerous. You keep telling me how you were the nicest female on a bike in New York, but you couldn't even lose an out of town cat in a truck. You must be slipping," Dakim said.

"Well, just give me what I came here for," Toni said.

"Alright and I'll give you an extra $500 for the trouble, but next time, follow instructions. Here is $1,500 dollars. I guess you can take *your little girlfriend* out or something."

"I'd like to hang out with Toni and her girlfriend. That has always been my fantasy, two women," Pop stated giving Dakim dap. "I wonder if Lil Man will ever find out that it was us that robbed him," asked Pop.

"Nah," they all said in unison.

****

Christopher Forster was born in New York City. In 1990 he enlisted in the United States Navy where he served his country until 1992. In August 2001 he successfully earned a Business Technology Certificate from Allegheny Community College. He continues to work daily on his writing in Petersburg, Virginia where he now resides.

COMRADERY
Alexander K. Morfogen

Ten minutes into the chaos, the bullets kept flying. M-16 assault rifles and other assorted caliber slugs, shattered the windows and screamed through the walls of the Inner City Liberation Program (ICLP). Out of the six people who were in the office when the melee began, two were dead. The other four remaining were balled up in fetal positions behind two large desks.

George and Amy were tucked behind one desk while another sheltered Sonja and Ernesto. Through his tears, George thought it was sheer luck that his lawyer had given the community program the old solid steel desks for their office. He silently wept through the turmoil as he looked about seven feet to his left where his fiancee's, Funatti, body contorted in a nightmarish position on the old brown carpet which had turned a much darker brown from her blood.

"Oh, my Funatti," George mumbled. He couldn't keep his eyes off of her body. She lay on her back with her arms and legs pointed outward in every imaginable angle. Her beautiful brown eyes had a grayish glaze over them. George counted the number of bullet holes on her chest, which had stopped flowing with blood only minutes ago. He counted no less than eight holes on her body and two on her face, both of which were on the right side of her cheek. Even covered in blood, she was still so beautiful.

George had met Funatti in 1994 when he had first come home from Attica after doing a five year armed robbery bid. One afternoon George was going to see his parole officer in midtown Manhattan and saw Funatti with her cousin, who had just finished serving time in Olster facility.

She and George made eye contact. As it turned out, Funatti had run a community program for ex- inmates to help keep young people out of the clutches of street life. Their conversation began with Funatti telling George he should come by the office in

Harlem. They needed people to work with the organization, it didn't pay much but it was something. George's stint in prison had solidified his ideology of helping the people. Before George was incarcerated he had been intent on working to eradicate poverty and suffering in his neighborhood of Harlem. He had gone by the office later that day and he and Funatti ended up being the only two left in the building after talking for hours early into the A.M. That was the day they fell in love. They've been floating ever since.

The pigs had taken Funatti away from George and he was in a state of agony. The gunfire was now more spaced out and occurred in intervals. George looked over at Amy, who was right next to him. Amy stuttered through her pale face, "I... I think John-John is dead."

George glanced over at the old black leather couch 15 feet from them. John-John lay positioned upright, like he was almost sitting up, but his head was bent back over the top of the couch with a hole in it the size of an old silver dollar.

"Yeah, Amy," George said with his jaw clenched, "I think he's gone."

"I'm really scared," Amy said.

George grabbed her forearm tightly to comfort her. Amy was about 23 years old. She was a blonde hair white girl with pretty freckles all over her face. Amy had graduated from Columbia University 10 months ago. Last year she had seen George speak to the students at the college about the horrible conditions of inner city life in New York. George had instilled in the audience that only a small park had separated the two worlds of the comfortable and the impoverished.

Days later, Amy had strolled through Morning Side Park into Harlem and absorbed the sights of the ghetto like a sponge. After graduation, she came to work with George and Funatti. Amy was very dedicated. Sometimes George and Funatti smiled simultaneously when the petite five feet five inches blonde hair blue eyed white girl strolled up the Harlem block looking like an orange goldfish in a big pool of blue fish.

As George held Amy's arm he peered slightly to the right at the other steel desk that was about ten feet from them.

"Ernesto," he called, "Sonja, are you okay? Talk to me."

"Yes, George were still here," Sonja chirped out in her shrill Puerto Rican voice.

"I'm hit in my arm, Hermano," Ernesto said, "but I'm okay, bro."

"Where's Amy and Funatti?" Sonja continued.

"I'm here too, Sonja," Amy responded.

There was a pause and the gun shots resumed. Seconds later George responded, "She's gone."

"Shit, no!" Sonja screamed. "My poor sister, Funatti, my poor girl. Damn it all."

"You fucking peurkos!" Ernesto yelled. "Fuck you all."

When Ernesto finished his sentence the police pumped dozens of more rounds into the street level office in the direction of the voices.

Ernesto and Sonja had been married for 10 years, since they were both the age of 18. O n this Tuesday night, they had come over from their east side organization called the Young Geuveras, to help their comrades at the I.C.L.P get ready for a big rally on 125th Street this coming Sunday.

Sonja and Funatti were like sisters. Both women had gone to performing arts high school together and had both been dancers. Sonja had jet-black hair and eyes. She barely stood five feet three inches, but had a bite to go along with her sharp tongue.

Ernesto was the chairman of the Young Geuveras. He was tall and thin, about six feet two inches with tanned skin and a pointy nose. He had always worn a beret like the hero his mother named him after Ernesto "Che" Geuvera.

"George," Ernesto said, "we're not going to survive the next round, brother. It looks like we have two choices, we can..."

"I know man," George cut him off, "but if we walk out with our hands high those pigs will probably cut us the fuck down anyway. They snipped the shit out of John-John and it wasn't a lucky shot."

119

Ernesto and Sonja glanced at the couch where John-John's body lay. The hole in his forehead seemed like a dot that was drawn there accurately.

"Where's the gun cabinet, George?" Ernesto asked.

George didn't answer. He just looked sadly at John-John. "Only 18," he thought. John, John had lived on the same block as the office. Funatti had watched him grow up. In the last four months a series of teenage girls had been getting raped in Harlem. Through various witness descriptions the pigs had known that the rapist was a middle-aged man, and the press was putting extreme pressure on the police department to catch the perpetrator. The last teenage girl who was raped lived in the same building as John-John. A couple of officers had seen John-John talking to her earlier that evening, hours before she was assaulted. The two racist cracker pigs decided in their sick power hungry minds that John-John was the rapist.

An all points bulletin had been put out for him and soon after he was seen going into the ICLP office. George knew that John-John wasn't responsible for the rapes. The night that the last victim was raped, John-John was in the office helping lead a creative writing and poetry class with Amy. It was something he and Amy did three times a week.

At the time of the terrible attack on the girl, John-John, had been nearly an hour into the class at the office. George clenched his left fist tight. This was another frame up, another fucking lynching, another young person of color set up for a fall and all because the filthy pig police couldn't and wouldn't serve the poor community properly. John, John was their latest scapegoat. Now he was assassinated and it was too late for his defense to be stated.

John-John, had received a full scholarship to the Boston school of the arts. He was a talented young man who started giving to his community at such an early age. His life had just started only to be returned to the essence by the pigs.

"George, man," Ernesto pleaded, "the gun cabinet, where is it?"

Ernesto interrupted George's thoughts. George raised his voice loudly over the sporadic gunshots and shouted, "It's in the back office!"

"No," Amy blurted out. "George, Ernesto, let me try something for us."

"What can you do baby?" Sonja shouted.

"Let me use my white skin as an advantage. Let me talk to the police and try to get us out of here. If we all die, who will carry the torches? Please, trust me. Let me try this. I love you all."

George thought for a minute. Amy had a point. Funatti was dead and he was internally on fire. He wanted to kill every pig in sight but he knew they hadn't a chance. The odds were against them, but the community needed them and the ICLP.

"The office," George thought to himself. *"It's in shambles."*

Glass and bullet holes where everywhere. Throughout the years they had put in a great deal of work building the place up for the needs of the people in the community. If he went out in a blaze of gunfire, he'd be responsible for the other's lives also. George would rather have died himself than be responsible for their deaths.

The gunfire ceased and a voice from a megaphone blared, "You, in the office, anybody alive? Come to the front door with your hands above your heads! Give yourselves up or we will proceed to tear-gas the entire place! You have two minutes to surrender!"

George looked at Amy and smiled.

"Okay, sister, its on you," he said.

Amy loved when the tall stocky black man called her sister. It made her happy to know that George cared for her and that he and everybody there looked past her white skin.

As Amy slowly unraveled herself from under the desk, she grabbed the long black broom that lay in the walkway between the two desks. As she crawled forward down the aisle towards the front door she saw a long strip of white drapery that was torn off of the windows by the gunfire. She pulled on the cloth and began to fasten it around the straw part of the broom, making a makeshift white flag. As Amy eased herself up she yelled out to the police,

"Were coming out. Please, don't shoot. I'm coming to the door. I'm coming now, please, don't shoot us."

Amy raised the broomstick flag and slowly walked to the bullet-ridden front door. Bright rays from the police spotlights danced through the holes and kept Amy from seeing straight. George, Ernesto and Sonja peered over the side of the two steel desks as Amy reached the doorknob.

As Amy turned the doorknob with her left hand, she awkwardly held the broomstick cradled in her right arm. The front door slowly opened and Amy took a single step out of the office. Before her foot touched the ground, the bottom part of the broom, which held the makeshift flag, caught the upper right side of the doorframe. The long black broom handle swung upwards in Amy's arm like a rifle being raised. The three comrade's jaws dropped as the tragedy unfolded. The police saw the supposed rifle swing upwards and before the girl could correct her mistake, they opened fire on her.

Sonja screamed in horror "Aaaaammmmmmmyyyyyyy!" The high powered M16 bullets hit Amy low at her knees, causing her legs to snap like dry twigs as she collapsed. Before she fell, another round of slugs ripped into her chest cavity and danced up to her neck, blowing her throat open spraying blood outwards like a water hose.

When the first shots hit Amy, George and Ernesto instinctively lunged from the desks towards Amy. Ernesto was quicker on his feet and broke out ahead of George. Before George could follow behind him something jerked him backwards harshly. He turned around and saw that his shirt was snagged on the corner of the metal desk. While he struggled with his shirt he looked back to see Ernesto. As Ernesto reached Amy a police voice had bellowed "fire the tear gas." Ernesto grabbed for Amy but it was to late.

Amy crumpled forward exposing Ernesto's tall frame to the police. With unnatural speed he turned to run back down the aisle towards George and Sonja, but the tear gas canister had already been fired. The heavy scorching metal canister struck

Ernesto on the temple crushing the entire right side of his skull. Already dead from the blow he fell forward. Before his body hit the ground, the police had riddled his back with gunfire.

As Ernesto hit the floor George freed his shirt from the desk and dove across the aisle to where Sonja was looking on in shock. George grabbed Sonja with both arms and pulled her out from the desk. George was 225 pounds so Sonja's small frame made it easy for them to make a break for the back office. George was practically carrying her like a bundle of laundry.

George ran hard to the left and lowered his shoulder into the bullet shattered door. The weight of the two carried them clean through the damaged wood. They both slid across the floor and were stopped abruptly as they banged into the long metal cabinet that leaned against the back wall of the room.

Sonja quickly sat up leaning against the cabinet as George lay on the floor staring upwards. He turned towards Sonja seeing her sitting with her head in her hands sobbing heavily. George pulled himself over to her and held her against his big frame. Sonja tried to talk through her tears as sweat ran down her face into her mouth.

"Those fucking pig, animals," she spit out. Those dirty, foul, devils pigs of the Earth. Oh, my Ernesto. George, oh George, those murderers."

George screamed out at the top of his lungs, "Motherfuckers, you fuck'n pigs."

He had gone with Amy's plan and it failed. Ernesto was slaughtered for nothing and John-John was assassinated. Funatti, oh his sweet and beautiful black queen, his Earth, his life and his universe, laid dead as well. They were all ripped from him, his culture, his woman, the Inner City Liberation Program and his comrades, just like everything else black folks ever had in their lives that was beautiful. So many before him and so many after him would end up dead or become political prisoners, doing 30 years to life on some bullshit trumped up charges.

As he looked at, Sonja she stared back at him and they had an unspoken understanding. George dug in his pocket for the big silver key ring with a dozen keys on it. He sorted through them, finding the gun cabinet key. The office slowly began filling up with smoke from the tear gas. George fingered the small oval key and fitted it into the gun cabinet. As he opened the door, Sonja leaned over and reached for the 38 Caliber Revolver that hung on the hook. George grabbed the Remington Pump Action shotgun. It was ironic. The pigs would never think that the gun cabinet was filled with legally registered guns. Funatti had a gun license and purchased the guns by legal means. The two checked their weapons and made sure that they were fully loaded. The police megaphone broke the cloudy silence once again.

"Any survivors, exit the building immediately or we will continue with the tear gas!" an officer shouted.

"Fuck you, pigs!" Sonja shrieked.

Before George could curse the pigs, more bullets whistled into the office and through the back walls, clanging into the gun cabinet. George and Sonja crawled on their bellies from the back of the office to the smashed door. They both eased up on their knees. Both of their faces were becoming red and irritated from the tear gas. From the office doorframe they could see the two desks, which had provided them with shelter during the ordeal. Looking up through the smoke filled office aisle they could see the destroyed front door. Glaring lights cut through the mist of tear gas. They eased through the door.

George went first. As he moved he pointed to the left, and without words, Sonja crawled in that direction past the desk where she and her husband had hidden earlier. She leaned against the wall and readied herself.

George was already closing in on the right side of the office. Before he reached the wall, he crawled over to Funatti's body. Through the gas he saw her bloody face and looked at her big brown eyes.

"My wife," George whispered. "I love you."

He leaned down and kissed the side of her cheek that was untouched by the bullets. He kissed her cold cheek and touched her thick curly natural hair. A tear escaped from his eye but his

124

nostrils flared and his face was grim. He leaned on the wall and looked across the room at Sonja, who had witnessed her friend's cloudy figure have a final moment with the love of his life.

Even though the room was foggy it seemed that George and Sonja were visibly clear to each other. They both had a mental clarity. Sonja pointed forwards gesturing them to move ahead, each against their side of the room. As they eased on, Sonja passed Ernesto's corpse that lay in the aisle. She bit her lip to hold back the tears, but anger had engulfed her. George looked across at Sonja. He saw her black piercing eyes and saw a fury he had never seen in another human being.

They both crouched and gripped their weapons tightly. As they stared at each other the police barked on, unheeded by George and Sonja. They were connected. Comrades, together with the same goal. One cause and one purpose. In these final moments, George had understood, comradery.

His brothers and sisters, who died in the office that night, had devoted their lives to something beautiful. A strong human effort to change the lives of the poor and the oppressed. Every human being there that night lived for the people. Human beings of different colors, who fought for the liberation of the impoverished people that lived in the jungles of New York City.

"Comradery," George said the word in his mind. He had never come across such a closeness and unity with others at all in his life until now. Not in prison, not growing up, but here, here tonight with the people he loved and worked with. He wondered why folks could never achieve this feeling he had? Why people of color couldn't see what he came into realization that evening?

As he and Sonja tensed up for their final move he clenched his right fist and placed it against his chest looking at her with endearment. Sonja returned George's clenched fist, putting hers across her breast. She mouthed the word, "comrade," to him. George mouthed the same back to her and smiled. Almost as if reading each other's minds the two lunged upwards and diagonally ran to the front door side by side. As they came together in the spotlights at the doorframe of the I.C.L.P. they both raised their guns and fired.

Sonja had emptied the whole revolver in the direction of the sound where the police megaphone was coming from. She heard the painful shriek of the same police officer whose voice had been heard through the course of the night.

George pumped the Remington 12 gauge into the sea of pigs and heard screams as the buckshot dug into the murderous officer's faces and bodies. The police returned fire immediately with a non-stop barrage of bullets that was enough to drop a herd of elephants.

George heard Sonja grunt from his left as he felt his own body burning all over. His limbs had become numb. He looked over to see where Sonja was but his eyes were clouded and blurred, He was totally blinded. As he fell backwards, he felt nothing at all.

He managed a weak smile as his eyes closed to sleep. He knew his comrade was there next to him. George knew that with everything he believed that they died together, side by side...Comradery.

****

Alexander Morfogen currently resides in New York City where he continues to write moving tales.

𝒯ℋℰ 𝐵𝐿𝒪𝒞𝒦 𝒫𝒜𝑅𝒯𝒴
Trustice Gentles

It's the second Saturday in July. That's when we throw our annual Hunter Houses Block Party. It's the day people from all over the projects come together to have a good time and enjoy the activities that bring all of Hunter alive with action. We have basketball tournaments between people from the Eastside of Hunter against people from the west. These games get quite heated at times. With everyone watching, nobody wants their side to lose. Whichever team wins gets a trophy and bragging rights until the next year.

Needless to say, there is a lot of food available. It wouldn't be a block party without it. Residents each bring out their own grills and the smell of hamburgers, hot dogs, chicken, fish and spareribs permeate the air. The food vendors come around and try to position their trucks in the best possible locations to maximize customers. Alongside the playground seems to be the most preferred spot. Vendors sell ice cream, Spanish food and hot dogs just to name a few. Today you can get just about anything you want to eat.

DJ C-Boogie is a resident of Hunter Houses and he's been playing his set all day. He makes and sells his own hip-hop mix CD's. He is considered a ghetto celebrity in our projects. He has people moving to his music as he does every year. He's rocking it. There is a dance contest and a M.C. battle where everyone and their mama try to prove who's the best. Kids are running around and having a good time participating in all of the events.

All in all, it's a good day in the projects. There is minimal beef and fights, which is always a good thing. People who do have conflicts with each other squash it on that day only. By not having to look over my shoulders as usual, I'm comfortably enjoying one of the basketball games. It's good as hell. People are shoulder to shoulder as the sidelines are packed. Little kids are pushing to the

127

front so they can get a better view. Everyone watching the game is into it and showing support for their respective team. There is also non-stop trash talking, both on the sidelines and in the game. I notice people turn their heads and stare at the opposite side of the street and I look to see what has everyone's attention. A caravan of six luxury cars and trucks drive slowly towards the basketball court. The yellow Hummer in the front I recognize as Primo's.

Primo is the leader of the Shoot To Kill Crew (S.T.K.). They have been known to do just that in maintaining their business of selling crack cocaine in and around Hunter Projects. S.T.K. is about 50 thugs strong. They are feared and hated in the community.

When Primo and his crew jump out of their respective vehicles, like celebrities at a movie premiere, everything stops. The basketball game stops, conversations cease and parents pull their children close. With S.T.K. around, anything can jump off. Many people leave just in case something does. Even though most residents dislike S.T.K., some younger kids and teenagers are in awe of them. They gravitate towards the money, cars and power and want to be just like them. To these impressionable kids, S.T.K. are heroes. That's how fucked up the world is.

Primo and his crew double-park their cars and trucks. You'd better believe they won't get parking tickets. Twenty members deep, they roll up onto the court and politic with the referee. When Primo, who is from the Eastside of the projects, takes the court, the team that had been representing the east walks off to the sideline. When S.T.K. wants to play, you don't tell them no.

Primo's chain and diamond-encrusted S.T.K. pendant sparkles against the bright afternoon sun catching every eye on the court. Too heavy for him to run up and down the court, he unhooks it and hands it to a slim, a brown-skinned woman.

"That's his moms," I overhear someone standing close to me say. The woman looks no older than 37 years old, and I know Primo is 21. Even though Primo is a little taller and heavier than she is, they could easily pass for brother and sister.

"Y'all motherfuckas are not winning today," Primo announces boldly and loudly. "Y'all don't want it. We're gonna beat y'all Westside niggas' asses. This is my house. You hear me? This is my fuckin' house!" His arrogance is overwhelming and no one from the opposing team dares respond.

The S.T.K. team plays dirty ball. Gunz, Primo's right hand man who resembles a Puerto Rican Tupac, grabs a rebound and elbows an opposing player in his head. There's no retaliation. Another S.T.K. player trips a Westside player in front of the referee and laughs. Once again, there's no retaliation. The whole S.T.K. team talks mad shit while throwing elbows and grabbing jerseys, intimidating the Westside team. The fear is visible in their eyes and in their play as they play half speed, avoiding physical contact with the S.T.K. team. The referee is shook too. He doesn't call any infractions against Primo's team. He knows better. It was surreal the way the kids watching the game cheer all the dirty plays from S.T.K.

I look back over to the sideline and notice that Primo's mother is gone. My attention turns back to the game when someone from the west team slams a reverse dunk. The next time up the court, Gunz drives hard to the basket and throws down a Tomahawk dunk that has the crowd screaming.

Right about then I notice something brewing on the S.T.K. sideline. Primo's mother is animated, talking to someone in his crew's face. The game stops and Primo walks over to her. With his back to me I couldn't see his face, but other people from his crew look at his mother intently. Their body language screamed their increasing anger. Suddenly, all of S.T.K. runs to their respective cars and trucks and speed off. The entire crowd follows behind in the direction of S.T.K.'s traffic.

"Did you hear what happened to Primo's mom?" says my man Red, reaching out and grabbing me as I approach the DJ table.

"No," I responded.

"Somebody robbed her of Primo's chain," he says. "They punched her in the back of the head and took it as she was opening the door to her apartment."

"Get outta here," I say in disbelief. "Somebody is gonna catch a bad one once Primo finds out who did it." Just then a rumble approaches us. Primo's voice reaches me before he and his crew do.

"Somebody knows who the fuck took that!" a member of S.T.K. yells. "Someone better speak up!"

Other members of the crew grab people by the shirt and try to rough the information out of them.

"Word to the mother," Primo says. "Once I find out who stole my chain, they are dead!"

Each word comes out of Primo's mouth like spit. He didn't even mention his mother getting punched. You would think he'd be more pissed off about that, but the chain was his first concern.

"Word to mother. Somebody better tell me something," Primo says in a calmer but no less threatening tone. "I will light these motherfuckin' projects up until I get my shit back."

"Somebody better tell us something!" Gunz chimes in.

The music is dead and I noticed the fear in DJ C-Boogie who was standing still trying not to make a move. He must have thought that if he didn't move no one would notice him, but he has the perfect alibi. Everyone knows he's been playing music all day and couldn't have had anything to do with the robbery.

Red and I look at each other and know it's time to bounce. Other people have the same idea and file out with us. A group of young dudes ahead of us walk straight into a S.T.K. swarm. Primo must have taken it as disrespectful that they were walking away while he was addressing his issue. He and his crew start stomping them out. Rapid-fire punches go flying as S.T.K. kick the shit out of them. One of the boys holds one of C-Boogie's speakers over his head and smashes it over one of the guy's head. At the sight of blood that covered the block, everyone scatters.

Red and I calmly step away as to not bring attention to ourselves. S.T.K. tore shit up. From a distance we see C-Boogie enduing a beat down in a heap in the middle of his broken turntables and equipment.

Walking through the projects kicking over barbecue grills and beating down anyone unlucky enough to be in their path, them boys roll like a violent urban tornado. Police sirens quickly approach and Red and I move even faster to my building.

Needless to say, the block party's over, but the beef was only getting started. Knowing Primo and his crew, they meant what they said about not stopping until they found out who took Primo's chain.

"Who the fuck would have the nerve to rob Primo's mom?" I ask Red in astonishment. "That's total disrespect."

"Hell yeah," he responds. "That shit is crazy. He shouldn't have his mom living in the projects anyway. With all the money he's making, he should at least move her out of Hunter. Now look at all the problems the robbery done caused."

Walking up to my apartment Red is out of breath but not out of words.

"There's only a few people I can think of that would have the nerve to do something like that," Red continues. "Supreme and Little K.O. are still locked up so it couldn't be them. Maybe Big Derek, but I haven't seen him in a few months. I can't think of anyone else from Hunter that would do some shit like that."

"That's about it," I respond, opening the door to my crib. "I can't think of anyone else either who would have the nerve to do it. But someone did."

Let's not get it twisted though. Primo has many people that don't like him. He's gained an incredible amount of enemies with all of the dirt he's done over the years.

There was one incident where Hector, who used to be down with S.T.K., was skimming money that was supposed to be going to Primo. I heard the amount was as much as $10,000 over two years. One of the crack head customers snitched on Hector trying to get some "rock." Once Primo found out what he was doing, they shot him 10 times then cut off his hands, feet and head. They then burned the rest of his body and left it on a park bench on the Westside of the projects. His brother, Jose, told us on the low that he was going to get revenge. That was two years ago.

Then there was the incident last year when Damon had a fight with an S.T.K. member and beat him down. In retaliation, Gunz gave Damon a "Cuban Necktie" from ear to ear. They shot him in both hands. Then they cut his penis off, put it in his mouth and left him in the back of Building 10.

Arguably, the most infamous incident is the one with Mason. S.T.K. gauged out his eyes, put them in the front pockets of his jeans and threw him off of Building 4. He landed on the seesaw in the children's playground. It happened at night so there were no little kids out there. His head was crushed and his skull and brain fragments covered the ground. Blood poured out of his head like water out of a water bottle. I actually saw the body in that incident because we were shooting dice on the benches only 10 feet away. The reason that they killed Mason was because he had a car accident with Primo's, then brand new, Chevy Tahoe. Even though it was Primo who caused the crash by speeding and cutting Mason's car off, it didn't matter. Primo's brand new truck was fucked up so he did what he did. S.T.K. are like urban legends in the projects and that mystique built up Primo and S.T.K. to mythical proportions. They are hated by most, but feared by all.

"POP POP POP POP POP POP!"

Out of nowhere a rapid succession of automatic gunfire rang out. Red and I drop to my apartment floor, as is the custom around here whenever shots are fired. After a few silent moments, we slowly get up and look out of my apartment window. Three housing cops are running towards where the gunfire must have come from.

"Let's go outside," Red says.

"You are mad," I reply to his outrageous request. "You don't know what the fuck is happening out there. I'm keeping my ass right here."

Red always wants to be in some shit. I see the look in his eye. This whole situation has him so amped that he wants to be a part of it in some way. He wants to see and know what's going on and what the latest is. I don't have time for all that bullshit. Being possibly shot or jumped doesn't work for me.

"C'mon man," Red says trying to convince me.

"Naw, I'm chillin'," I say more definitively. "You can go though."

After a pause, he answers, "I'm out then."

He must think I might change my mind. When he realizes that I won't, he gives me a pound and bounces.

Alone, I turn on the local news to see if there's any talk about the playground incident. Nothing. I fall asleep waiting.

"BANG BANG BANG!"

The knock on my front door awakes me. I run to open it and break on whoever is knocking like they're the cops. It's Red. He rushes in, closing and locking the door behind him.

"What the fuck, Red?" I said detecting that the anxious look in his eye from before seems satisfied.

"Yo," Red says, moving his arms for emphasis. "I just saw Primo's mom in the staircase. She was dead."

"What?" I said.

"She was shot in the head, right there on the second floor."

"Of this building?" I ask incredulous.

"Yeah," Red confirms with a nod of his head. "I was going to Dave's house. The elevator wasn't there so I was going to walk up to the third floor. I entered the staircase and there she was. I was buggin' when I saw her there. I just stopped and looked at her. Her mouth was wide open like she was shocked. Her eyes were open and it looked like she was staring right at me. There was a puddle of blood around her. It was fucked up."

"How do you know it was her?" I ask.

"I told you, I looked right in her face. Plus, she was wearing the same clothes that she had on today. It was her."

"Then what happened?" I ask.

"I got the fuck outta there," Red replies like it was the dumbest question in the world. "What the fuck you think? I wasn't sticking around, especially with po-po all over the place today. I went back to the first floor and waited for the elevator. Then I came here."

"Hold up," I say trying to register the whole situation. "First, they rob her for Primo's chain and then they kill her? That doesn't even make sense."

"You think?" Red asks sarcastically. I ignore him and continue, "I really don't know what's going on now. I can't call it. I have no idea of who could've done that shit."

"What did you find out when you went outside?" I asked.

"There really wasn't anyone out except for the po-po, and they were fucking with any niggas they saw. They stopped and searched me. Then they asked a bunch of questions about what happened today and told me to get the fuck off the street. Please believe that's just what I did," Red said.

"So you don't know who was shooting or if someone got shot," I say as more of a statement than question.

"No, not yet," Red responds.

"Did you call the cops about Primo's mom?" I ask.

"Hell fuckin' no!" Red exclaims. "You know I don't fuck with cops. They'll find her eventually."

"That's fucked up," I tell him with an uneasy smirk on my face.

"But you should at least let them know there's a dead body there."

"Fuck that," Red says emphatically. "I'm not getting into all that. You can call if you want to." The phone rings and interrupts us. It's Dave.

"Guess what?" Dave says.

"Primo's mom is dead," I respond before he can speak.

"How did you know?" he asks deflated.

I explained to Dave what Red had just told me. Dave explains that the cops found the body and were going door to door asking residents of the building if they heard or know anything about the shooting. Dave and I exchange dead end theories of who, why and how until he hangs up to go to the bodega for cigarettes.

"Be careful," I tell him before he hangs up. "Cops are stopping everyone they see."

"You know me," Dave replies like he was a big shot and cops couldn't fuck with him.

"Yeah, I know you," I respond. "That's why I'm saying be careful."

"Alright then," he chuckled.

"Later."

The clock reads 10:00 p.m. and Red and I are fixated on the Bronx News Channel News 12. Ten thirty comes around and still no mention of the drama in Hunter Houses. I guess when something happens in a neighborhood like ours, mainstream media doesn't give a fuck about it. They feel that we're just animals killing each other.

My doorbell rings. Red is laid out and I'm so comfortable on my couch that I almost don't answer it. It rings again before I reach it. Annoyed I yell, "Who is it?" Whoever it is doesn't want to answer. Dave's head is visible through the peephole. I let him in. He walks straight to the couch and plops down without saying a word. Red and I look at him, then at each other as if to ask, "What the fuck is wrong with him?"

"What's up Dave?" I finally ask. Being dramatic, he looks at us for a moment without answering.

"Well?" Red asks anxiously.

"I found everything out," he replies at last. "I know the whole story. I was speaking to Tone from the Westside and he told me what he knew."

Red and me lean in as he starts his story.

"This is what happened," Dave says. "Remember when Primo gave his chain to his mom to hold when he was playing that basketball game? Well, she didn't really get robbed for it. She made that whole story up. Unknown to Primo, his mom had recently started smoking crack. He had no idea though. If he did, of course. he wouldn't have given her his chain."

"Get the fuck outta here," I say in amazement.

"Word to mother," Dave says. "But that's not even the whole story. Guess who she gave the chain to?"

Red and I don't say a word as we anticipate his answer.

"Gunz," Dave says.

"Hell no!" I exclaim in disbelief.

"I'm telling you," Dave reiterates. "Gunz started hustling his own product and Primo's mom was getting high off of Gunz's shit. Tone said he thinks that Gunz turned her out in the first place. He's been selling his own product for a while but Primo didn't know about it. I guess Gunz was tired of being the second in charge and wanted to be the top man. Primo's mom finally admitted to him that she gave the chain to Gunz for crack. Primo quickly had her killed. He was then going to kill Gunz but there was a problem. There are S.T.K. members who are loyal to Gunz and members loyal to Primo. The members that are loyal to Gunz told him that Primo found out he had the chain and was selling his own product. They then told Gunz that Primo was planning to kill him. Gunz and his loyalists shot and killed Primo right by the community center. Those were the shots you heard earlier. Now more than likely there's going to be a war between loyalists from both sides. S.T.K. is now fractured down the middle. I don't know what's going to happen with them."

That whole situation is ironic. Primo was the leader of the infamous drug selling S.T.K. crew. His right hand man, Gunz, supplying "rock" to his boss' mom. Primo has his own mother shot and killed and left in the staircase of my building like she was nothing. Then Primo, who thought he was invincible, is killed too.

S.T.K. may be dead but that is yet to be seen. At the end of the day, the product that he made lots of money with and destroyed lives with, destroyed him.

No wonder the media don't cover the shit that happens on my block. Who would believe it?

****

Trustice Gentles is the author of *Rage Times Fury* (1st Books Publishing), a novel that asks "What would you do if your child was gunned down in the middle of your street?" Trustice was born and raised in the Bronx, NY.

14 DAYS
Kiki Swinson

Rude Boy Trevor, who's of Jamaican decent, is locked away in a maximum-security penitentiary. He's awaiting an appeal to come back from a twenty-year sentence that was handed down to him after he was found guilty by a circuit court judge for murdering one of his lieutenants execution style. His lieutenant arranged for some local thugs from one of the projects across town to rob Rude Boy Trevor.

Rude Boy Trevor's wife, Venus, is three days fresh out of Federal Prison after serving a four-year bid for trafficking one hundred ten pounds of marijuana across highway I-95 coming from the Sunshine State. To this very day Venus believes this chic that goes by the name of Elena had something to do with her getting busted.

Elena knew too much. Trevor trusted her with almost everything. She had knowledge of how many pounds of smoke came in every week, how much money was generated from it and where all the stash houses were. Trevor and Elena were close, too close as far as Venus was concerned.

As Venus sat in the waiting area of DC's Federal Probation office for her first meeting with her probation officer, she thought back on the entire fucked up incident.

About two days before Venus was to leave to pick up a package, Trevor called her from Jamaica to give her last minute instructions. During most of their conversation Venus could clearly hear Elena chanting to a reggae song playing from the car radio. Listening to her you would think she was from the West Indies. Like Venus, her roots are from the capital of Virginia. They were both born and raised there, but were from two different sides of town. Without question, their personalities showed it.

Elena is more soft spoken, whereas Venus is cocky, outspoken and a daredevil. As far as the physical, they have light skin complexions and are very pretty, but were shaped differently. Venus was closely proportioned as a full-figured woman and Elena is known to others as being *"Thick like a Luke Dancer."* This attribute of Elena has always made Venus feel insecure even though Trevor constantly makes it known how he loves oversized mum pies.

When the conversation between Venus and Trevor was about to end, Venus overheard Elena in the background suggesting to him how he should have Venus take the whole package instead of splitting it up into two deliveries. That meant that instead of picking up fifty-five pounds, she would have to pick up one hundred and ten pounds of marijuana.

Hearing this made Venus cringe. She hated it when Elena made suggestions to Trevor about how things should be handled, especially when she would not lift a finger herself. Venus expressed her concerns about this to Trevor all of the time. The normal rebuttal was always, *"Venus, baby you know you are my girl. Bu, Elena is like a sister to me. She and I been friends since she used to be wit' Screw. So, I value her advice and ting."*

"Sister my ass!" is what Venus would always say. So the day of the pick up, Venus knew she had to do everything as planned. That meant always flicking on the blinkers when she was getting ready to switch lanes or turn corners. But most importantly, make sure the head, break and tail lights worked. She couldn't give the police any reason to pull her over.

As the drive began, Venus started to feel leery of something. But every time she tried to think of what it could be, she always came up with no answer. After three hours into the drive she looked at her wristwatch and noticed it was nine in the morning. As she approached the Georgia State line, she saw that there was a McDonalds restaurant just a few feet away. Venus decided to pull over for a breakfast sandwich. Meanwhile, as she waited in line to order her food, she noticed two undercover police vehicles pull into the parking lot and park right beside each other. Immediately Venus' heart began to race sixty miles per second.

"Where the fuck did they come from?" she said to herself. "And why the hell are they just sitting there?" her thoughts continued.

"Can I take your order?" the young woman behind the counter asked.

Startled, Venus looked ahead as if she was at a lost for words. "Umm...what did you say?" Venus asked.

"Are you ready to order?" the young woman said.

"Ahh...let me get a big breakfast."

"Is that for here or to go?"

"For here," Venus uttered without hesitation.

After only a few seconds of waiting, Venus was handed her meal on a tray. As she proceeded to take a seat at one of the tables, she noticed that the two police vehicles were still parked outside. Without looking suspicious, she desperately tried to look into both cars in hopes of seeing how many men were in each, but the tint from the windows made it impossible. Suddenly anxiety crept into her stomach, along with visions of her being handcuffed and hauled off to jail. But somehow a sense of boldness came over her. A feeling of being invincible.

"Just be cool Venus," she started telling herself. "It's going to be okay, girl. If you look nervous then that's when the po-po likes to fuck wit' cha'. So just finish eating and get on down the road. Everything's going to be alright."

Finally getting all the gumption she could possibly muster up, Venus threw the remains of her food into the garbage and took a leap of faith by walking back outside to her vehicle. The walk seemed to grow longer with each step forward. Through her peripheral vision she managed to see the cops' reaction while she was opening the car, and to her surprise, all their attention was right on her.

"Oh my God!" she thought to herself. "They gon' try to lock my ass up!" Her thoughts continued as she closed the door and started up the ignition. "Just be calm and drive off slowly. Don't give these motherfuckas anything to go on."

Driving slowly pass both vehicles, Venus took one hand off the steering wheel and used it to snap her seat belt into place, but somehow she lost control of the steering wheel making the car jerk. From that very moment Venus's life took a major turn.

The cops flashed their lights and turned on their sirens before she had a chance to get out of the parking lot. Four men hopped out of the cars and walked over to her vehicle. They were all dressed in the normal blue jeans and T-shirt attire with their badges and guns in full view. At the sight of them, Venus saw her whole life flash before her and knew that there was no turning back.

"Can I see your license and registration?" the biggest cop asked as the other three stood around her car and watched.

Venus remained silent and immediately handed him her driver's license and registration.

"So, Venus, you're from Richmond, Virginia, huh?" the cop asked.

"Isn't that what my license says?" Venus replied.

"Yeah, that's what is says. But now a days people are coming up with fake identification all the time."

"Well, mine isn't fake. Now can you tell me why you're holding me up?"

"Are you in a rush?" the cop said.

"Is that any of your business, Mr. Police Man?"

"Well, that all depends. See, now if you're passing through our town legit then it ain't our business. But if things aren't right, then it is our business."

"Look, if you're going to run my name then go ahead because I don't have all day to chit-chat."

"I'm gonna run it. But I want you to step out of the car first."

"For what? I ain't did nothing for you to tell me I got to get out of this car!"

"Listen, mam, I'm gonna only tell you one more time," the cop said becoming a little agitated with Venus' attitude.

"And then what? What's gon' happen if I decide not to?" Venus asked in a frustrated manner.

"I would have to use force, mam."

"Look, don't keep calling me mam. My name is Venus," she told the officer as she began to remover herself from the vehicle. "I hope this shit don't take long," she continued in a sarcastic manner.

"Come stand right here," one of the other undercover officers instructed her.

Venus looked in the direction of the officer who had just given her instructions to stand beside him. The distance was only a few feet from where she was already standing. So she walked over to him and stood right beside him. The officer who had her license handed it to the officer she was standing next to and instructed him to run it while he had a talk with Venus.

"Venus, are you traveling with any illegal drugs or firearms we should know about?" the officer inquired.

BAM! He finally popped the question. Venus had been waiting patiently for those words to depart his lips. So with the most sincerity, she answered him, "No, I don't."

"Are you sure?" he kept pressing.

"Yes, I'm sure."

"Well Venus, me and my partners got a tip informing us that you were gonna be traveling through our town with a huge shipment of marijuana."

Extremely nervous, Venus laughed very loud, hoping this tactic would throw these men off.

"You gotta be joking!" she responded.

"No, I'm sorry but I'm not," the cop said.

"Well, I don't know what to tell you 'cause I ain't traveling wit' no marijuana."

"Are you sure?"

"Yeah, I'm sure!" Venus replied, as if she was getting frustrated again.

"Well, do you mind if my partners search your vehicle?"

"Do you have a search warrant?" Venus asked

"No," the cop responded.

"Well, you gon' have to get one."

"Are you sure you want us to do that? The longer it takes for us to get that warrant, the longer you're going to have to sit out here and wait."

"You must be crazy if you think I'm gon' sit out here while you try to get a warrant to search my car."

"Look Venus, if you want to make this difficult for us then we will treat you in the same fashion."

"That's bullshit! You can't hold me here unless you're going to arrest me."

"I'm sorry to inform you, but I can hold you up to three hours if I've got probable cause."

"What kind of probable cause you got?" Venus asked.

"I've got more than you know."

"You ain't got shit!"

"Listen, now I'm going to warn you just this once. So if you don't reframe from using obscenities, then I'm gonna arrest you for that."

"Yeah, what the hell ever!" Venus uttered in a low tone as she leaned back up against one of the police cars looking out at the early morning traffic passing by on the highway.

After waiting another five minutes the officer with her license got out of his car and began to walk towards Venus. She immediately noticed he had a grin on his face. Her heart started pounding. She knew she was caught red-handed. No turning back now she thought.

At that very moment she wanted to escape, make a run for her car and do a Jeff Gordon on them. She wanted to create a highway speed chase with the result of her getaway.

"*Oh hell nah! I'm too big for that shit. It'll never work.*" she thought to herself. "'Cause by the time I try to make a run for it, these muthafuckas gon' tackle my fat ass and slam me on this hard ass concrete. I might ass well just sit my ass still and deal wit' this shit they getting ready to dish out to me. Fuck it! I'm a trooper!" Venus's thoughts continued.

"Did you know your license are suspended?" the other officer asked her.

"I don't know where you got that information from 'cause that ain't true," Venus told him with certainty.

"I'm sorry, mam, but it is. I had the dispatcher check it twice while she was running your name for warrants."

"Look, this is crazy!" Venus said as she began to walk towards her car.

At the blink of an eye all four officers were on Venus's heels. "Freeze and put your hands up!" they all said simultaneously as they drew their weapons.

Caught in her tracks, Venus stood still and raised her hands in the air. The officer who had initially confronted her by asking for her license and registration was the one who grabbed her, handcuffed her and escorted her to the back of his vehicle.

"This shit ain't right! Y'all know what the fuck y'all doing. Y'all just trying to make up some ol' bogus ass shit so y'all can search my fucking car!" Venus shouted.

"Just shut up!" the officer yelled to her as he slammed the car door in her face.

"Fuck you cracker! Y'all some crooked ass muthafuckas!" Venus continued as her voice got louder.

Sitting in the back seat of the police car, Venus could see every move the officers made. She knew they were lying about her license being suspended, but what could she do. Officers of the law use the same dirty tactics everyday, especially if they're hungry for a bust. Venus knew they were going to find her stash.

In a huddle, all four officers stood with their arms folded and began to talk. Venus sat back in the seat with desperation as she tried to read their lips.

Not even three minutes after they formed their huddle, all four police officers were opening the doors to her car and searching through the trunk. Venus knew it was going to take these men a while before they run across the marijuana, so she laid her head back against the headrest as she thought about how her life was going to change.

After thirty minutes of searching the car thoroughly, one of the officers approached Venus and said to her, "Where are the drugs?"

"I don't know what cha' talking about," Venus told him in a nonchalant manner.

"Look, Venus, I can make this really easy for you if you tell me where they are," the officer said.

"Look, man, please stop bothering me and do your fucking job!" Venus told him as she laid her head back up against the headrest.

Livid and highly aggravated, the officer walked away and headed back into the direction of Venus's car. He called for back up from his radio. Less than fifteen minutes later a uniformed officer, along with an officer in a K-9 truck, pulled up to the scene. Immediately after they arrived, Venus sat and watched the K-9 officer and his dog as they were escorted over to her car. Seeing this, Venus's heart started pounding. She was reminded that her freedom was about to be interrupted. She knew that any second that dog was going to sniff out all of the marijuana that she was transporting. What joy that would bring for those four undercover narcotic officers.

As the dog hopped into the vehicle his senses began to run rapid. Nothing of the sort got the dog excited until it jumped out of the car.

"I think we got something!" yelled the K-9 officer. "He's barking at the back tires."

Hearing this, all four officers gathered around the left back tire.

"Whatever it is, it's stashed in that tire," The K-9 officer told them.

"Get the jack out of the back of the car," one of the officers said.

As the officer retrieved the jack out the back of Venus's car, her heart seemed like it had stopped beating. She just sat there lifeless as she watched the officers pull retrieve marijuana from each of the car's tires.

"Venus Walters," said an unfamiliar woman's voice.

Snapping back into reality, Venus began to blink her eyes and focus in the direction of which her name was being called. Realizing where she was before she drifted off into her past, she raised her hand.

"I'm Venus Walters," she told the woman.

"Can you come with me?" the woman asked her.

"Sure," Venus replied.

Venus got up from her seat in the waiting room and followed this black woman, who stood at about five feet eight inches with heels, down a long hall. The woman weighed in at about one hundred and forty pounds. She was dressed in executive type attire; wearing blue slacks and the matching jacket.

"Are you my P.O.?" Venus asked.

"Yes I am," The woman told her.

"What's your name?" Venus wanted to know.

"My name is Mrs. Ramport. Now, come in here and take a seat," she told Venus as they entered her office.

"Are you prepared to take a drug test today?" Mrs. Ramport wanted to know.

"Yeah. I guess so," Venus replied as she took a seat in a chair across from Mrs. Ramport's desk.

"Have you spoken with your husband since you've been home?" Mrs. Ramport asked.

"No. Why?"

"I just need to know."

"Is there a reason?" Venus said.

"It's just a standard question."

"Oh. Okay."

Mrs. Ramport looked down at her desk, wrote something down and then looked back up at Venus.

"Have you moved from the address you were released to?" she continued as if she was reading from the document in front of her.

"No. I'm still there," Venus replied.

"Have you started looking for gainful employment?"

"Not yet."

"Well, you need to put that on your "to do" list starting tomorrow. I'm giving you two weeks to find one."

"Why so little time?" Venus asked in a curious manner.

"Don't take it personal, but everyone who comes before me gets the same time frame."

"Were they successful?"

"Some were. Some weren't."

"And what did you do to the ones who weren't?"

"I made examples out of them," Mrs. Ramport said smugly.

"Well, I guess you can't be more direct than that, huh?"

"Listen, Venus, I am as fair as it gets."

"Are you sure about that?" Venus asked uncertain.

"Yes, I am. As a matter of fact, I'm one of the more lenient probation officers in this entire building. However, I do have a strong pet peeve for no nonsense."

"I believe that."

146

"No, I'm serious," Mrs. Ramport said.

"I know you are."

"And everyone only gets two chances with me, not three, but two."

"What is it that you expect from people on your case load?"

"All I expect is that you follow all of your probation guidelines."

"And what are those?" Venus asked.

"I'm going to give you a list of them. But the ones I want you to carefully follow is having no contact with other convicted felons and staying out of drug infested areas. You must tell your employer that you are a felon. You must pass all of your random drug test and there is absolutely no traveling out of state unless you get approval from me first."

"Dag, you mean I gotta get permission to leave the state."

"Yes, you do. And another thing, I'm gonna give you some monthly reports and financial sheets that are self-explanatory. So all you have to do is fill them out and make sure they get to me before the fifth of every month," Mrs. Ramport said.

"What happens if they get to you after the fifth?" Venus asked curiously.

"Just remember my two chance policy and that should be enough incentive for you."

"I get the picture!" Venus said sarcastically.

As Mrs. Ramport continued on with the do's and don'ts, Venus listened. When the visit was over Venus hopped in a taxi and headed home to her grandmother's house, which was across town. On the way Venus decided to make a detour into a near by housing project just a couple of blocks away from home. This place was called Wickam Court. It is considered to be one of the roughest sections in the East Side of Richmond, Virginia. Venus knew everyone who lived and hung on the streets surrounding these projects. Her husband, Trevor, controlled everything walking and running. And since his departure into the penal system, his control was relinquished.

Venus knew there was money out there to get, but who could she trust was the question.

"Pull over right here and wait for me," Venus instructed the taxi driver.

"Wait, honey. You gotta leave some money first," the driver told her in his foreign accent.

Venus reached into her front pants pocket and threw the taxi driver a folded bill.

"Look, take this and chill out please. I'll only be two minutes," she said.

After she closed the back door to the taxi, Venus began to walk towards a group of guys stooping down and rolling dice on the ground.

"Yo, Bink!" Venus shouted at the crowd.

"Yeah. What's up?" replied a short young guy who looked to be in his early twenties.

"What, cha' just gon' stand there or can I get some love?" Venus asked as she extended her arms.

"Oh, shit! Is that you Venus?" he asked in an excited manner as he began to greet her.

"Hell yeah it's me, nigga! What the fuck is up?" she asked him while they were embracing one another.

"Nothing but the same ol' shit! You know! Just another day."

"Who making money out here now?" Venus inquired.

"Some local cats. Why?"

"Nothing. I just asked."

"Why? You trying to get your husband's shit back up off the ground?"

"Nah," Venus said.

"Why not? I mean, shit, it's plenty of money out here to be made 'cause ain't nobody got no good smoke or heroin out here."

"You lying!" Venus said.

"Well, this nigga named Diesel got some of that shit. But it ain't hopping and popping. So, if you got a hold to some of that good shit your man used to have out here, girl you would have these muthafuckas going crazy, especially some of that shit that ain't never been cut."

"I bet I would," Venus replied giving Bink a slight grin.

"So, how long you been home?" Bink asked.

"Three days," Venus answered.

"How does it feel?"

"Shit, it feels good as hell!"

"Damn, how long you been locked up?"

"Shit, Bink, I did a four year bid."

"Boy, the longest I been locked up was eighteen months and that damn near killed me!"

Venus laughed and replied, "You are still crazy as hell!"

"So, did you get cha' fuck on with any of them fine ass women up in there?"

"Hell nah! You know I ain't no damn butch!"

"Shit, you ain't gotta be a butch to fuck another woman. I know that's what I was told," Bink said.

"Oh, the hell with you!" Venus responded by hitting Bink on the shoulders.

Before Bink could respond the taxi driver blew his car horn.

"Damn, that muthafucka must be in a rush!" Bink said.

"I see. But look, let me ask you something," Venus said.

"Yeah. What's up?"

"Have you seen Elena around."

"You didn't hear?"

"Hear what?"

"That bitch got pulled in that murder beef with your husband."

"When did this happen? 'Cause when he first got locked up, ain't nobody say shit about her."

"That's because her ass just got picked up about a month ago."

"What did she have to do with it?"

"They said she was the one driving the getaway car after Trevor tortured and killed that kid from Church Hill."

"To do some shit like that she must've been fucking Trevor," Venus said.

"Shit, Venus, everybody knew Elena was fucking Trevor."

"What?" Venus replied as if she was disgusted as well as surprised.

"Yeah. She made it known."

"Look, I'm gon' get outta here. But you keep in touch."

"Are you gon' try to get back on the scene?"

"I'll let cha' know, Bink."

"Do that," he told her as she walked back towards her taxi.

The rest of the ride home was kind of bumpy and uneasy; especially on Venus's stomach. Hundreds of knots began to turn rapidly at once. Venus knew these feelings stemmed from Bink's comments about Elena and Trevor's relationship.

"That's what that bitch gets! Fucking my husband behind my back!" she said aloud.

"You talking to me?" the taxi driver asked.

"Nah, I'm talking to myself," she assured him.

Later that night Venus decided to lay down early, considering she had just eaten one of her grandmother's hot southern meals. Meanwhile she also decided to call a couple of her old friends.

"Hello," Venus said. "Is Dana home?"

"This is she. Who is this?"

"It's me, Venus."

"Get the fuck outta here! You home girl?" Dana asked.

"Finally," Venus replied.

"So what's up with you?" Dana wanted to know.

"Nothing much. Just doing me."

"You went down to the jail to see your husband?"

"Nah, not yet."

"Why not?" Dana questioned.

"If you wanna know the truth, I ain't really got shit to say to the muthafucka!"

"What did he do?"

"Well, everything was all lovely until I got sentenced. But after that, his ass got ghost! He wouldn't ever be at my grandmother's house when I would tell him to be there to get my calls. Plus he stopped sending me dough."

"Girl, you lying?" Dana said in disbelief.

"No, I'm not. Now look at his sorry ass, in the same predicament I was in. But the only difference is, he got more time."

"Don't he got an appeal out there?"

"So, I heard. But trust me, them crackers ain't gon' let his ass get out."

"I know you heard the police just arrested Elena because she was tied into that killing shit with your husband?"

"Yeah, Bink told me. And he told me Elena and Trevor was fucking too. That explains why his sorry ass left me hanging. I just can't believe you kept that shit from me!"

"Look, Venus," Dana said, "you're my girl and all and you know I love your ass like you're my sister, but jail ain't no place to be telling people shit like that."

Venus fell silent.

"You feel me?" Dana said.

"Yeah, you're right. So forget about it. Just let me ask you something."

"What is it, Venus?"

"Do you think you could get your son's father to front me some shit?"

"Who, Ty?"

"Yeah, Ty," Venus said.

"Girl, Ty's ass was sent up the road about a year ago."

"You lying!"

"Shit, I wish I was lying 'cause I sho' miss that nigga hitting me off with all kinds of expensive ass shoes and bags, and not to mention the dough he used to give me for holding his shit at my house. Now all that shit is cut out. You know I ain't use to this."

"Shit, how you think I felt being up in the Fed joint without all my money and jewels?"

"Girl, I couldn't imagine," Dana said.

"I know that's right! That's why I'm gon' get my shit back."

"How you gon' do that?"

"I'm gon' get my hustle on!"

"Ain't you on paper?"

"Yeah, but so what."

"Girl, I wouldn't fuck around with that shit if I were you. Niggas getting sent back to prison everyday behind them crazy P.O.s downtown. Shit, you better get your ass a damn job!"

"I'ma get me a job. But I'm gon' do my thang too," Venus said.

"Your ass better be careful, Venus, 'cause dem muthafukas out there on the streets ain't cha' friends. And the worst part about it is you ain't gon' know whose dropping salt on your ass either."

"Shit, I'll find out."

"Yeah, that's what Ty said. Now, look at him," Dana said.

"Dana, I know you care and all, but I don't need to be hearing all that negative shit right now. I'm broke as hell. And on top of that, my grandmother needs some help with all these fucking bills she's got piled up to the ceiling."

"Well look, let me see what I can do because I know this cat named Tony who probably needs somebody to run his shit up and down the road."

"Yo, I ain't trying to travel nobody's shit," Venus said.

"So, what cha' want?"

"Is he fucking wit' that smoke?"

"Yeah. That's all he got," said Dana.

"Well, see if he'll hit me off with about a pound of it."

"A'ight. Let me see what I can do."

"Yo, tell him I'm your sister or something."

"Chill out and let me handle this."

"You gon' call me back?" Venus asked.

"Yeah. Give me about ten minutes."

"A'ight," Venus said.

After Venus hung up the telephone she sat patiently beside it and waited for Dana to call her back. And just like she promised, Dana was back on the horn ringing Venus's telephone not even five minutes later.

"So what did he say?" Venus asked eagerly.

"He told me to bring you by his spot tomorrow night," Dana replied.

"Did he say he was gonna do it?"

"Come on. You know niggas ain't about to talk about that crazy shit on the phone."

"So what did you ask him?" Venus asked.

"I asked him if he could do a female friend of mine a favor."

"And?"

"And he wanted to know what the favor was? So I told him that you wanted to work."

"And what did he say?"

"That's when he told me to bring you to his spot tomorrow."

"What time?"

""Probably about eight o'clock."

"You fucking him?"

"Nah, not yet. But I'm letting him sniff my pussy every now and then," Dana said as she burst into laughter.

"Yo, Dana you are off the chain!" Venus replied as she chuckled.

"I know."

"Well, look, I'ma get my ass some sleep. So just holla at me tomorrow," Venus said yawning.

"Take down my cell number?"

" What is it?" Venus asked scrambling for a pen and paper.

"You got something to write with?"

"Yeah. Go ahead."

"It's 555-7243."

"Okay. I got it."

"Alright," Dana said.

The following day Venus knew she had to include job search on her "to do" list for the day. But somehow all she could think about was her meeting with the guy, Tony, so this agenda of hers took number one on her list. As nightfall rolled around, Venus met up with Dana as arranged and they both headed out to meet Tony. Tony was from Newark, New Jersey so his northern accent was thick. He was a very tall guy and he looked like he weighed in at about two hundred ten pounds easy. He was very fashionable as well with the latest brand in clothing and the huge diamonds in his watch and ring.

"Come on in and take a seat," Tony told Venus and Dana as they stood at his front door.

"Tony, this is Venus. Venus, this is Tony," Dana introduced.

"How you doing?" Tony asked Venus, as he extended his hand to shake hers.

"I'm fine thanks," Venus replied.

"So, you the one who wants to work, huh?"

"Well, actually I was hoping you could front me something."

"Front you something like what?" Tony asked with curiously.

"I was hoping you could let me get a couple of grams of some pure shit."

"Well damn! I see you're straight to the point. I like that. But, I don't think that's going to be possible," Tony said. You see, a couple grams of pure heroin is a lot of money to just sit out in limbo not knowing whether or not you're going to get paid."

"Look, I know what you are saying," Venus said. "But a couple of grams ain't a lot to me. But it will help me get back on my feet."

"What cha' mean a couple of grams ain't a lot? Shit, girl, niggas would love to get a hold of the shit I got."

"Look, Tony, no disrespect but I'm just coming home from doing a four year bid behind 110 pounds of smoke and right now I'm hungry and I want to eat. Now, will you help me? If not, then I don't want you to waste anymore of my time."

Hearing this, Tony immediately looked over at Dana.

"Shit, where in the hell did you get her from?" he asked Dana.

"I told you we were family. Why?" Dana asked.

"Yo, I love her attitude. She's raw as hell."

"So, are you going to help her?"

Before Tony spoke he looked back over at Venus, who by this time was staring directly into his eyes awaiting a response.

"Look, I'll tell you what. I'll hit you off with a couple grams of some killer shit. But, I wanna know where you live and where you hang out at," Tony said.

"That won't be a problem," Venus told him in the most sincere way.

"So, what cha' gon' do with it? I mean, are you gonna bag it or cap it?" Tony asked Venus.

"I'ma cap it," Venus answered.

"Sounds like a plan to me," Tony said as he rubbed both of his hands together smiling.

"So, tell me how much you fronting this shit to me for?" Venus asked.

"Bring me back fifteen hundred," Tony said.

"Damn right! Good looking out!" Venus said all excited. "So, when can I get it?"

"It'll be in Dana's car by the time y'all leave," Tony replied.

"Well, whose gonna put it there?" Venus asked.

"Look, sweetheart, you asking too many questions. Now, just chill out and let me handle everything."

About fifteen minutes before they departed from Tony's house, Dana handed Tony her car keys and from there the deal was done. As Dana was about to drop Venus off, Venus retrieved the package from the glove compartment and stuffed it into her shoulder bag.

"Yo, Dana, thanks," Venus said.

"Venus, you my girl. So you know I ain't gon' see you ass out."

"Yo, why you ain't fucking that nigga? I mean, shit he looks hella good!"

"He's alright, but, the reason why I haven't fucked him yet is because he's on some controlling type shit. So you know if I give him the kitty cat, his ass is gon' be crazy!" Dana said laughing.

"How old is he?" Venus asked.

"I think he's about thirty-five or thirty-six," Dana answered.

"He got kids?"

"I don't think so. But if he did, do you think he gon' tell me? Shit, you know dem out of town niggas ain't about to tell you every thing about them. Shit, if you ask me, I don't even think Tony is his real name."

"Oh yeah. You know I know what cha' talking about. 'Cause Trevor tried to run that same shit on me, telling me his name was Donavan."

"Oh yeah, I remember that. So when did you find out Trevor was his real name?"

"When he took me to Jamaica about seven months after we got together?"

"Niggas are a trip ain't they?" Dana said.

"You know I know," Venus said as she stepped out of the car. "Holla at me later."

"You know I am," Dana said. "Especially since you fuck with that nigga Tony. You seen all them muthafuckas up in the spot with him, right?"

"Yeah. And?"

"I would hate for him to send a couple of them niggas behind your ass," Dana said.

"Shit, you know a bitch like me ain't sweating that shit!"

"You just better be on point!"

"Trust me! I will. 'Cause I'm trying to get back on top."

"I hear ya," Dana yelled out the car window as she drove off.

The following night crept in quietly. It was a Thursday and Venus knew there was some money out there to get. She suited up for the forty-degree weather and headed out on the block. She had the taxi driver drop her off back out at Wickam Court. The streets were pitch black but busy as ever. No one in particular was visible, but you could hear their voices.

"Seven, baby! Seven!" a guy kept repeating from a group of men huddled over a dice game under a very dim streetlight.

"Is Bink over there?" Venus yelled, as she approached them.

"Nah, but who that?" the guy wanted to know.

"It's Venus," she said.

"Yo, Venus, he's right over there talking to his girl," the guy said as he pointed.

"Thanks," Venus replied.

Venus walked across the street in the direction Bink was standing. About half way there she decided to get his attention.

"Yo, Bink," Venus yelled.

"Yeah. Who that?" Bink answered.

"It's me Venus."

"Ahh, shit, what's up?" Bink asked as he began to walked towards Venus with his girlfriend along his side.

"Trying to get some dough."

"Me too! So, what's up? I mean, you holding now or what?"

"Yeah. I got some killer on me now," Venus answered.

"How much?"

"I got it capped."

"Did you step on it?"

"Nah, but I ain't pack the caps either."

"It don't matter 'cause you gon' kill a muthafucka tonight. These fiends gon' love your ass!"

"What cha' getting ready to do?" Venus asked Bink.

"I'm getting ready to let niggas know that I just ran across some killer so follow my girl to the crib before the good-o-boys roll through while you standing out here dirty."

"Yeah, he's right," Bink's girlfriend interjected. "'Cause it's been kind of hot out here today."

Taking the advice that was just given, Venus turned in the direction Bink's girlfriend was leading her.

"Yo, wait!" Bink yelled. "Give me a tester," he instructed Venus.

Venus pulled out a small clear capsule with a powdery substance and handed to Bink. He took a quick look at it, then he cuffed it in the palm of his hand and walked off.

"Let whoever know that we ain't taken no shorts," Venus yelled.

"Yo, trust me. You ain't gon' have to if this shit is missile!" Bink yelled back as his voice faded out.

Throughout the whole night, Bink escorted customers in and out of his girlfriend's domain to make their purchases from Venus. And before she even realized it, every cap she packed and sealed up was sold.

"I can't believe all that shit you brought over here is gone," Bink commented as he let the last customer out of the backdoor.

"I can't either," Venus replied as she sat at the kitchen table and began to count all the money she had. "What time is it?" she continued as she began to separate the tens from the twenty-dollar bills.

Bink looked over at the clock on the VCR and answered, "Umm...it's almost three-thirty."

"Damn, it's that late."

"Yep," Bink replied as he took a seat at the kitchen table alongside of Venus.

"Well, I gotta hurry up and count this dough so I can get my ass to the crib. I'm tired as hell."

"Shit, me too. You see my girl done took her ass to bed hours ago."

"Shit, if I ain't have to make this money, my ass would've done the same thang!"

"Yo, it looks like you did good tonight."

"Nah, we did good," Venus corrected him.

"How much you make?" Bink asked.

"Umm, I think I got about three gees."

"Yo, you cleaned up tonight."

"Tell me about it. I hope shit be like this every time I come out this piece."

"I keep trying to tell you how much money is out here. Dem fiends love that shit you got. All you gotta do is keep that same shit rollin' and you gon' be a paid ass bitch!"

"Yeah, baby! That's what I wanna hear," Venus said as she stood up and gave Bink a high five. Before Venus left she handed Bink some cash and headed out the front door with Bink by her side as he carried a cocked thirty-eight revolver in his right hand, awaiting anyone who might have had the intentions to rob Venus of her profits.

Venus' visit back to Tony was a very pleasant one. She handed him the cash she owed him and had another package waiting for her in Dana's car once again. This time the quantity was double the size. As planned, Venus did her usual to prepare for another all nighter out at Wickam Court. And as expected, the next several nights went smoothly. That meant she was able to return home in one piece. And after only being on the bricks for seven days, word was already on the street how she was taking over the scene by making plenty of money and holding down her spot. Through this sudden transition, she started attracting a lot of attention from other jealous dealers from around the way. They wanted her out of Wickam Court through any means necessary. It did not matter who Venus' husband was because he was on the inside. Venus finally got word from Bink about how other people felt about her being out there. He gave her the names of every individual who had bad blood for her.

"Damn, niggas hating on me like that?" Venus asked Bink in an astonished manner as she listened to Bink on the other end of the telephone.

Bink sighed and responded, "I know that shit sounds crazy, but I had to tell you 'cause you my dog."

"You know I got love for you too," Venus said. "But them niggas must be crazy if they think they gon' run me out of Wickam Court. I mean, what kind of shit is that? What? They hate seeing a woman come out in their hood grinding real hard and getting hers?"

"Come on Venus. You know how other niggas get if they ain't eating as much as the next person. Yo, the streets been like this since that nigga Al Capone was out on the streets getting it."

"So what cha' think I should do?" Venus asked.

"It's up to you, shorty," Bink replied.

"I know that sounds silly, but what would you do?"

"Well, if it was me, I wouldn't let any nigga tell me when and where I can make me some dough. But you're a female so niggas look at you as being soft."

"Yeah, but you know I ain't soft. Before it's all said and done, I'll probably blaze one of dem cats you just mentioned," Venus said.

"I don't think so. 'Cause that nigga Diesel is living foul. I remember when this nigga named Izzy owed Diesel some dough and kept lying saying his girl had the money. Yo, do you know that nigga Diesel went up to Izzy's girl's job and pulled out his burner on her and told her Izzy sent him up there to get his dough. Now, you know she was straight bugging off this nigga 'cause she works at a daycare center."

"Ain't nobody help her?"

"Hell nah, dem workers didn't have her back," Bink said.

"What they do to her?"

"They fired her."

"For real?"

"Hell yeah. They told her she had to go."

"So you don't think I can handle myself?"

"Look, all I gotta say is if you do decide to keep coming out here, bring a burner with you 'cause the one I got ain't enough."

"That ain't no problem," Venus said.

"So, you coming?"

"I'll be there."

"A'ight," Bink said.

$$$

Venus instructed the taxi driver to make a detour to the Richmond City Jail before her final destination to Wickam Court. Upon her arrival, she handed the driver a crisp fifty-dollar bill and asked him to wait for her return. He happily obliged. Venus hopped out of the cab and headed towards the visiting room. To her surprise, there was one other visitor in the waiting room besides herself. She immediately walked over to the glass window, said a few words to the deputy, showed her ID and then signed her name into the logbook. Waiting only for about ten minutes, Venus' name was called by the deputy behind the glass.

"Mrs. Walters, go to the door that says nine and wait for me to lift the switch, then push it open," the deputy said.

"Are they bringing my husband down now?"

"Well, he should already be in that room waiting for you."

Hearing this, Venus got an instant case of anxiety. Having not seen her husband for over four years somehow took its toll. Wondering how he was going to look or react to the visit was another factor. To end the feelings she was having, she entered the room and looked straight ahead. Sitting on a chair behind a glass petition wearing an orange jumpsuit was Trevor, looking straight at Venus. Without hesitation, Venus stepped up to the glass, took a seat on the stool and grabbed the telephone receiver from the wall panel. Trevor smiled.

"You look good," Trevor said.

"Thanks," Venus replied.

"How long you been home?"

"A little over a week or so," Venus replied.

"You missed me?"

"Yeah, I did when I was doing time. But you know how shit changes when you're on the street."

"Look 'V', I'm so sorry, Star. I know I was suppose to be there for you, but shit got kinda hectic after you left."

160

""How hectic did it get, Trevor? I mean, damn, is that all you can come up with?"

"It's the truth," Trevor said.

"Look, I ain't got time for all your fucking lies. All I came down here for is to tell you that I'm filing for a divorce. But I'm sure you don't mind since you and Elena had y'all's fun while I was on lock."

"What?" Trevor yelled as if he was surprised at Venus' remark.

"Oh, nigga, don't act like you wasn't fucking that hoe! The shit is all over the streets."

"Look, baby...." Trevor started to explain but nothing else came out.

"What? You ain't got nothing else to say, huh? Yeah, I know. You busted muthafucka!"

"But, 'V', it wasn't like that."

"Oh, shut the fuck up with the lies. And don't be coming with that I love you bullshit either. You proved to me how much you loved me by leaving me in the cage for four years. So kiss my muthafucka!"

Giving Trevor no chance to respond, Venus hung up the telephone, got up from the stool, walked out of the room and not once did she look back for an expression on Trevor's face.

On the way to Wickam Court, Venus sat back and laid her head up against the headrest as she counted the stars in the sky. During the entire ride all she could think of was what she should have said and then her heart started fluttering. She knew deep down inside she was still in love with Trevor. To see him after all of those years sparked a flame in her heart. But unfortunately, the flame died out immediately after he opened his mouth to speak.

As the taxi driver entered Wickam Court, Venus requested for him to circle around the block, giving her some insight on who was out there selling their product. After he circled the place, Venus instructed him to drop her off in the back of her designated area. As she got out of the taxi, only then did she remember that she had left the gun at home that she was going to use to protect herself with.

"Damn!" she said in a low whisper. "How in the hell did I forget the burner?" she continued as she walked to the back door of Bink's girlfriend's apartment. It only took two knocks to get Bink to answer the door.

"Yo, Venus. Wuz up!" Bink asked.

"Shit, you tell me," Venus commented as she entered through the back door.

"Well, I ain't heard nothing else."

Venus took a seat on the sofa in the living room and said, "Have you seen that nigga Diesel?"

"Nah, but I heard he was out here."

"Any money been through here?"

"Hell yeah. You missed about a good four hundred bills."

"You lying!" Venus said.

"Nah, I ain't."

As they continued to converse, someone knocked on the back door. Bink saw that it was a customer and opened it.

"Yo, what cha' need?" Bink asked the man.

"Give me ten of dem thangs," the guy answered.

Bink walked over to Venus and retrieved ten capsules. "Yo, here you go," Bink said to the guy. They exchanged the money for the drugs.

"Oh yeah, the good-o-boys just kicked up in that nigga Bay-Bay's spot a few minutes ago," the customer informed Bink.

"For real?" both Venus and Bink said simultaneously.

"Hell yeah. Them crackers went up in there full force. So, y'all better be careful," the customer said as he exited the back door.

"Damn, you hear that shit?" Venus asked Bink.

"Hell yeah."

"You think I should get my ass out of here?"

"Nah, but to be safe, we'll just close shop until dem crackers leave."

Sticking to the plan, Bink turned away a lot of customers and sometimes he wouldn't even answer the door. Once they got word that the coast was clear, both Bink and Venus got the show on the road. At about five o'clock in the morning Venus' supplies had finally ran out. Like always, she sat at the kitchen table and began to count her profits. About half way through her count, someone knocked on the back door.

"Who is it?" Bink called.

"Yo, it's me, Bink," said a male's voice.

"Who is me?" Bink asked.

"It's Poogie."

"A'ight, wait a minute," Bink told him as he looked back at Venus. "Yo, put that dough up for a minute. I'm gonna go see what this nigga want."

Venus began to stuff the money into her jacket pockets as Bink left the room to go answer the door..

"Yo, nigga, come on!" Poogie yelled from the other side of the door.

"I'm coming, man!" Bink assured him.

Bink opened the back door for Poogie. As Poogie entered into the house, three other guys followed in behind him.

"Yo, what's up niggas?" Bink asked not knowing what answer he was going to get.

"Where that bitch at?" Poogie asked.

"Yo, she just left," Bink replied in a manner hoping these guys would be convinced.

Poogie, who's notorious around Wickam Court for robbing people of their money and personal belongings, pulled out a Smith & Wesson forty-five and pointed in the direction of Bink.

"What the fuck is you doing, Poogie?" Bink asked as if he was pleading.

"Bink, didn't Diesel tell you not to let that bitch come up in this spot again?" Poogie asked Bink as he walked closer to him.

"Yeah, but I ain't get to tell her until tonight when she got here."

"But you let her stay and make some money, though," Poogie said.

"She ain't make no money outta here," Bink said.

"You lying muthafucka!" Poogie yelled as she took a shot directly at Bink's chest.

"**POW! POW! POW!**" Was the sound of the shots fired. The force from the bullets picked Bink up off of his feet and carried him a few feet backwards, landing him landed on the floor. After the shots were fired everyone, including Poogie, fled from the house. Nervously Venus sat quietly on the floor in the hall closet. She was very numb and ambiguous as to what she should do.

Meanwhile, Bink's girlfriend came running out of the back bedroom after hearing the gun shots fired. Seeing Bink covered in his own blood, she screamed at the top of her lungs.

"Somebody help! My baby's been shot!" she cried.

Hearing this, Venus somehow conjured up some gumption and crawled out of the closet. When she saw Bink lying there, her eyes instantly became watery.

"Is he dead?" Venus asked, as she walked closer to take a better look.

"He ain't breathing no more," Bink's girlfriend answered, still sobbing.

"I'ma go call the ambulance okay," Venus said.

"Okay."

Venus ran straight out of the back door. The nearest pay phone was about two blocks up the street. Once she reached it she dialed 911. Not knowing what to do from that point, she decided not to go back to the Bink's house considering she was on probation.

Venus called for a taxi and headed home. By the time she reached home, the sun had started to rise. Venus' grandmother was up cooking breakfast when she walked through the front door.

"Now I know you ain't just coming in from last night," her grandmother commented as she sat her plate of food on the table.

"Look, grandma. Now is not the time," Venus told her as she headed towards upstairs.

"I hope you ain't hanging out with the same old crowd," her grandmother said.

Venus refused to respond as she continued on to her room.

The next day seemed like a very long day. It was Venus' fourteenth day of freedom. But through all of the bullshit, on this fourteenth day of freedom, Venus wasn't really free at all.

****

Kiki Swinson is the author of *Mad Shambles*. She currently resides in Virginia Beach, Virginia where she is working on her latest *novel After the Shhhh Hits the fan*.

CHOICE
Angel Hunter

"Sophie, get up. Somebody is at the door," my mother said. She is always paranoid about something.

I get up big and pregnant to answer the door. By the time I start to walk towards it, there is very loud banging as if someone is beating the door with something. As I looked through the peephole a man shouted, "This is FBI. Open up!"

I did the cordial thing and I opened the door. I stuck my belly through because I had left the chain on and the only way my head could get through the crack was for my belly to show too.

The man said, "Sophie we really don't want to take you in handcuffs pregnant, but we have a warrant for your arrest. Here's what we can do for you; We suggest that you turn yourself in today before 10 a.m. or we will come back and get you, handcuffs and all."

I was shocked, but I already knew what it was all about. I promised the man that I would turn myself in and I closed the door.

First I ran to the phone and dialed frantically. As I listened to the ringing I looked out of the window. I saw about 12 marked cars outside, and all of them were Feds. Handcuffed in the back of each of the cars was someone I knew. They had my entire block on lock. People were hanging out of their windows, on their fire escapes and on the rooftop of their buildings. Some were in nightgowns and robes watching the action go down.

"At six o'clock in the morning, this better be good," I heard my lawyer say as she picked up the phone.

"This is the worst day of my life," I said as I proceeded to tell her of the events at hand. She told me to stay calm and go ahead and surrender myself to the FBI. After listening to her reasoning I agreed.

I took a shower, oiled my belly and surrendered to the FBI. At the Federal Plaza I was finger printed, taken pictures of, read my rights, and cuffed to a chair in a huge board room. An agent was sitting next to me asking me if I needed anything.

"*What an ass*," I thought. "*Yeah, I need to go home.*"

As I searched the room, embarrassingly I noticed everyone I had grown up with. There were people I worked with, people I went to school with, and I even spotted the cop that stopped my man from almost killing me a while back during a domestic situation.

I was scheduled to be arraigned, but following my lawyers advice I signed a waiver of speedy arraignment and went to the hospital claiming all types of labor pains and what not.

The Feds escorted me to the hospital and then home. I talked to them in the car asking them to explain to me exactly what I was being charged with. My attorney had attempted to explain it to me in layman terms, but it was all still confusing. I was told that the warrant was for conspiracy to commit mail fraud, insurance fraud, money laundering and child endangerment. I couldn't believe it.

When the Feds contacted me six months ago, I thought that the situation would go away, but they wanted me to roll on my people and I know that the code of the streets, the code of my life, would never allow me to do such a thing. So I played stupid as they ran our entire scheme down to me. I acted like I knew nothing. I even cried stating that I was totally innocent and had no idea that what they were saying was true.

The Feds were questioning me about a man I knew to call daddy since I could remember. Not that he was my mother's man or my dad, but just because he took care of us, all of us kids in the hood. When we needed jobs, money, cars, hideouts, you name it, he was there. You could look to him for anything. I put him on a pedestal in my statements about him to the Feds. I acted as if he was a saint instead of the ringleader of our criminal outfit that he was.

The Feds knew they needed me to somehow pin him to the ring. I knew they needed me, but I wasn't telling them nothin'. I didn't know how many others they had contacted or who might get to snitchin', so I went straight to the source to tell him all that was going down.

I explained to daddy how the Feds knew his whole operation inside and out and how they knew who his soldiers were. Everyone's phone had been tapped, including mine. I told him that he should check on all of our insiders on payroll (cops, lawyers, doctors, etc...). I think that by the time I got to him he was tired and had given up the fight.

I know we could have all avoided jail time if he had done what needed to be done, but his ass just gave up and took us all down with him, the entire family. He left all of us out in the cold, his biological children, his nephews, his cousins and all of his extended family members, which is the entire neighborhood damn near.

My attorney did her best for me, but because I was charged in a conspiracy, I was tried in a group. This means that I was treated the same' as the others...same crime same time. She tried to get me severed so that I could stand trial alone, but the judge denied her request. And if that wasn't enough, there were statements given about me to the Feds and they were from daddy's real daughter. She was going to testify that I was the ringleader, the one who set everything up. Meanwhile, she and I are on trial together.

I stayed quiet about her dad and she rolls on me. Pissed is an understatement. I wanted her dead. This bitch made a deal and used me in the process. I knew I couldn't make any moves during this trial so I just prayed during the entire ordeal for strength.

I gave birth to a baby girl and two weeks later I was on lock down. My bail was set at $100,000.00 and one of my girlfriends had access to my stash and set it for me. No one, not even my family, knew about my dealings with these people or that I had accounts in fake names set up all over the state.

I thank God almighty that the Feds didn't know either, otherwise I would've been fucked. I had to report once a week, via telephone, to a pretrial officer. I had to submit monthly statements to him as well. I went through this bullshit for two years. Finally, after all of the testimony from cops, witnesses, lawyers, handwriting experts, etc..., it was time for the verdict. Too late to make or take a deal , it was time to hear my fate.

My mother and brothers sat behind me in the courtroom along with my children. My baby's daddy sat in the back trying not to be seen and next to me was my fucking idiot co-defendants who dropped as many dimes as they could and still ended up without a nickel.

"Will the Defendants please rise?" said the court officer.

We stood up, the judge motioned to the jury and said, "Have you been able to reach a verdict?"

The foreperson replied "yes" and then handed a piece of paper to the court officer.

This had to have been the longest couple of minutes in my life. Everything was in slow motion. As the court officer handed the verdict to the judge I realized that that one piece of paper determined the rest of my life.

The judge looked at the paper and began to shake his head. He then gave it back to the court officer who returned it the foreperson. After that, all I remember hearing were the words "guilty". Every last one of us, my co-defendant's and myself, were found guilty.

"Sentencing is to be held one month from today" said the judge.

The courtroom was noisy with wailing, shouting, sniffing and cries of "Lord have mercy".

I looked at the gallery and all I saw was a blur of crying young women and their babies. All I could think was how are these babies going to eat ? How are these young women going to maintain a roof over their heads? Most of these women never had a job in their entire life and now the family that they devoted all of their time and energy to was going to be ripped apart by the justice system.

What was I going to tell my kids? My son was seven-years-old and didn't understand what was actually going on. The baby was two and very attached to me. I looked at my moms and I cried. I cried for all that I had done and all that I was going to have to do.

Some of us were not remanded before sentencing. We just continued to report weekly. I began to make my moves. I only had 30 days to make some shit happen and I was not about to be stuck again. I pulled together $50,000.00 and put a hit on that fat bitch that gave statements on me. She was done in two days. I also put one on daddy, who I had later found out made a deal on me too. His hit was easier because he was in jail. It only cost me $20,000.00 to have him done.

I phoned my pretrial officer and told him that all of my co-defendants were being murdered and I was afraid for my life. He also became concerned and asked me to come in to see him. I immediately jumped in my truck and went to his office. After all of the killings, the Feds were brought in to investigate. I wasn't concerned that they might be
able to connect the killings to me. I covered my tracks.

The government had played games with my life for over two years and now it was my turn. They decided that I would be sentenced to probation with restitution set at $80,000.00 because there was a concern for my safety (you know all they wanted was the money). I was sent to live out of state with my children, the Feds flipped the bill.

The first year no one was allowed to contact me, and vice versa, but after that I was allowed to contact my loved ones.

Life will never again be the same, but I guess in the end all I can say is don't hate the players hate the game. If you ain't ready to play, don't come on the field.

I took my sentence and now I am dealing with it, but for those who could not handle it, well I took care of them too. Was I wrong? Maybe. Do I regret any of it? Yes. Would I choose to do it all over again if I could? What do you think? That's the game of life.

****

Angel Hunter was born in Atlanta, Georgia and moved to New York in 1982 where she now raises her son and daughter. Angel is a high school graduate with an Associates Degree in Business Management. She has been writing since she was 11 years old.

𝒜𝒱𝐸𝑅𝒯𝐸𝒟 𝐻𝐸𝒜𝑅𝒯𝒮
John "Divine G" Whitfield

Daquan Smith sat in the far corner of the crowded bullpen wondering how things would look in another week. There was no doubt he was going way up north, probably somewhere near the Canadian border. The smell of stale bologna sandwiches and funky armpits merged together to form a depressing aroma that only increased his tress. The wooden bench seemed extraordinarily hard, but Daquan knew this was all in his mind. He was well aware that human nature required the human mind to perceive things in an exaggerated fashion when abnormal situations arose.

This was his second bid for possession of drugs. Daquan still believed he could get rich and make a livelihood out of selling drugs. During this zip five year bid, he intended to use the time learning how not to get caught the next time his feet hit the bricks. I

"If only I had moved my spot a couple of weeks earlier," Daquan pouted to himself. "I could have pulled it off. The next time I'll be more precautions instead of taking things likely," he insisted.

But there was something inside him that was struggling to be listened to. It was like a little voice trying to be heard amongst crashing sounds, hallowing shrieks and ear battering explosions.

The bullpen gate opened and the C.O. ushered three new prisoners into the already standing room only pen.

Daquan's eyes landed on the second prisoner. The face jumped out at him with intense familiarity. After a moment his memory bank correctly placed the face. It was Shawn Wayne.

"Yoh, Shawn!" Daquan shouted.

Shawn turned his head with nonchalant smoothness. It took him a few seconds to recognize Daquan. He struggled not to express his happiness to have bumped heads with someone he knew. With rock-hard firmness, Shawn bopped pass a couple of prisoners as he approached Daquan.

172

"Daquan," Shawn said standing a few feet from Daquan. "Jefferson High School, right?"

"Yeah, with all those games we lost, ain't no way we should ever forget each other," Daquan said cracking a smile.

Shawn laughed and said, "The ole bum ass Buckstormers."

Shawn shook Daquan's hand.

"Yeah, at least we was famous for getting' our asses pounded out on the regular."

"More like every single game we ever played."

Daquan scooted over for Shawn to sit next to him.

"Come on and chill," Daquan said.

Shawn sat down. It was a tight fit, but close contact in their environment was as common as crooks in a political arena.

"It's been some years, man, but I see you still looking like you holdin' it down," Shawn said.

Daquan and Shawn talked, reminiscing about the past and bringing each other up to date on the new developments in their lives. Shawn was an aspiring rap artist who thought he was the ultimate thug. Like Daquan, he too resorted to selling drugs, claiming it was his way of getting money to pay for his demos and other hip-hop adventures. Shawn was doing a zip four years for possession of heroin.

"While I'm here, son," Shawn said. "I'm gonna get buffed. By the time I see the board, I'm gonna be so big and cut up that they gonna be callin' me swolla-might. I'm gonna write about eight albums too."

"Let me hear you spit some raw, man," Daquan urged. "The way you sound, your shit gotta be gutter."

"No doubt, son. Check it." Shawn began to kick rap lyrics. Everyone in the bullpen stopped what they were doing and started listening. Next they began bobbing their heads and moving their bodies to the rhythm of the spoken word. Suddenly, a prisoner sitting next to Shawn provided a beat. He banged engagingly on the wooden bench, and before they knew it, there were handclaps.

When Shawn finished, almost everybody in the bullpen was giving him big ups, pats on the back and much dap.

"Yoh, Shawn. Your shit is genuine, man. How you ain't score with thug lyrics like that?" Daquan asked.

"Man, I think them dudes that checked my tapes out was hatin'. But it ain't nothing. When I get out, I'll be all right. By then my brother will have the entire East New York locked down with heroin. "I'll be able to buy my own recording studio, son."

"sounds like a plan to me," Daquan agreed. "When my shit falls into place, I'll even invest in you. I always wanted to get into that rap producing stuff. I want to get into some behind the scene type of thang, you know, like Suge Knight. We gotta make sure we stay in touch. Here's my name and number."

Daquan wrote his name and number down on a matchbook cover and handed it to Shawn.

"Here's mine," Shawn said writing his information down and giving it to Daquan.

The C.O. approached the bullpen and opened the gate. He started calling names. Daquan's name was the fourth to be called.

"Yoh, son," Daquan said hugging Shawn. "You maintain and I'll see you when we hit the town."

Daquan exited the bullpen without looking back.

*   *   *   *

Daquan landed in a facility about four miles from the Canadian border, just as he expected. The place was like another world beyond another world. Boredom and rampage foolishness seemed to be the order of the day. Watching rap videos, working out, programming and striving diligently to stay out of the box was all he did. Then he met an old timer named Wise Intellectual who was an instructor for a Black Studies class held on the weekends in the school building. Wise tried constantly to convince Daquan to attend the classes. Finally, our of boredom, Daquan agreed to check out one of the classes.

Daquan was impressed by the topic that were taught and returned the following week. By the time the fifth class rolled around, Daquan was wide open and thirsty for the information the class had to offer. A door was not only opened inside of his mind, but inside his heart as well.

Wise taught about blacks in science, amazing accomplishments made by blacks and many great things that would never be taught by mainstream educators. What really touched Daquan deeply was the class regarding how drugs were used as a weapon against the poor masses of the world. He was shocked to discover drugs such as opium and heroin were premeditatedly used against the Chinese; the American Indians were bombarded with alcohol and African American communities were flooded with crack, heroin, PCP and all the other poisons.

Daquan thought Wise was pulling his leg when he claimed there was proof that showed the CIA assisted international drug dealers with shipping drugs into the United States. If it wasn't for the publicly documented speech made by Congresswoman Maxine Waters, condemning the CIA's reprehensible acts, he would've never believed it.

Daquan laid on his bed starting at the dirt spot on the ceiling. Daquan felt like he was severely scarred by the information Wise passed on to him. All of these years he thought he was the man, but reality showed conclusively that he was nothing more than a puppet; and idiot being used as an instrument to facilitate the mass destabilization of his own community. He was directly and indirectly responsible for hurting other innocent people and his conscience (that little vice now loud enough to be heard) was letting it be known that it wasn't happy at all.

Daquan always wondered how this country was able to detect a small animal running through the woods with satellites, but couldn't stop millions of tons of drugs from entering the country. They didn't stop the drugs because they had no incentive to do so. In fact, they had every reason to make sure that drugs were fully available to certain communities. Daquan felt himself changing, becoming angry. He hated to feel like he was being used, abused, disrespected and pimped like a retarded skid-row prostitute.

Within a year after this awakening, Daquan made a 180-degree turn around. The way he viewed life was altered in a monolithic fashion. He acquired his GED, became a bookworm and sought to enhance his discipline with fanatical vigor. Wise was his guru and trainer, guiding and advising him every step of the way. Daquan had read over a dozen books on the music industry and just as many on Record Contract Law and Business Management. His mind was made up. He would never sell drugs again and would give his all towards breaking into the hip-hop industry.

In another facility, on the other side of the state, Shawn was catching and raising hell. He made many changes, but they wall were for the worst. Education of any sort was the furthest thing from his mind. Although he aspired to get into the rap industry, he did nothing to enhance his knowledge of the business. Instead, he relied solely on rap radio and fashion magazines that showcased the rich and wealthy. Despite his continual efforts at writing rap songs and kicking out albums with shocking ease, Shawn had no discipline, was irresponsible, reckless, arrogant and afraid of hard work. He believed that merely because he was able to rap very well that the limelight, instant fame and glamour were fully with his grasp.

Years later, Shawn ended up in a facility closer to the city. Daquan had arrived a this same facility three months earlier.

Shawn was on his way to his new program (a school porter). Daquan, who was a teacher's aide, jumped out of his seat and headed out of the room when he saw Shawn walk pass the his classroom.

"Yoh, Shawn!" Daquan called.

When Shawn turned around, Daquan saw that his face was covered with battle scars. After talking for a few minutes, Daquan saw that it was evident Shawn went from being a thug to a cold-hearted savage. It was nothing short of a miracle that he had made it this far without catching a new bid or getting himself killed.

Daquan signed, "Why don't you get your head together, Shawn. You got all those rap skills, but you throwing it all away by letting the time do you instead of you doing the time. Messing with them drugs is not what it's all about."

"What's this, you on some flip shit?" Shawn's anger was clear. "So, you ain't slinging no more?"

"No, I don't sell that stuff anymore. Nor will I ever do it again," Daquan said.

"Well ain't this some shit?" Shawn giggled. "You got soft and crossed over."

"This ain't about crossing over," Daquan replied. "It's about using some intellect and being educated on the devastating impact of drugs on our people. We gotta stop allowing ourselves to be victims of our own vices and stupidity."

"Oh, so now you calling me stupid?" Shawn said clenching his fists. "Now you tryin' to dis me."

"No, I'm not calling you stupid. All I'm saying is that we gotta get away from all that life destroying nonsense and start opening out minds."

"My mind is open motherfucker?" Shawn said moving towards Daquan in a threatening fashion. "The last dude who dissed me left out leakin'. You want some?"

Daquan saw the rage in Shawn's eyes and body gestures. The fight or flight chemical kicked in.

"Everything I said is all love, Shawn. I can't force you to see what I see, so when you're ready to get your head right, come see me," Daquan said as he tried to walk away, but Shawn took a swing at him. Daquan ducked and the blow struck him on his shoulder. Daquan continued walking.

"Fuck you, Daquan!" Shawn shouted a Daquan's back. "I don't fuck with cowards and cross-over niggas."

Daquan slowed his pace and considered going back to confront Shawn. His pride and ego sizzled with boiling intensity. A crossroad popped in his mind. The two roads he could travel down were vivid and clear. Forcing himself to continue walking, Daquan struggled every step of the way not to go back into that world he fought so successfully to get out of.

The days that followed tested Daquan's foundation like no other challenge. Shawn was bent on getting at him and even sent some of his thuggish hounds to harass him. If it wasn't for the intervention of numerous sideline observers who knew Daquan was a good due, Daquan might have been forced to fall completely off his square. Shawn kept the pressure on until Daquan was released from prison.

*   *   *   *

Daquan saw that time sure had a way of slipping by when the mind stayed preoccupied. Daquan couldn't believe he was walking out of the front gate. He felt he was as ready as he was going to get. Daquan even felt blessed because he made several connections with individuals who had people in the rap game. In numerous correspondence, Daquan had convinced the director of a small record label called "Rappertron" to give him a shot at managing, promoting and searching for talent. As he rode the southbound train, Daquan vowed he wasn't going to mess up this chance of a lifetime.

Within six months, things were starting to look good. Daquan had firmly planted his foot in the door and the boss was feeling him. The two acts he brought on board, Sha-real * TGONG were lyrical wizards and had styles like no other rap act on the market. Both groups were considered conscious rappers. They used rap as a means of educating the masses. They had the craziest beats that would make anyone move to the rhythm and had an excellent relationship wit Daquan.

When one of TGONG's songs was played on the radio, it started a process of raining good things. Daquan was scared to death by all this good fortune. Things were almost too good to be true, but Daquan quickly learned how to take it all in stride.

One late September afternoon, Daquan was sitting at his desk sifting through a stack of distribution inventory logs of TGONG CDs sold to date. He was cruising high on the debutorial success of TGONG and was planning to move his mom and two sisters out of the projects.

There was a knock on the door and Debbie, the secretary, stuck her head in the office.

"There's a dude out here demanding to see you," Debbie stated. "He said he's a personal friend of yours."

"Tell him to come back tomorrow," Daquan said.

"Listen, Daquan, this cat is acting real crazy. If you don't talk to him, there might be some drama."

"Send him in," Daquan said. "Who in the hell was this barging in demanding shit," Daquan said under his breath. He rose to his feet and stood in front of his desk with his arms folded across his chest. Shawn then entered his office.

Daquan shook his hand pitifully. Shawn looked like he changed form a savage to a straight up deranged monster.

Shawn smiled and held his hand out for a handshake.

"Daquan, my brother. What's happening, Home Team?" Shawn said.

The two shook hands, but Daquan let Shawn do all the talking and didn't even offer him a seat. As expected, Shawn had heard about Daquan's involvement in the rap game and was looking for some airplay. Obviously he wanted Daquan to give him a shot, sign him up to cut a couple of tracks.

"Damn, Daquan, say something, man," Shawn said. "I know you ain't still twisted over that little bullshit misunderstanding we had back in the joint are you?"

Daquan locked eyes with Shawn's. It was amazing how people were able to conveniently downplay their blatant wrong doings. Three years ago, this man attacked him like he was his ultimate enemy. Now he was standing in front of him pleading for a favor. To make matters worse, the fool didn't have the intelligence or decency to at least apologize for the foul things he had done to him.

Daquan wanted to blaze him, kick him out of his office and shatter his high strung attitude, but his discipline told him that wasn't what this was all about. How else were ignorant folks supposed to act? Empowerment wasn't about being vindictive and letting negative emotions dictate your behavior. He would help Shawn, but he wasn't going to give him a handout because he definitely didn't deserve it. But he would make him work real hard for it and hopefully in the process help Shawn to change his foul ways.

"Listen, Shawn," Daquan said. "This is what I'll do for you." Daquan went behind his desk and took a seat in his chair. "If you figure out this quote, incorporate the principles into your own life, your behavior, the way you deal with people, the way you think and produce evidence of this fact, then I'll put you on. No holds bar. I'll go all out for you, get you a sweet record deal with this label. Do you agree?"

Shawn was enthralled with excitement and replied, "Ain't no doubt I'll do it, Big Dee." He instantly saw stardom lights flashing across his mind.

Daquan leaned back in his chair.

"Here's the quote: What direction you choose to avert your heart is entirely up to you. But rest assured, the avenue you select will reflect in your behavior whether you avert negative or avert positive, the decision to turn away lies solely in the heart." Daquan said as he watched Shawn standing before him squinting his eyes. "Don't worry, I'll write it down for you."

Daquan pulled out a sheet of paper from the top drawer of his desk. He wrote down the quote and gave it to Shawn.

"Now, here's what you have to do," Daquan said. "Avert your heart from all that toxic bullshit. Become a man of principle and integrity and come see me with proof of all this." Daquan picked up his pen and continued his work as if Shawn wasn't even there.

Shawn was about to say something, but he turned around and simply walked out the door. When the door closed behind him, Daquan looked up and laid his pen down. Shaking his head, he hoped Shawn knew that in order to avert his heart he had to take a serious introspective look at himself without debilitating distractions. Sad to say, change of this magnitude required time, seclusion and an inner desire to want to change. Whether Shawn knew it or not, when he failed to take advantage of the opportunity to change while he was incarcerated, he missed the best opportunity he would ever get to attain such a transformation.

****

John "Divine G" Whitfield, has written seven (unpublished) novels, four of which have been adapted into screenplays. He has written four plays, two of which were performed before the Sing Sing prison population. He is also the first place winner of the 2003 PEN award for the Drama category for his play entitled Pro-Se. He is currently the star fiction writer for the Sing Sing Chronicle.

TWISTED
Regina Thomas

The clock on the bedside table read 2 a.m. I glanced at it as I reached for the ringing telephone. My stomach was in knots because only bad news came in the middle of the night.

"Hello," I said.

"Kayla, it's Mrs. Jordan," she nervously responded.

"Mrs. Jordan, what's wrong? Has something happened?" I asked gripping the receiver tightly, expecting the worst.

"Kayla, I haven't heard from Yollie since last week and she doesn't answer her phone. I'm worried that something terrible has happened to her. I know she's out there in the streets all night long doing God knows what. I just know something is wrong," Mrs. Jordan cried.

"Don't worry, Mrs. Jordan. I can check out a few of the places she might be. I'll call you back when I have some news."

"Bless you, Kayla. I don't know what I'd do without you. Since her father died I don't have anyone else to call on."

"You know I'll do whatever I can."

"Thank you, Kayla," Mrs. Jordan replied breathing a sigh of relief.

I hung up the phone and got out of bed searching for something to put on.

"Who was that, Kayla, and where are you going at this hour?" my husband, Derrick, asked.

"That was Mrs. Jordan. She hasn't heard from Yollie since last week and she's worried sick. I told her I'd go out and look for her."

"Kayla, you can't go rushing out at all hours of the night every time Yollie's mother calls," Derrick said.

"I have to," I told my husband.

"No you don't. It isn't safe. Why can't she call someone

else?" Derrick questioned.

"There is no one else, Derrick. Look, don't worry. I'll be careful."

"Wait, I'll go with you," he said rising from the bed to get dressed.

"Derrick, we both can't go. You stay here with the baby. I'll be back soon. I promise," I said in a reassuring tone.

I rushed out of the house before he could stop me. If he knew where I was headed he'd be furious. I desperately hoped that this would be the last time I would have to do this, that this time I could finally convince my friend to get her life together. How could things have gotten so out of control for someone whose life was as full of promise as Yollie's was?

I met Yollie when we were both 11 years old. It was the day my family moved on the block where she lived. Her house was directly across the street from ours. I remember how she sat on her stoop watching the movers carry our belongings into the house. Being new to Queens, I wasn't used to being openly stared at and immediately took offense because in the Bronx we didn't play that.

"Well," I said to her giving her my best head roll.

"Well what?" she responded.

"Why you hawkin' me? You act like you ain't never seen anybody move in before. You better stop staring so hard."

"It's a free country so I can look wherever I want to," she proceed to tell me, opening her eyes as wide as she could to emphasize her point. She looked so funny I couldn't help but laugh.

"What's your name?" I asked her. I was curious about this girl because she stood up to me. Back in the boogie down I was the terror of the sixth grade so I wasn't used to being challenged.

"My name is Yollie," she said.

"What kind of name is that, Swahili?" I asked.

"No, it's short for Yolanda. What's your name?"

"Kayla."

"You wanna come over and watch videos, Kayla?"

My mother had already sent me outside claiming I was in the way. So I agreed to watch videos with Yollie.

"Yeah, I'll come over. I just have to ask my mom first."

Yollie waited for me while I went inside to ask for permission. We then went over to Yollie's house. Yollie's house was the nicest one on the block. Her room was done up in pink and white and she had every stuffed animal in creation.

"Dang! It looks like a zoo in here," I commented upon entering her room.

"My daddy brings me home a stuffed animal every time he goes away on a business trip," Yollie said sadly.

"From the looks of it he must travel a lot."

"Yeah, he does. But I'd much rather have him home instead of all these stuffed animals. It seems like the only time he ever talks to me is to say goodbye before he's off on another trip."

"What about your mom?" I asked her.

"She's used to him not being around much. She says in time I'll get used to it too, but I don't think I ever will. Sometimes I think he travels so much just so he doesn't have to be here with us." she confided.

I felt bad for her when she told me that. My father drove a bus and he was home every night. My parents worked hard to get us out of the tenement we lived in and sacrificed a lot to get the house we were moving into. I used to complain all the time about not being able to get everything I wanted but what I hadn't realized until that day was that I'd always had what I needed. She and I spent the rest of the afternoon in her room watching videos, eating the snacks her mother fixed for us and enjoying each others company. When it was time for me to leave she walked with me outside.

"I had fun hanging out with you, Kayla. See you later."

"Goodbye, Yollie," I said.

"No, Kayla, never say goodbye. Always say see you later."

"Why?" I inquired.

"Because it means you forward to seeing that person again."

"Okay, see you later, Yollie."

From that day on Yollie and I became best friends. Since

neither of us had any siblings we forged a sisterhood between us. Yollie and I were like night and day but the differences between us only made our bond stronger. She was a tall and skinny girl with a big heart and bigger dreams.

"I'm going to be a famous model one day," she used to tell me all the time. I didn't doubt it because even at eleven she was beautiful. Her dark skin was as smooth as glass and her short black curls were soft and glossy. She wore pretty dresses, matching barrettes and nail polish. People always noticed her. She excelled in her classes and believed that the world would someday be hers.

I was short and curvy for my age. My light skin and long hair used to make me a target for the viciousness girls like me had to endure until I started fighting back. I always wore jeans, tee shirts, ponytails and a bad attitude. I didn't have stars in my eyes like Yollie. I just wanted to get through high school. Unlike my best friend, school was harder for me but I managed to get through it. I got a job after I finished high school as a receptionist at the local crisis center. It was there where I met and later married, Derrick, who was the Assistant Director at the time. He encouraged me to further my education and obtain a degree in psychology. It was a struggle but I did it. Yollie was there for me every step of the way. She tutored me, pushed me whenever I felt like giving up and cheered the loudest at my graduation. When Derrick proposed to me, Yollie helped me plan my wedding and when I was pregnant with my daughter, Yasmine, she threw me the biggest baby shower in history. Having her in my life has always been a blessing to me.

I often reminisce about those days, especially when I'm out here in the middle of the night looking for her. I hate driving through the streets of Hunts Point. It's so depressing to see so many young women out there selling their bodies to feed their addictions. It breaks my heart even more because Yollie is out here among them. Just a few short years ago she was well on her way to realizing her dream of becoming a model. She was signed with the modeling agency, Urban Empress, straight out of high school. Everything seemed to have been going so well for her; she was featured in magazines, print ads and even did a few runway shows. It was all good for a while until she got caught up in the game.

Yollie was partying all the time and hanging out in the clubs with the so-called ballers, wanna be players and hustlers. Yollie started drinking heavily and using cocaine. It wasn't long before her lifestyle began to affect her work. She would miss important appointments and not show up for bookings. The agency stopped sending her out on calls because she had become so unreliable and ultimately they let her go. It was around that time that she met Mack, a drug-dealing hustler, at an industry party. He filled her head with his plans to put her back on top, filled her nose with cocaine and pumped her veins with heroin. She went from the cat walk to the strip clubs and ultimately out onto the streets of Hunts Point.

I've made this trip countless times and will continue to come down here as long as she does. I pulled my car over and rolled down the window when I spotted one of the girls who worked the same area as Yollie.

"Sparkle, have you seen Yollie tonight?" I asked.

"Naw, she ain't been around the last two nights. She's probably with Mack. He came down here a couple of days ago wildin' out. She got into his car and I ain't seen her since. When you see her tell her tricks out here are thirsty. They keep asking for her and shit. She ought to know a bitch can't make no money if her ass ain't out here on the track," Sparkle said.

"Sparkle, if you see her will you tell her I'm looking for her?"

"Yeah, whatever."

I drove off filled with a sense of dread. Yollie couldn't see past Mack's image but I could. Outwardly he was all shine, diamonds, designer labels and a flashy car, all ill gotten gains made off of the sale of my best friends body.

"God, please let her be all right," I prayed as I headed for Mack's house.

Mack was a mean son of a bitch. He used Yollie, abused her and treated her as though she owed him a living. I've tried so many times to get Yollie away from his influence but I could never convince her to leave him. She claimed he took care of her and gave her what she needed. Being a counselor at the crisis center, I recognized the issues she was dealing with. Yollie became my personal crusade. I loved her and I knew all too well where trying to fill the void in her life could lead. She was vulnerable and Mack took advantage of her weakness. He made her dependent upon him and manipulated her into becoming part of his hustle.

I pulled up in front of his house. I didn't see his car parked anywhere on the street as I walked up to the door. My fear was replaced by anger towards Mack for whatever he had done to my friend this time.

My husband pleaded with me constantly not to go chasing after Yollie every time she went missing, but I couldn't turn my back on her. She was lost and I wanted so desperately to help her find her way back. She had always been there for me. I didn't know how to not be there for her if she needed me.

I rang the bell and waited for her to answer. After a few minutes, when she didn't answer the door, I stepped out onto the curb and looked up at the windows that were facing the street. They were all dark so I knew no one was home. I walked back to my car trying to figure out where else she could be. Just as I was about to drive off I noticed Mack's car coming around the corner. As soon as he was parked in the space behind me I jumped out of my car prepared to do battle.

"Where the hell is Yollie!" I screamed at him.
"Whoa, calm your ass down. Who the fuck you think you talkin' to, huh? What did I tell you about coming around here," Mack said.

"Your trick ass don't scare me, Mack. I'm looking for Yolanda. What did you do to her?"

"You know, Kayla, you're a feisty little bitch, Kayla. I like that. Why don't you let a brotha put you on? A woman as fine as you could make a lot of money with the proper guidance." Mack said.

"Fuck you, Mack. If you really want to do something for me just tell me where I can find Yollie."

"Relax, ma. She's in the car."

187

He walked around to the passenger's side and opened the door. I was so relieved. I pushed past him to get to her myself.

"Yollie, are you okay? Your mother called me. She told me that she hasn't heard from you in over a week," I said to her putting my arms around her once she was out of the car.

"Hey, Kayla. I'm fine. Tell mama not to worry about me. Tell her I'll call her in a couple of days," Yollie replied hugging me back.

When I stepped back I noticed that she had a black eye and bruises on her face.

"My God, Yollie! Did he do this to you?" I demanded to know looking at Mack's smug face.

"It was an accident, Kayla," she said.

The glazed look in her eyes told me she was high.

"Yollie, come home with me, alright? You don't have to stay here with him. I'll help you get yourself together," I begged.

"Come on, baby. Let's go upstairs. I got a few of them thangs for you," Mack interrupted.

Yollie looked from me to Mack, then back to me again.

"Kayla, I gotta go," she said turning away from me and heading towards the apartment.

"Yollie, please don't go with him. Let me help you," I pleaded with her.

She turned back to me and said, "You can't save me, Kayla. Go home to your husband and your baby. I'll be fine."

"Yollie, wait!" I cried.

"I'll call you tomorrow, Kayla. I promise."

I started to go after her but Mack stepped between us.

"She said she'll call you tomorrow, now get the fuck out of here before I forget I'm a gentleman," Mack said.

"Yollie!" I screamed. She turned around again and smiled at me.

"See you later, Kayla," Yollie said.

I stood there feeling helpless as I watched them disappear into the building. When I got home my husband was waiting up for me.

"Kayla, you can't keep doing this!" Derrick said.

"Derrick, you don't understand. Yollie needs me. I have to help her."

"You can't help someone who doesn't want to be helped. I only wish you were as devoted to me and Yasmine as you are to Yolanda."

"That's not fair, Derrick," I said.

"She doesn't need you, Kayla. We need you. All your good intentions won't do Yollie any good until she's ready to help herself."

"But I can't turn my back on her."

"I'm not asking you to turn your back on her. I just don't want you to sacrifice everything for her. Every time she gets into trouble you drop everything and go running off after her and a few days later she's back on the streets again. I'm sorry that your friend's life is so out of control but it's her life. Your life is here with us. What if something happens to you while you're out there trying to save Yollie. What do I tell our little girl? Why is she so much more important to you than we are?"

"Derrick, I'm sorry. Nothing is more important than you and Yasmine, but for as long as I can remember Yollie and I have taken care of each other. She means a lot to me and I feel like I've failed her somehow. I feel like I have everything now and she has nothing. She deserves so much more Derrick."

"Kayla, you can't feel guilty because your lives have turned out so differently. Yollie made her choices, unfortunately for her they were mostly the wrong ones but that's not your fault. I hope she does get her life together but it's going to be up to her to take the first step."

I knew he was right but that didn't make it any easier. I vowed to always be there whenever she was ready to make a change. I knew I was endangering myself by driving down to Hunts Point alone and by confronting a thug like Mack. I had a husband and a child to consider and although I knew I'd do anything for Yollie the decision to change her life had to come from her. I called her mother and told her I had spoken to Yollie and that she asked me to let her know that she'd call in a couple of days.

Three days later the ringing telephone woke me up. It was after midnight so I wasn't surprised that it was Mrs. Jordan calling.

"Mrs. Jordan, is everything all right? Is Yollie missing again?"

"No, Kayla, not this time. The police just left, they found my daughter's body in an alley in Hunts Point. You won't have to go looking for her any more," she said before she burst into tears.

"NO!" I screamed. My husband managed to take the telephone from my trembling hands and get what details he could from Yollie's distraught mother. He tried to console me but the only thing I could think of was that my friend was gone.

"It is with a heavy heart my brothers and sisters that we commit our dearly departed sister to the earth today. She will be missed by all who loved her but take comfort that God loved her best."

The preacher's eloquent benediction gave me no comfort as I watched the casket being slowly lowered into the ground. My tears silently ran down my checks as I shut my eyes in a futile attempt to wish it all away. My best friend was lying in there. This was all a terrible dream. It had to be. But the reality of it hit me as the wails of her mother filled the air.

"Oh Lord, my baby! Sweet Jesus she was my baby!"

The family could barely restrain her as she attempted to throw herself onto the casket as it disappeared into the ground. Some believe death is final. I guess in a way it is, but only for the deceased. Those left to mourn carry the grief of that death forever. I will miss my friend terribly. I know in my heart that I did everything I could to help her but in the end she was right, I couldn't save her. As we prepared to leave the cemetery I looked back at the grave where my best friend lay.

"See you later, Yollie," I whispered.

I didn't want to leave her buried in the ground. I'd give anything to have her with me again but I knew she wouldn't be coming back.

Her existence on this earth was over now and mine would continue for as long as the Lord would allow. I knew I had to be strong, for myself, for my family, for Yollie.

****

Regina Thomas was born February 25, 1964. She is a native of Queens, New York where she resides with her two teenage children, Dawn and Leon Ladson III. From the time she could hold a pencil, writing has been a passion of her, a legacy passed down to her from her father, the late William Earl Thomas who was a gifted storyteller in his own right. Regina credits her father with inspiring her to pursue her dream of becoming an author.

FREE MONEY
Freeze

It was about 2:30 in the afternoon when my phone rang. I was in the bed with wifey, Sonya, and that' where I had planned to stay since it was Sunday (her day). Besides, it was raining outside. The kids were with Sonya's mom, so it was on.

"Hello," I said.

"What's up nigga?" the caller said.

"Where you at?"

"I'm still up top. I need you to do me a favor."

"What?" I asked.

"I need you to pick me up from the airport in Norfolk."

"Damn, yo. Why you can't catch the plane straight here?"

"Cause I would have a long ass layover in Charlotte. I got *food*."

When I heard that shit, I knew what time it was. That's my man Boogie on the other end of the phone. I met him through his cousin, Chomba, who is a supermodel type and one of my bitches.

Their family is Panamanian but they look black. I had flown to Panama with her last year and met Boogie and a bunch of her other peoples. Boogie was the only dude there, besides myself that lived in the states. Boogie lived in Brooklyn. He and I hit it off and hung out. Now, whenever I go to New York to re-up, he always comes to the crib that I share with Chomba in the Park Slope section of Brooklyn, which is the same block that rapper Foxy Brown lives on with her moms.

I let Boogie come back to Greenville with me once because he was fucked up in the game and needed to flip a Big Eight (four and a half ounces) a few times. That was a few months ago. The nigga got a crib down here now and we're closer than ever. My kids call him Uncle Boogie.

"If I run out of food, Boogie will sell me a ki for the same thing he paid for it. That's my man, so I couldn't leave him hangin'.

"What time does your plane land?" I asked him.

192

"Six o'clock. I'm on US Air," Boogie said.

"Aiight. I'll be there."

"Peace," Boogies said hanging up the phone.

I looked at the digital clock on the nightstand next to the bed. I had about three and a half hours before Boogie's plane landed. I know wifey is about to flip.

"Boo, I've got to make a run," I said to Sonya. "I'll be back either late tonight or early tomorrow morning."

"No you not!" Sonya replied. "I ain't tryin' to hear that shit. Today is my day."

"It's important," I said.

"So! I don't care," Sonya replied.

"I've got to pick Boogie up from the airport in Norfolk. His plane arrives at six."

"I'm going with you then."

"You can't, ma."

"Why not?" Sonya demanded to know.

"Cause he got drugs with him. You know I don't have you around that shit," I explained.

Sonya sucked her teeth and crossed her arms. I could clearly see she was upset. Since it was only a two our drive from my house to Norfolk International Airport, I had about an hour and a half to kill.

I walked up to Sonya, who was in pout mode, and put my hand around her waist. I pulled her close to me.

"Get off me," she said trying to push me away.

"Don't act like that, ma. You know this is business. What did I tell you about business?" I said.

"I know. I know," Sonya sighed.

"You know business pays the bills and keeps you living in this nice house. It keep you from wanting anything."

"I don't need all this shit," Sonya stated. "I just want you to start spending more time with me and the kids."

"I will. I promise. As a matter of fact, plan a trip for us," I told her as I kissed her on the neck.

Sonya didn't respond to the kiss so I started playing with her nipples as I pushed down my boxers. She likes that shit. She reached down and grabbed my dick, raised her leg and put me inside of her. She loved it this way. She liked to watch my dick go in and out of her. After 15 minutes of changing positions and love making, she was ready to cum. By this time I had her legs cocked up on my shoulders. She wanted me to go deeper and hit that spot.

"You ready?" I asked her as I plunged in and out of her.

"Yeah," she replied.

"Tell me when."

"C'mon, now!"

"Oh, oh, oh, oh," we both cried out as we came together. I just laid there in her arms, still inside of her with sweat running everywhere. I felt my dick going soft. She must have felt it too because she started grippin' my shit with her pussy muscles and throwin' it at me at the same time. We went at it again. That's why we got three kids now...her nasty self.

We both got dressed after taking a long hot shower together. Sonya decided that she was going to pick up the kids since I wasn't going to be home. I suggested that she take my car, the Benz, and I'd drive the Escalade since it wasn't as flashy. I kissed Sonya goodbye and we went our separate ways.

Once Boogie's plane landed it took him about 15 minutes to make his way outside to passenger pick-up. I flashed my headlights when I saw him. He got in and threw his bag in the back seat.

"What you got with you?" I asked.

"Nothin'," Boogie said. "There's been a change of plans. I've got a new connect from around the way and he's coming down with a few of them thangs. He wants to see how fast I can move them down here. I told him shit was sweet out here. His flight lands in an hour."

"I'm not staying out here to wait for him."

"Nah, let's go 'head and bounce. I gave him your 800 number. He's going to hit you as soon as his plane lands."

While driving through Norfolk on our way to my apartment in Virginia Beach, I called Tonya, one of my freaks. Actually, she was more than that to me. Tonya had a face and haircut like Halle Berry and a body like Mary J. I really liked shawty a lot. She worshipped a nigga like a God whenever we were together.

I had Tonya go pick up dude from the airport for me. I described him to her with the description that Boogie gave me. He was a Spanish and his name was Hymito. I told Tonya to bring him back to my crib.

Shortly thereafter I received a page. I showed Boogie the number and he confirmed that it was Hymito so he called him back. I told Boogie to tell him to look for a light-skinned girl in a black Lexus.

Tonya, along with Hymito, arrived safely to my apartment. Right out of the gate, there was something about Hymito that I didn't like, but I couldn't put my finger on it. Maybe it was because dude talked too much. Yeah, that was it. That little fuck talked too much.

Boogie and Hymito went on and on with words. At first I wasn't involved in their conversation, but Hymito put me in it talking all this Big Willie shit. He was saying that if I helped Boogie get rid of the five bricks that was coming down by car in the morning, that he'd come back with twenty more bricks.

We discussed a price for the five bricks. Hymito wanted 17 grand each. That was a good price. I made a mental note that if the coke was any good, I might make him my new connect too. My connect up top was still charging me 20 grand for a ki of powder. Boogie and I could cook up the five bricks that were on their way and put the whip on each one. That would bring us back a brick and a half, which would give us an extra two and a half bricks. That's an easy ass fifty grand for a day's work. Boogie and I would split.

In the morning I was supposed to be going to Jamaica with this broad named Zorona. That's another reason why I had planned on chillin' with wifey so hard. I had to call Zorona and let her know that something had come up and Jamaica would just have to be rescheduled.

I went into the kitchen and called Zorona on my cell phone. She talked mad shit, but what could she do? She ain't pay for shit anyway. I told her to pick another date and call the airline and hotel to reschedule. After hanging up with Zorona I called a couple of niggaz

I knew in Norfolk about weights. They liked the price at 20 grand a pop.

Later on that night, Boogie and I dropped Hymito off at his hotel, which was down the block from my apartment. When we got back to my spot, Tonya was coming out of the kitchen with a bowl of Applejacks. She was barefoot and didn't have on anything but one of my T-shirts.

Boogie saw all ass cheeks hanging out and said, "Damn, yo. What's up with shawty?"

Tonya had gone into the bedroom and shut the door. I knew what Boogie was getting' at so I replied, "Ain't nothing. She don't get down like that."

"How you know, nigga? All bitches got some freak in 'em."

In order to test Boogie's theory I called out, "Tonya, c'mere.

Tonya walked into the living room, ass-cheeks still hanging out. She sat next to me on the couch and asked, "What's up?"

"My man Boogie here wants to hit that," I said.

Tonya stared at me for a moment. Not believing that I had just said some shit like that to her, she got up and walked back towards the bedroom.

"You better call that bitch, Zorona," Tonya said slamming the door.

"I told you, nigga," I said.

"Damn, that ass is phat," is all Boogie could say.

We laughed and smoked a blunt before going to bed. I knew Tonya was mad at me so I had to give her some make-up-dick. The next morning Hymito's driver paged me to let me know he was in town. Boogie and I met up with him and too him to Hymito's hotel.

Hymito and the driver spoke in Spanish throughout each of their conversations. I sensed something was wrong, then that's when Hymito dropped a bomb on us.

"The price is going to be 25 grand each," Hymito said.

"C'mon, man. That's some bullshit. I've already got them sold for 20 a piece," I told him.

I looked at Boogie who wasn't saying shit. He saw that I was upset. He finally stood up and said, "Yo, let me holla at them for a minute."

I walked outside and got into my truck. Boogie came out and got in the car with the bricks.

"What happened with the 17 grand a piece like he said last night?" I asked.

"I don't know. They trippin'," Boogie said.

"That means we got to go up on our price then."

"Guess so."

We went back to the crib and Tonya whipped one up for us, bringing back a little over a ki and a half. The coke was like that. I fronted the half to my man, Blu, in Norfolk. He had a spot that pumped 50's all day over on the 31st Street.

The next day Boogie and I were on the interstate on our way to see Blu. Blu had called and said he had 12 grand for me. While driving my pager went off. I looked at it and saw that it was Hymito. I told Boogie to call him back. I was glad that we were going to pick up this money so that I could give it to this nigga. I was getting tired of him stressing us out.

I could hear Boogie's side of the conversation with Hymito. It didn't sound as though it was going too good. When Boogie hung up with Hymito he didn't say anything.

"What's up, you?" I asked, breaking the silence.

"You know what that nigga just said to me?" Boogie said.

"What?"

"He told me that we were taking too long with his ends. He told me to wait for you to go to sleep tonight, get the drugs and any money and bounce on you. I'm then supposed to go to his hotel and shoot back to New York with him."

"Oh, he was gonna play me like that?" I said.

As I continued driving the beats of the music filled the car. I thought long and hard before I said anything else. Boogie hadn't said anything either. I guess he was thinking too. Finally I turned down the music and spoke.

"Check this out, yo. I ain't giving that nigga shit. Fuck him! I'm keeping all that shit. That nigga don't know me. What you gonna do?" I said pissed off.

"I'm with you, but he knows my family, dawg."

"Aiight, we'll think of something. Let's go pick up this money. You still tryin' to get at that broad, Sharon?"

"Yeah, I'm gonna call her now and tell her to be ready, that we about to come scoop her," Boogie said. "I need my dick sucked and ass licked. That bitch is a big freak. Maybe we can get her and Tonya to eat each other."

I looked at Boogie like he was crazy, but neither of us couldn't help but laugh.

We handled our business with Blu, picked up Sharon from Roberts Park and went back to the crib. Boogie made Sharon go in the second bedroom and watch TV because Tonya was still in mine. I watched Sharon walk away and I swear she's got to be the phattest bitch in Norfolk. I thought to myself, "When Boogie leaves, I'ma double back and hit that." got to. I heard she was a beast.

Boogie and I sat in the living room and put our heads together. We came up with a plan to fix Hymito's ass: I took the coke and bounced with it in the middle of the night. All of it, the coke and the money collected. Boogie would claim that he woke up early in the morning to bounce on me, but I was already gone. I left a note behind telling him that I took everything because his man tried to play me with the fucked up prices and shit.

Boogie called Hymito while I was sitting right there and fed him the story. Boogie should have gotten an Oscar he played it so well. His best performance was yet to come.

Hymito told Boogie to come to the hotel. Boogie caught a cab to the hotel. It was only a matter of time before he and Hymito beeped me. I stepped outside on my terrace and phoned them.

"What's up?" I asked once Hymito answered the phone.

"Yo, freeze up," Hymito said. "It ain't even got to be like that man. I was just..."

"Shut up, bitch!" I said, cutting him off. "You tried to play me so I took your shit. Do you know who you fuckin' wit? By the time you get back to New York, get your squad together and head back towards my turf, I'll be long gone. As a matter of fact, fuck it! You know what? I'm bout to call my mans and them and we'll be over there to get at you. If you're punk ass is still there by the time we roll up, you and that nigga Boogie is dead!"

I hung up the phone. I should have gotten an Oscar for Best Supporting Actor.

I went back to bed. I told Tonya what was going on and she laughed. I asked her whether or not she was scared and if she was if she wanted to go home. Tonya replied, "Hell no!" I love this gangsta shit."

That shit right there turned me on. My dick got rock hard. Tonya and I immediately went at it. Tonya must have been turned on too 'cause she was extra rough with me.

After Tonya and I got down I sent her out to make a few runs for me. That gave me time to call wifey. I knew I was getting ready to get an earful from Sonya. I told her that something had come up and that I would be gone for a few more days. That was my regular routine, so she didn't go off to bad on me. I told her to go into my safe, something she never did without permission, and to get a grand out for her and the kids to go shopping. That would occupy her for the next few days.

$$$

A loud knock on my door startled me. Tonya and I both jumped up from out of our sleep. I looked at the clock and it read 8:25 a.m. I eased out of the bed and slipped my boxers on. Tonya did the same with her thong and T-shirt, then she took the Ruger P-90 9mm out of the nightstand drawer. I usually kept it a shoe box in the closet, but I had Tonya place it in the nightstand drawer the night before just in case them niggaz tried to pull a sneak attack and kick the door in or some shit.

Tonya took the gun and went and hid in the second bedroom closet. We had gone over the plan the night before so she know if she heard shots, to come out blastin'. I had my Heckler & Kock 45 in my hand as I crept to the front door.

I could see whoever was out there's shadow through the bottom of the door. I had the gun pointed at the peephole. I figured their head should be right in that area. A shot from the four pound would have gone through the door and left a hole the size of a silver dollar in their face.

As I took a step a spot on the wooden floor creaked. A voice came from the other side of the door.

"Yo, it's me!"

"Who wit' you?" I asked.

"Nobody!"

I looked through the peephole and saw that it was Boogie. I let him in and he gave me the 411 on how I scared Hymito's punk ass so bad that he demanded he and Boogie leave the hotel on foot. They found a pay phone and called a cab to the airport. Boogie said that once they got back to New York, he had to play the nigga close so that he wouldn't think anything was up with him and me.

Boogie told me that Hymito wasn't trying to come back at me over no five ki's. He said he'd catch me up top one day. Boogie and I split 10 of the 12 grand I had collected from Blu and I gave Tonya the other two. Tonya whipped up the rest of the food for us and we went along with the original plan.

Once the drugs were sold Boogie and I split the pot and he headed back up top. He had to show his face to avoid suspicion. Me, I sent Tonya home and went home to spend a couple days with wifey and the kids. I then got my money together and went to see my connect, Norm, in New York.

I had these two girls I know, Kecia and DeRonde, drive my Quest mini van up top for me that had over $200,000 dollars in the stash boxes. I flew up and met them. Since Norm was waiting on his big shipment to come in, Kecia, DeRonde and I chilled at me and Chomba's apartment in Brooklyn for a few days. We were only a couple of blocks from Hymito's block. I didn't care though. Fuck that bitch ass nigga! That was free money.

****

Freeze currently resides in Petersburg, Virginia where he just completed his first novel. He is currently seeking publishing opportunities and hopes to see his masterpiece on bookstore shelves soon.

MAMA'S BOY
Roy L. Pickering Jr.

The plan was perfect, simple and effective. It was so dependable in outcome that you could set your watch to it. The four adolescents had pulled this scam off numerous times previously, always without a hitch.

Rodney had the deepest and most mature sounding voice of the group. So it was always he who placed the call and always to a Chinese take-out restaurant for a variety of important reasons. Reason number one was that the delivery guy would always be small, frail and scared to death of black people (at least when he was surrounded by four of them anyway). Reason number two, they never arrived in a car, always on a beat up old bicycle so they never tried to run for it. The third and fourth reasons were that all four of them liked Chinese food (who doesn't?), and there were about half a million Chinese restaurants in the area. This might seem odd to some since no Chinese people actually lived in their neighborhood, but the four young men didn't spend much time contemplating this enigma. They tended to accept things as they were, without excessive questioning.

"What's taking this guy so long?" asked Cognac, who was named after the beverage responsible for his conception. He often joked that if other parents in the neighborhood used the same method of name giving as his parents, there would be a whole lot of Malt Liquors running around.

Cognac was in love with gold. It adorned his fingers, wrists, neck, ears and one tooth. His nickname, as if someone named Cognac needed a nickname, was Glitter.

"If he doesn't show up in the next two minutes, I say we don't tip him," Coletrane said. As usual, Coletrane's joke cracked up none other than Coletrane. His laughter was a sight to see due to a great quantity of loose flesh that bounced and jiggled in every which direction. He claimed to not really be fat, merely too short for his weight. Coletrane planned to correct this situation by having a growth spurt to go along with his newly grown chest hairs.

If somehow this did happen, he still wouldn't be much taller than Jerome, who seemed to grow about a foot per month. Jerome held a basketball in hand, his trademark. The game of hoops was the most important thing in his life. It was his school, his church, his lover, his mother and his child. Jerome could recite from memory the statistics of just about any player in the NBA.

Rodney's memory was equally impressive, only with a different subject matter. Roaming around in his head were the lyrics for pretty much every rap song ever recorded, as well as close to one hundred songs he had composed. The headphones around his neck were as constant as a tattoo.

The four friends killed time by bragging about the numerous girls who would allegedly soon be theirs, and recycling insults at each other all in the name of fun. Any moment now their latest victim would arrive, supplying them with much needed (or certainly wanted) cash, an antidote for their boredom, and some never to be taken for granted free food. What more does a growing boy want?

"Here he comes," Coletrane muttered.

The deliveryman approaching appeared to be about a thousand years old. He looked too antiquated to walk ten consecutive steps, much less be peddling a bike laden with food uphill. As soon as he hopped off the bike (yes hopped, the man was startlingly agile) and started looking for the fictional address Rodney had given, the four young thieves made their move. Their move was simply to surround the deliveryman. Nine times out of ten, food, money and the bike were willingly offered without them having to say a word or make a single threatening gesture. Their mere presence was sufficient. They never actually wanted the bicycles, being that they were always pieces of crap, and often the most difficult part of the crime was convincing the deliveryman of this fact. Occasionally they had to be a bit more menacing in order to convince the guy to forfeit his goods. Once Rodney had to pull his knife, but that was as dramatic as things had ever gotten.

Coletrane didn't look particularly menacing on this day. His mother dead and his father wherever he was, he had been raised by his grandparents on his mother's side and taught to respect the elderly. He didn't have the nerve to threaten someone who made his grandparents look like teenagers, but he didn't want to appear cowardly to his friends. He walked up to the delivery man along with the others, but instead of staring into the man's eyes as was custom, Coletrane looked sheepishly down at the ground.

The four of them waited patiently for the old man to realize he was in the same shoes that Custer had found himself in, probably during this guy's childhood.

"Food for you?" The deliveryman asked.

"Hell yeah, food for us," Jerome growled.

"Twenty-two fifty."

"How about for free, and we let your old ass live?" said Rodney.

"Twenty-two fifty," the deliveryman repeated.

"How about one ass whipping?" said Cognac. "Or you can just hand over that food and the money in your pocket, and we'll call it even."

"You boys should be shamed of yourselves," the deliveryman scolded.

"Who you calling boy?" asked Jerome, who towered ridiculously over the little, fearless old man.

"You boys need a spanking. Your mamas raised you better."

"Now I know you ain't talking 'bout my mother," Rodney said taking a step forward with intent to intimidate.

"Give me money or we make trade," the deliveryman said.

"What? You senile or something, Grandpa? Hand over my motherfucking Moo Shu now," Rodney yelled as he was clearly getting agitated. He had a nasty temper that could ignite quickly when situations unfolded unexpectedly.

"Money or trade," the delivery mans insisted.

"Fine," said Cognac. "We'll trade you those bags and whatever cash you have on you for your life. Sound good to you?"

"No good," the deliveryman said shaking his head.

"You ain't 'fraid to die, fool?" Rodney asked.

"I seventy-seven years old. Sometime I think death scared of me. Twenty-two fifty or trade," the deliveryman said.

"Trade what?" asked Cognac.

"I take one of your gold chains, your Walkman, your basketball, and ... What you have for me round boy?" the delivery said making his way down the line of boys.

"Let's just let the old guy go," said Coletrane, still studiously examining his sneakers.

"I'm getting tired of this bullshit," said Rodney. "This is a robbery, not a negotiation." Rodney tried to grab a bag of food from off of the deliveryman's bicycle, but his hand never reached its destination. The old guy quickly and firmly slapped it away.

"Not a smart move, Gramps. Now I'm gonna have to jack you up," Rodney said.

"Let's just leave the man be," Coletrane said.

Rodney raised his fist and started walking towards the old man. "No, I don't think ..."

Suddenly Rodney was laying on the ground in fetal position, his statement left incomplete. His hands were between his legs covering the very vulnerable area he had just been kicked in. That alone was ample cause for amazement on the parts of the three would be robbers who remained standing. What really shocked them though, was the old man removing the headphones from around Rodney's neck.

"This pay your share," The deliveryman said turning towards Jerome. "Now you."

Jerome was very unsure of himself, that much was apparent by the look on his face. Cognac and Coletrane half expected him to run off. Instead he started to bounce his basketball.

"You want it, take it," Jerome said.

Jerome was an excellent ball handler for his height, for any height in fact. On the basketball court he was unstoppable. He would come racing down the floor dribbling the ball with the dexterity of a Harlem Globetrotter, then he'd go soaring over his lesser opponents in Michael Jordan-like manner and slam the ball through the hoop with Shaq-like authority. He was a shoe in for a college scholarship, and would probably end up being one of the rare success stories from their neighborhood.

Cognac and Coletrane watched Jerome expertly dribble the ball at a dizzying speed through his legs and around his back. They were rather surprised to see the old man assume a defensive position. They were stupefied when he cleanly stole the ball from Jerome.

The old man tucked the ball under his arm. "This pay your share," he confirmed.

A dejected Jerome hung his head in embarrassment, but did not protest. Anyone who could humble him in the game of basketball deserved no disrespect. As much as he cherished that ball, he knew that sometimes in life you have to pay what you owe.

The old man turned towards Cognac, but before he could even say a word he was being handed a gold necklace. Cognac had seen enough to convince him that it was preferable to glitter a few karats less brightly than to deny this old man his due.

"This pay your share," the deliveryman said to Cognac.

The deliveryman placed his newly acquired goods on the ground next to his bicycle. He then he turned towards Coletrane who was still determined to avoid the man's gaze.

"What you have for me?" the deliveryman said to Coletrane.

Coletrane remained silent. His shame at harassing such an elderly, although quite spirited, man placed a heavy burden on his tongue.

"You no deaf or dumb, so you answer me. What you have?"

Coletrane raised his arms helplessly and said, "I don't got anything. What you see is what I have...nothing."

The deliveryman stepped towards the rotund lad and lifted his chin so that their eyes may meet.

"What you tried to do to me was wrong. You should know better. You should never do anything that don't make your mama proud."

"My mother's dead," Coletrane replied.

What would she think if she could see him now, about to do what he was about to do? She'd kick his butt good and toss it into the streets with no more hesitation than if he were the garbage. His mama would be ashamed that he was her son.

But she wasn't seeing this and he didn't have a choice in the matter. He had wanted to be down with the Crypt more than anything. Now he was. Being down brought responsibilities along with it. The lesson most stressed by his mother was that you live up to your responsibilities, no matter what. That was how she had managed to raise half a dozen kids in this neighborhood with no man around, and had done just fine.

Ricky was the last of those children to grow up, and the most difficult to get there. His older siblings had made Mama proud by graduating high school, getting jobs with the city and marrying before kids were on the way. They made things easy for their mother, because they bent to her overpowering will. However, she had not been able to go six for six. Ricky fought with his mother from day one, when he had to be forcibly removed from her womb. A clear omen of things to come.

When his mother commanded that he eat his vegetables, Ricky screamed for candy. When she told him to get to bed early, he wanted to watch late night talk shows. When she demanded he hit the schoolbooks, he read comics. She insisted that he clean up his act and stop getting detentions in school, so he got himself expelled instead. His mother had dreamt the impossible for all of her children, that they would go to college. Ricky was her last hope. He had not placed college very high on his list of priorities and at the age of thirteen, he joined a gang.

That was six weeks ago. Since then he had done a lot of things his mama wouldn't have approve of. He had consumed alcohol and ingested drugs. He had engaged in sex. Ricky had robbed, fought and hurt people foolish enough to resist. He had hurt people who didn't resist at all.

If there was anything in his mother stronger than her will, it was the love she held for her children. Ricky knew that despite the things he had done in the past, she would forgive him. But after what he was *about* to do, he didn't think so. This crossed the line not even a mother's love would venture beyond.

Nevertheless, Ricky had chosen his path so now had to walk it. He wasn't willing to travel the long arduous road his mother had tried to direct him towards. He was in too much of a hurry. Out on these streets is where he would stake his claim, where he would immediately be paid in full.

That's why Ricky was leaning against a fence, waiting to fulfill his latest duty as a member of the Crypt. Any moment now his prey would be coming home, basketball in hand, cap turned backwards on his head with one pants leg rolled up to his knee. And Ricky would make his first kill.

He patted the gun that was held securely in the waist of his jeans, hidden from view by his overlapping shirt. Ricky wondered what it would be like to kill a person. What else was there to think about at such a time?

Would he feel like more of a man, or less? Would he feel regret and remorse? Or would he feel only relief that he had accomplished his mission? Would he like it? Would he like himself? Would he be able to do it? If so, would any of the other questions matter?

Here comes Ricky's prey. Ricky could set his watch by him. He was alone as usual. The sun was down, the nearest streetlight out, no witnesses to be found.

Ricky moved closer. It was necessary to be as quiet as possible because if seen, his intentions would be instantly known. But he couldn't be too far away. Missing was not a luxury he could afford.

When Ricky's foot accidentally kicked the discarded soda can, a dozen car alarms and a marching band could not have made a more resounding clamor. Surprise was no longer his ally and neither was time.

Ricky raised his arm and fired. The bullet harmlessly flew over the left shoulder of its target, eventually imbedding itself in a wall of the tenement building behind him. The second bullet released sunk deeply and with finality into soft flesh. Its victim crumbled to the ground, his hands useless as a dam to hold back the flow of blood.

"Did you see that?" a voice asked. "He just smoked that nigga."

Apparently there had been people around. Ricky hadn't noticed them. Who could blame him? He was new to this. Killing was a skill like any other. One has to practice to get good at it. Doing it right, doing it perfect wasn't easy to achieve the first time out. Novices tended to be sloppy. They made amateurish mistakes like not observing witnesses; making unnecessary sounds that gave them away; missing their first shot, which could turn out to be their only one. Cause if your mark was wearing a piece himself, then he would get a chance, and you could end up lying on the ground bleeding your life away...just like Ricky was.

He would never know what it was like to kill a person, but he would learn how it felt to be killed. Voices around him slowly growing softer, the stars in the sky becoming fainter by the second. The pain, overwhelming at first, then fading as well. No chance to even be afraid, for Ricky had allotted his precious remaining moments to asking himself a question.

The police would come, the news would spread, and the sordid tale would be told. Ricky Tate, thirteen-year-old gangbanger, tried to pop someone and got popped himself.

What would his mama say?

****

Roy L. Pickering Jr. is a freelance writer living in New York City. He has been gaining exposure for his prose through appearances of his short stories in anthologies and is seeking publication for his debut novel, *Patches of Grey*. One of his short stories is slated to appear in the anthology *Proverbs for the People* in June 2003.

THE CHOSEN ONE
Destin Soul

"I told you to freeze!" the officer shouted.

"Suck my dick you pig motherfuckers!" yelled Kareem.

"We got tuh spilt up nigga," said Julius looking at his partner, since childhood, in the eyes as they ran for their lives, knowing it was the last time he'd see him.

"Aiight nigga, one love!" Kareem said.

As Kareem leaped over the hood of the red Maxima that was stopped at the traffic light, a specially issued piece of lead tore a hole in the back of his right shoulder, monkey flipping him onto the concrete. This would have slowed the average person down, but it didn't stop Kareem. He hit the ground running. The drugs he ingested had his body numb and the blood that spilled from his wound didn't shake him. It just made him angrier. This was one of those days when Mother Nature didn't seem to respect a nigga's hustle or his getaway.

The rain that fell made it difficult for Kareem to get traction, especially with the forty-nine dollar Timberland's he had strapped to his feet. So Kareem cut through familiar project buildings trying to lose the police. Separating was the best decision Kareem and Julius, his partner in crime, could have made.

Julius, the faster of the two, decided to skip the projects and attempt to outrun the officer who was on his ass like sweaty boxers.

"Stop running and give up! You're making it harder on yourself," the officer yelled.

The rain had no affect on Julius. It seemed to make him sprint faster, and as he reached the ninth block, the police officer started to fade. Tired of chasing the track star, the officer shouted one last time, "Stop, freeze!" When Julius didn't comply a slug from

211

those specially issued 9MM burners made him tumble in front of Jose's, the local bodega. The people on the sidewalk spread like Hispanic hips trying to find a safe place to stand. Julius screamed, "Ah-shit! It burns! Fuckin' pig. Jake ain't gon' take me down, fuck that. I'm a warrior motherfucker."

Julius dragged himself along the concrete semi-paralyzed.

"Yuh hear me?—a motherfuckin' warrior!"   Julius reiterated.

Even in Julius' last minutes he felt compelled to put on a tough show for the urban onlookers who didn't care whether he lived or died.

The officer, giving Julius a break, told him to toss his weapon to the side and lay flat on his stomach.

"C'mon, no one else needs to die out here. Toss the weapon and put your palms to the ground," the officer shouted.

Following directions, where Julius was from, was something that pussies did. Being that he wasn't going to go down as one of those, he sat up and reached for his 45. Although the officer felt Julius deserved what he was about to get, his face saddened as he squeezed the trigger. The first shot exploded in Julius' chest causing his arms to fold across his body, and the second made his skull tremble as his body went limp, melting to the ground.

Kareem knew that the cops wouldn't shoot with all of the innocent bystanders around, and with their uniforms wet, it added another five pounds causing them to slow down a taste. For the most part, he knew police were out of shape and it was only a matter of time before the sugary snacks caught up with them.

Kareem ran inside the Eastside building, his destination being his cousin Monica's apartment. He didn't want to hide, but to exit out of her kitchen window and down the fire escape. His thinking was that while the officers searched every apartment in the projects, he'd be gone in the wind, doing the bird. As soon as he entered the building he saw both elevators sitting in their B-boy stance, empty, and he quickly hit all of the buttons in them and broke for the stairwell. After buffaloing his way pass a crew of baseheads, Kareem took four steps at a time making it to the fourth floor in record time. Exploding through the door he lost his footing and slipped on the floor, falling on the shoulder that had his entire arm soaked with his blood. It was those Timbs again. Instead of the normal tree that was found on the heel of Timberland's, his more closely resembled a bag of weed. Although he stumbled, he managed to hold on to his pistol like a Spanish female holds onto her family.

His shirt was so covered in blood that when he hit the floor, the force pushed it out of his shirt and painted the wall. Kareem still felt no pain but lifting his arm pass forty-five degrees was easier said than done. He came up hobbling; a twisted ankle was all he needed.

Kareem refused to get busted, and if he had anything to do with it, he wasn't going back to the pen. After limping over to apartment 4H and before knocking on the door, he took a second and had his first deep breath since he started running. His eyes darted around like a crackhead's. Taking in air woke up Kareem's nerves and he began to feel the damage the flaming projectile did to his shoulder. Wiping the perspiration from his burning eyes he heard his cousin unlocking her door.

Monica opened the door quickly, pulling her blood relation into her apartment and immediately locking it behind him.

"Kareem, what the hell y'all did? The whole force is lookin' for y'all. It's on the news, nigga, look," Monica said.

Monica pointed to the big-screen television Kareem had purchased for her after selling his first package. When he saw himself on the news, he knew he was living on borrowed time. Killing a pregnant woman, three officers, and seriously wounding another meant if the police didn't fill him with metal when they *did* catch him, he was going to get juiced.

"You can't stay here, nigga. You got to get the fuck out of here. I got my son in here too. C'mon, Kareem, hurry up. What choo gon' do?"

213

"Stop bitchin' and let me breathe for a minute. I ran at least two and a half miles, top speed. Get me some water. Damn! I think they got Julius," Kareem said out of breath.

Monica was in full panic mode.

"Look at your shoulder. Kareem, you bleedin' all over my floor."

Monica threw newspaper at her cousin's feet, pushing him on it like a dog.

"Get me a T-shirt. Nah, a sweatshirt. C'mon, I don't have all day," Kareem ordered.

"What choo gon' do? You crazy, Kareem. They gon' get yuh ass this time. They not playin'."

"Just get me that sweatshirt and water. I'll worry about the rest."

After Kareem peeled off his blood-soaked shirt and put on the red St. John's sweatshirt, he headed to the window looking through the curtain posing like Malcolm. Thinking the coast was clear, he walked out onto the fire escape quietly making his way down. Feeling his was home free, Kareem got arrogant and added a bop to his walk only to then freeze like Simon told him to. Why? By the time he made it to the second floor he was surrounded by police.

Normally the police would have tried to talk him down, but killing innocent bystanders and members of the force threw that procedure right out of the window.

Kareem was a soldier and if he was supposed to go out like this, then so be it. He looked up at his cousin who was watching his escape from her window. Kareem blew her a kiss, hoping that it would make it through all of the drizzle.

"Freeze! Drop your weapon and slowly put your hands in the air!" an officer ordered.

Kareem reached for his gun and before he could get it completely out, bullets screamed through the air, ripping holes in his body and taking out one of his knees, which caused his body to fold over the edge of the fire escape, almost falling.

The crowd that had gathered gasped. Choking, Kareem looked at the police below and cracked a bloodied smile. Dying on a fire escape never crossed Kareem's mind. He always saw himself meeting his maker attached to some pussy. Hanging over the edge of the fire escape while losing his life, he still had enough strength to spit two slugs that were lucky shots cutting into an officer's throat. That's when the entire force unloaded rounds, Swiss-cheesin' Kareem until he fell two stories to the ground.

The spectators said, "Whoo" , in unison. At least that's what I heard happened. A lot of times stories are embellished. It's hard to know what exactly went down, but the one thing that was for sure was that I was going to be chosen soon and get my chance at combat.

"Who in here is ready to be chosen? Raise your hands! We Nition strike fear in the hearts of everyone we meet, crippling their style. No one has the courage to stand against us unless they're protected, *and even then*, they act like pussies. Ammu, are you prepared to represent us? Are you equipped for that kind of power, boy? Are you willing to put your life on the line and ready to get used for whatever people want? We've been here hundreds of years. We're *needed*. We ain't goin' nowhere."

Everyday elder Cannon gave us these speeches and made sure he instilled in us that to be "chosen" was everything. When educating us, he could barely stop shaking from the excitement and he would raise his voice as loud as he could as if the louder he yelled the more we would understand. The consensus was that when Cannon spoke about being selected for battle, he was overly excited because he loved beef, and in all of his years, he had never been selected

Not being picked to hit the front-line was an embarrassment. Without any war stories, who are you? However, my intelligence told me that if everyone were picked, there wouldn't be anyone to school us, the new breed. Nowadays Cannon's too old; he's obsolete. This is something he will never get over according to the seniors who tell us new breeds stories.

My name is Ammu, but friends and family call me Bullethead for obvious reasons. It took a lot of conditioning to make my heart cold and if it were up to me, I would workout to chisel my frame making it hard like steel. Strangely enough, working out too much is against the rules. Using metals as an example, we're motivated to be hard but need to be able to give like lead. I never liked the nickname Bullethead, but with the shape of my shit, I can't lie, my shit looks like a slug. Actually, everyone I know has similar head shapes. In addition to having the same head shapes, our living conditions are all the same.

The house I stay in is similar to everyone else's too. It's cheap like a cardboard box and filled with at least, in my case, dozens of my closest family members on some Mexican shit. In our neighborhood the houses are so close together that the sides literally touch one another. We're like a cult. We all believe in the same thing, have the same values and the same morals or lack of. Everyone is taught from the point of his or her inception what to think and do in a given situation.

I've been told that once chosen, you'll end up in groups of six, sixteen or even more depending. That's when it's the *most* exciting. One of the seniors told me, "Don't get your hopes up. Sometimes we're wasted, only given air time, cutting through the wind until we lose steam and fall. Not being able to be used again sucks, boy. It sucks—no action."

Rumor has it that seniors protested against being wasted, but of course it was to no avail, something about this thing called government. I guess it's a case of being so powerful that you're powerless. Ask any so-called African American.

"But when we're used right, *boy* it's fun!" said the senior.

I attended lectures about how fun being drafted for wars was; splitting wood, tearing through fabric and flesh, denting metal, blowing up gas tanks, being heated in fire, taking soldiers down and splittin' wigs on cold nights and bloody days. Although wars were "where it's at," it wasn't the best time or the most action a Nition could have because wars didn't happen that often.

I remember being told about human flesh and how good it tasted. The story started with a distant cousin of mine, Twenty-two. He was being held with five of his friends by a man...a man who had sweat pouring from his skin. Twenty-two said that before he was used, the salty liquid that soaked his face came from a human hand that shook because of anger.

"The bitch will never do it to me again. I'm gon' end this shit right now. I gave her everything and she does this shit to me...Not me! Not Sam Greene... fuck that," Sam rampaged.

The story was that Sam had been with his fiancé for six years and had plans to get married soon, but Jessica, his wife to be, enjoyed sex and loved it from Carlos Davis. Sam followed Jessica all day and watched how she strolled down the street with Carlos arm-in-arm, like he was the man who put three karats on her ring finger.

"Suckin' his dick, fuckin' him without a condom—look at these motherfuckers," Sam thought. "Carlos is my cousin, my blood. He betrayed me. He must go too. They gon' learn they can't do this kind of shit to me," is what Twenty-two said the guy who called himself Sam Greene whispered.

Out of nowhere, Twenty-two said he was elected and given the responsibility of flight. He described how his red-hot body rotated through the cool air, breaking through a window, tearing through cotton sheets, and entering flesh so fast that the hole could hardly be detected.

"The hole was so small that when my ass passed through it, it closed back up. While inside, everything became muffled and I tasted that great acidic liquid that we've been told about. I also was slowed down by all of the soft shit I bumped into," Twenty-two said.

What really stopped Twenty-two was something solid that we Nition know as bone. I don't know what bone is or what it's made of, but it's harder than a motherfucker. Unless you catch it on your way in, full steam, it usually stops you dead in your tracks except if you break it apart, but that knocks a dimple in your head.

Twenty-two's story was okay but the elders tell us that the most action that we'll ever receive is from what humans call police officers or niggas. The police officer's problem is that they choose too many of us causing them to end up with surplus. They're forced to make space for the new. Although the police give good action they don't have shit on niggas.

Nearly every one of them uses us. There was a time when niggas made us proud. They give us the most action. We're told it's by design, but we're taught not to give a damn. All Nitions wish they had eyes to see what niggas looked like so that they could thank them. That's all the seniors talk about was nigga this and nigga that. We were all told to praise niggas for thinking so much of us until . . . Federal police came in our neighborhood and hundreds of us overheard that niggas loved thuggin', killing each other, stealing, ignorance, the false sense of courage that owning firearms give, drug using and drug selling.

The tone of the officer's words let all of us listening know that these things were horrible and niggas were not to be praised, but in fact were bad people. They were people that were useless, had no purpose and needed to be erased from the planet. The officers also spoke of a drug sting that was about to go down and how they wanted so badly to just go in and kill all the niggas involved. What their orders were and what they wanted to do were totally different. If not for their CI (Confidential Informant), Calvin Whitney, who got pulled on a routine bust, members of Power would still be able to strut around like their over-sized denim had Teflon woven into them.

Officer Santiago was aware of the infamous drug team for four years, and with Mr. Whitney's insider information, he was finally able to learn the inner workings to take them down. All it was going to cost these federal officers was a small percentage of the bust they'd promised to turn over to their CI. This crew had already killed four officers and although the police had their orders, they were going to function slightly outside of the box for their fallen comrades. The drug deal was supposed to go down at one-thirty in the morning behind the new Macy's location in the Green Acres shopping Mall parking lot.

I overheard that the police took over two houses directly across the street from Macy's in order to stake out the area. In addition to that, there was a vomit green van that sat on the mall-side of the street that was full of officers ready to get revenge. The police, knocking our house around after lifting it from its foundation, felt like an earthquake and temporarily made if difficult to hear. But it was clear that they were going to shoot first and ask questions later.

Mr. Whitney went in wired and was supposed to get everyone on tape, and the icing on the cake would be to get any of the boys who trusted him to admit to murder, especially the leader, Shifty. As the deal went down, an officer ripped the roof off of my house and grabbed a handful of my family members, sliding us in something the elders told us was a clip. We were renamed, given numbers while we were forced to stay in line. My twin brother was six, my first cousin was called eight and I was now seven. Finally being selected for combat was as exciting as Elder Cannon told us it would be. We couldn't stop smiling. Now it was up to the niggas to make a mistake, which was almost a given, at least that's what the Feds were saying. Without an error in judgment, we'd be forced to sit in our new apartment praying for the time one was made, and nothing's worse than that. But still, we all prayed. We had faith in the niggas that were showing up.

Minutes after being moved into our new residence, we overheard that members of Power began to pull up to the meeting spot and when Mr. Whitney showed his face, the police hit the record button.

"Yo, Sam, you been actin' funny the whole night. What's happenin'?" Shifty said as he was suspicious of everyone and usually had good reason to be. He also never hesitated to kill, so when he started to question Sam's swagger, his body produced an unnatural amount of perspiration for a seasoned hustler.

"Ain't nothin', man. I'm just hotter than a motherfucker," Sam said wiping the sweat from his brow with his forearm, blinking like an eyelash had fallen into his eye.

"Then take some of that shit you got on off. You a little overdressed anyway, nigga, ain't yuh?" Shifty said prying and digging for information. Anytime he noticed someone doing anything abnormal a red flag went up in his head.

"I can't," Sam said.

"You can't," Shifty replied focusing on his worker's face while looking for the truth. "Why the fuck not?"

"I think I'm comin' down with somethin'. I feel sick. That's why I have on all of these clothes. I ain't tryin' to get pneumonia."

Sweating and putting on an extra layer of clothing didn't give Sam away, but his breathing and mannerisms did.

"Why you breathin' so hard? I know that you ain't scared," Shifty said.

"I don't know," Sam said. "I think that it's this cold I'm fightin'. It's kickin' my ass."

"Yo, Tah told me that you got pulled last week. How'd that turn out?"

Shifty knew that with Sam's record, what he got busted with should have put him under the jail. But here he was still on the streets, which meant one of two things. He either was working for the Feds as a CI or they botched up the bust and had to let him go because of a technicality. The way Sam acted was going to tell Shifty which one it was.

"It was some illegal search-and-seizure shit. They had to let a nigga go. You know how it is."

"Yeah, I know," Shifty said as he began to play around shadow boxing. "What you know about this, boy? These hands are like Ali's."

"C'mon Shift, stop playin'. This shit is about to go down," Sam said.

"What's up, nigga? You scared of this quickness ain't yuh?"

Shifty threw a soft jab that hit Sam in the chest and a slap that caught him across the neck to see if there were any wires around it.

"C'mon, man. Stop fuckin' playin'. You always playin'," Sam said.

"Stop bitchin', nigga," Shifty replied..

Sam saw the delivery that they were waiting for in the distance and announced I, making Shifty stare at his style. When Sam tried to get him to admit to murder, he got the answer he'd been looking for. Shifty began to scope out the area around where he stood and noticed the green van that stuck out like Khalid Muhammad at a Klan rally. When he saw someone pull the curtains in the window of the house across the street as he glanced in it's direction, he knew that one of the soldiers he trusted had set him up.

Shifty signaled to all of his boys to be out.

"What's up Shift? We need this deal man," one of his boys said.

"I don't know what you talkin' 'bout nigga. Deal? What deal you talkin' 'bout? The bitches ain't comin', huh? You had me believin' that I was gon' get some pussy. Where these females at, nigga? I'm starting to think you brought me down here for nothin'," Shifty raged.

Shifty's change in attitude told Sam and the police that he was onto what was going down, but with the delivery pulling up they still had him nailed with the help of Sam's testimony.

Shifty shook his head and gave Sam a handshake as he laughed. "You a funny-style nigga. I knew you was a sucker and against my better judgment I put you on. I should have listened to that little voice. Sam knew he was busted but continued to play stupid.

"What you talkin' about, Shift?" Sam asked.

"How much you gettin' nigga? I know they givin' you a percentage of the bust. How much do confidential informers make nowadays motherfucker?" Shifty said.

"Huh?"

"You know what the fuck I'm talkin' about motherfucker."

The police wanted to jump in and save Sam because they needed him to testify but they gambled on Sam being able to handle the situation, so they fell back.

Shifty pulled out his TEC-9 and rested it against Sam's teeth as he had another one of his soldiers rip Sam's coat and shirt off exposing the wire. That's when the police jumped out of the van with their guns drawn attempting to protect their rat.

"Freeze! You're under arrest! Drop your weapons and put your hands in the air!" the officers said.

Law enforcement came from everywhere and in seconds they had the parking lot where Shifty stood surrounded. When you hustle you risk the chance of something like this happening. Shifty had a strong eight-year run and that's pretty good. The average hustler could only dream about a run that long without ever being pulled, but all good things come to an end. Shifty was firm about not ever going to jail and if he was going to die he was taking as many people with him as he could.

"I said don't move! Drop your weapon!" the officer repeated.

Shifty eyeballed all of his boys, and with that signal, they tried to unload all the rounds they had, but the accuracy of the police had niggas dropping like the stock market.

After Shifty blew the back of Sam's head away from his skull, he ran for cover but not before getting hit in the stomach and in his left calve by two of my distant cousins. The officer that carried us went after Shifty telling him that if he cooperated they'd take it easy on him. Three of our next-door neighbors had been selected, but the damage they caused was minor and right in the middle of the conversation my brother and I were having, he was chosen. My brother tore into Shifty's back and ate as much flesh as he could until he was smothered by muscle.

Anticipating my turn made me sweat. I knew that as long as Shifty wasn't dead he was going to try and kill the officer that held us tight like a Jew does their wallet, which meant there was no doubt this was going to be my night to shine.

"Freeze!" an officer shouted.

Barely able to move, Shifty pointed his Tec at officer Kiernan and I finally had my chance. I was finally the chosen one.

I cut through the wind so sharp there was a whistling sound and as I spiraled, I aimed myself at Shifty's forehead. I knew banging into his head was going to dent mine, and for that, right before impact, I started to tumble. Cracking through Shifty's skull was easier than I thought and making it into the wet, mushy center felt good. I didn't have enough steam to exit out of the back of his head so I stayed embedded in the bone at the back of his skull, causing Shifty to collapse on the concrete.

After being shot, the life span of a Nition is short. Minutes after you're selected you start to feel the affect of death calling. It's inevitable, so I don't have much time left. Our whole life we're educated about and prepared for any sort of action that we're called to be a part of, and the build up at times is overwhelming. But as long as niggas exist we'll always have a job. Thank God for niggas and their hustles. Thanks for listening my time is . . .

R.I.P. Ammu

****

Known in some circles as the Jay-Z of black fiction, Destin Soul's (the exceptionally gifted author of "Who Took The Last Shot?", "90% Of Me Is You", "Sex, Lies & Big Mistakes", "Pubic Enemy", "Hump Day", "Abortion Money", "Sistergirls.com" and "Flava".) unique reality-based fiction style has a way of making even those far removed from the subject matter able to relate. Soul's prolific pen never stops as he is putting the finishing touches on forthcoming novels.

<u>*Out of Đa Game*</u>

After serving a combined 13 years in Federal and State prisons, we decided that we had had enough. Was it easy to say no to the lifestyle? Absolutely not. Was it easy to believe that we could live differently? Hell No! What it took was the courage to believe and know that we didn't have to live like that. We sincerely thank you for your support of our street tales. It is because of you that we now live legally. It is because of you that we are able to use our God given talents to reach a nation. We would like to take a moment to say a heartfelt THANK YOU!

In Biblical days, the story is told of how Pharaoh instructed the children of Israel to make **Bricks without Straw**. Well, very often in current society, the underclass or downtrodden is asked the same thing: Make Bricks without Straw. Get a decent job without an education, get off of welfare, live legally after years in prison and the list goes on. And as impossible as these accomplishements may seem, it can be done. Please remember the words *Bricks without Straw*. Because the children of Israel served an awesome God, they did it. You too can make Bricks without Straw. No one said that it would be easy. But it can be done. Here are the ingredients:

¼ cup of Consistency
2/3 cup of Humbleness
½ cup of Dedication
110% Belief in God

All these things mixed together make the impossible, possible. How do we know?
WE are living witnesses.

Making Bricks without Straw,

Triple Crown Publications

TRIPLE CROWN PUBLICATIONS

ORDER FORM

Triple Crown Publications
P.O. Box 7212
Columbus, OH 43205

NAME _____

ADDRESS _____

_____

CITY _____

STATE _____

ZIP _____

BOOKS AVAILABLE

#QTY	TITLE	PRICE
	GANGSTA **By Kwan**	**$15.00**
	Let That Be The Reason **By Vickie M. Stringer**	**$15.00**
	A Hustler's Wife **By Nikki Turner**	**$15.00**
	The GAME **Short Stories**	**$15.00**

SHIPPING/HANDLING (Via U.S.   **$ 3.50**
Priority Mail)

TOTAL   **$_____**

FORMS OF ACCEPTED PAYMENTS:
Postage Stamps, Institutional Checks & Money Orders